I0723219

Time Enough

Anne Louise Bannon

HH
Healcroft House, Publishers
Altadena, California

ISBN 978-1-948616-29-4

Library of Congress Control Number: 2023903635

Healcroft House, Publishers, Altadena, California, United States of America

Contents

For Stephanie Beverage and Susanna Apitz, my collaborators on the early versions of this project. I still remember those days fondly.

Acknowledgments

As noted in the dedication to this volume, my dear friends Susanna Apitz and Stephanie Beverage were instrumental in the creation of this story and But World Enough and Time. They listened for hours, read all of it, made excellent suggestions. Not to mention all the historical research Stephanie did so that I could get the historical bits more accurate.

But it doesn't end there. Years later, my daughter, Cornelia Ann Klarner, added her insight. As for my poor, beleaguered husband, Michael Holland… Well, let's just say that I'm surprised the man has ears left. Still, his comments have always been spot on and the few times I've ignored them, I've largely been sorry I did.

Thank you, one and all.

Chapter One

Sullenly, Robin Parker shifted her mouse, then clicked. Six of hearts on seven of clubs. She clicked again and the five of spades and four of hearts landed on the six, and the column cleared. She sighed. Nothing like being the queen of Free Cell.

Robin continued moving the mouse and clicking, aware that she had come into her office in Pasadena, California, for the usual weekly meeting only because she was one of the business's owners. Aware also that it was entirely possible that she would not be one of the owners for much longer. And she couldn't help wondering if it would make any difference whether or not she was one of the owners.

For the past year, it had seemed like she did damned little of the engineering she had spent six years gaining her bachelor's and master's degrees to learn. Most days, if she hadn't been holding somebody's hand, she was holding two other people apart. She and her partner had held the small company together through a tech sector meltdown a couple years before, and though business was picking up, she still wasn't doing what she really wanted to be doing. That was assuming she had ever known what she wanted.

Move, click. Queen of clubs on king of diamonds. Move, click. A whole column starting with the jack of hearts on top of the queen. Another click, and the cards went like magic into their cells and the game was won. Robin stared at the green field and debated starting another game.

She thought back to the small black box safely hidden in her house. It reminded Robin of an old wireless router she'd had. But all she had to do was hold it and think about where she wanted to go and it would take Robin not just to anywhere on the planet, but just about any time, as well.

A knock on the door to her office startled her back to her present.

"Still mousing it?" asked Steve Wasserman, Robin's business partner, as he wandered in and grinned at her.

Steve was of average height, slender, with brown hair, perfectly styled, and clothes that were always perfect.

Robin smiled and clicked the mouse next to her laptop. "I like antiques. So what? Have you finally gotten Garson to stop whining?"

"You should really cut him a break." Sighing, Steve plopped down in one of the two chairs in front of Robin's desk. He was wearing a burgundy tie, starched rose-colored shirt and flat front pants of ultra-fine wool and a perfectly sharp crease. "You can't blame him for getting peeved when every time he designs something, Petrie over-sells it and he has to re-work it." He looked at her with a wan smile. "Are you okay?"

"I'm fine."

"Like hell you are, kiddo. You haven't been fine since you left Rick. You were supposed to be spending all of July in

Europe, and you come in here not even halfway through the month, announcing that you're not here."

Robin shrugged. "I had some luggage to pick up."

"Which also meant you weren't in Europe like you were supposed to be. But were you here? No. You've been working from home since then and it's almost Labor Day."

"That's, what? Two weeks from today."

Steve shook his head. "That's not the issue, Robin. I'm perfectly happy with you working from home. You were a mess at the meeting this morning. I thought you were going to haul off and strangle Garson."

"He's a crybaby." Robin growled, then held up her hands. "I agree Petrie can't keep overselling things and expecting the team to turn it around in five minutes. But she's up against it, too, and when the team keeps coming through on their end, she's going to keep relying on that."

"We've talked that one to death, Robin. I'm going to take care of it with Petrie. This isn't about her or Garson. It's about you." Steve leaned forward. "We're best friends, Robin. And except for wanting to kill Garson, you've been fine on the business end of things. But I also know you've been damned frustrated with it and life and I don't know what all else. I thought Europe was supposed to fix that."

Robin laughed sadly. "I guess it did, in a way." She thought fast. "I'm in transition, Steve." Which was true enough. Only Robin had no idea what she was transitioning to. "Things got a little... weird in England. Made me think about a lot of things."

"Like what?"

"Well..." Robin briefly debated not telling Steve the planned story, but then realized it would be good practice for when she had to tell her mother. "You know I got stuck taking Dean to England with me. It's kind of complicated, but he'd been involved last fall with this young woman, Elizabeth, who suddenly broke up with him. Well, around the time I was breaking up with Rick, I found out that the reason that Elizabeth broke up with Dean was that she was pregnant with his baby. So, I ended up helping get her settled and back with Dean."

"So why didn't you say anything about that?" Steve glared a little.

She hadn't because that's not what had really happened. Dean had found Elizabeth in a hidden room in an old castle they'd been touring. Elizabeth had been in a state of suspended animation – or what appeared to be, at any rate. It turned out that Roger, who was from the future, had brought Elizabeth forward in time for some purpose. While escaping him, Robin had acquired the hand-held time machine, and used it to bring her, Dean, and Elizabeth back to Elizabeth's original time in seventeenth-century England. The intent was to get Elizabeth established some place other than her hometown, then leave.

Only it hadn't happened that way. One of Roger's colleagues, Donald, had tried to re-capture Elizabeth multiple times. Dean and Elizabeth had fallen in love and Elizabeth got pregnant. The machine had broken down, stranding them in eighteenth-century England for a time. They'd actually been gone for fifteen months, even though it had seemed like only two weeks to Steve and everyone else. Dean and Elizabeth were quite happy not to time travel anymore. Robin's appetite had only been whetted.

Robin sighed. "Dean swore me to strictest secrecy because he wasn't sure what he was going to do beyond supporting the kid. The thing was, Elizabeth really messed him up when she broke up with him because he was pretty serious about her. Anyway, Elizabeth sends us off to England because she's not due until August, but then we get this call and she's already had the baby. In fact, she had it right after we left, only she lost my cell phone number and didn't get through until two days before that time I came in. So, for the past few weeks, they've been bonding, and I've been taking care of all three of them."

"Gotcha." Steve chuckled. "So that's why you've been working from home. Why couldn't you tell me?"

"That." Robin reached over and tapped her screen to start a new game. She didn't think Steve would believe that she and Dean had to bring Elizabeth up to date on almost four hundred years of human and technological development before the young woman met their mother. "I need to re-think things, Steve. I'm just not sure where I'm going right now."

"Robin, you're only twenty-nine. The biological clock can't be ticking that loudly."

Robin shot him an annoyed smirk. "It has nothing to do with that." She paused. "It's different. In some ways, I've already achieved all I set out to do. So now what? Playing babysitter to a bunch of techno-geek crybabies is not what I envisioned for my life."

Again, it was a more truthful answer than Robin had planned.

Steve threw up his arms. "You want to know what your problem is?"

"Not really, but when has that stopped you?" Robin glared at him fondly.

"You want the fairy tale, the perfect relationship, the perfect career, the two-perfect kids. But you're not perfect,

Robin. And life isn't perfect. Okay, I was probably wrong about hanging in there with Rick."

"Probably?" Robin snorted. "Yeah, he liked Internet porn, but even without that, if he could have made love to his computer, he would have. He only needed me because I'm warmer than a plastic blow-up doll."

"But it's not about having a soul mate."

"Says the guy who found his."

Steve grinned happily. "Yeah, Rob is a great guy. But we still have to work at it. You've gotta be real and let somebody see it. You don't do that well, Robin. Especially with guys. Well, straight guys. Your biggest loves are always the guys who are unavailable."

Robin grimaced. "Yeah, I noticed that recently. Dean dumped some fear of intimacy crap on me."

Steve leaned over and plopped his forearms on the desk. "You know, Robin, maybe you need to just take some time and get comfortable in your own skin."

"Time." Robin smiled softly to herself. "That's exactly what I want."

Or more accurately, time travel. Robin still wasn't sure about why that held such an allure for her, but she knew she would be time traveling again soon. She just wasn't sure when she'd leave her time for that of Roger.

Roger had told her things would be bad when she got there. He also told her that he would see her when she arrived. But he also told her not to leave before she got Dean and Elizabeth settled and assured her they'd be safe from Donald while they were in Pasadena. So, Robin stayed on, pushing Elizabeth as hard as she dared to get the young woman adjusted to her new world, which was both a lot easier and a lot harder than Robin expected.

"Anyway," she said. "I've got to get things together." She yawned. "Dean and Elizabeth have been staying at my place while Dean looks for a job and gets his school stuff together, which means there's a new baby in the house, and we haven't been sleeping too well." She shook her head quickly. "So, what do we need to get on top of for the rest of this week?"

Robin pushed aside her laptop and got out a notepad. For the next two hours, she and Steve worked out plans and goals, which they'd been doing every week. Robin left the office shortly after noon and walked home feeling relieved and wistful and annoyed, all at the same time.

She took a deep breath as she walked up to the bungalow she was slowly restoring. She'd always felt a deep affection for the tiny place, an affection that had only grown as she'd worked on it. The house had been built in the early Twentieth Century for a working class-family. Too tiny for a family these days, it seemed perfect for a single woman who had achieved most of her life dreams but hadn't found herself yet.

Robin dropped her keys on the phone table next to the front door. The small living room was spare with polished dark wood floors and mission-style furniture finished in a rosewood stain and tan leather cushions. On one of the side walls was a fireplace and Robin had installed a flat screen TV covered by a cabinet over the fireplace mantle. The back wall of the room was bisected by the door to the dining room, with the couch on one side and bookshelves covering the entire wall on the other.

Dean had texted that he and Elizabeth were out taking baby Robin Mary to the doctor for a check-up. It was both Elizabeth's and the baby's first time, and the baby was coming due for some vaccinations. Robin hoped the visit would go well. They'd been putting it off as long as they could.

Robin had taken advantage of the little family's absence to take a quick detour to her favorite sandwich place. She dumped her laptop bag on the couch, then opened the paper bag she was carrying. The tantalizing scent of pastrami wafted out. Pastrami was one of the better parts of the Twenty-First Century. Robin carried her lunch into the kitchen to get a plate and some milk.

Robin's living room flowed into her dining room, which had only been finished a couple months before, with the same dark hardwood floors and spare mission furniture. Elizabeth had initially confused the dining room table with a worktable, so Robin had taken to keeping a tablecloth on to remind her not to cut things on its surface. A small nook off the main room opened out onto Robin's side yard, and Robin had squeezed in a worktable and filing cabinet for a small home office.

The kitchen door, at the back end of the dining room, remained shut most of the time because Robin hadn't started re-doing that room yet. It was a long room that reached to the back of the house. A small refrigerator occupied a niche that had been cut out next to the door from the dining room by an earlier occupant. A counter ran the length of the room, with a scratched-up porcelain sink in the middle. The top was beat-up formica framed by aluminum stripping, and the white cupboards were beat up and badly needed stripping of the many, many layers of paint that had built up over the years.

Nonetheless, the stove was almost new - or had been when Robin bought the house. It was backed up against the refrigerator niche. A small table sat nearby, almost in the way of a tiny corner cupboard that was open to the space under the house. Elizabeth had filled the shelves with bread, cheeses, cabbages, carrots, and potatoes. It had taken a couple weeks before she regularly remembered to use the refrigerator for any meats they'd bought. In fact, she was still getting used to the idea of having so much meat easily available. On Sundays, dinner would feature three or four different roasted meats and nothing else.

Robin dropped her bag on the table and got a plate from the cupboard and a glass. Neither she nor Dean had been able to teach Elizabeth much about modern cooking since neither of them cooked. Elizabeth had initially scoffed at the cookbooks they'd bought. After all, she knew perfectly well how to cook, and had taken over that task completely. But she had liked the glossy pictures of all the various dishes and was slowly becoming more interested in the recipes.

With her lunch dished out, Robin returned to the dining room, grabbed a reading tablet off her desk, then settled in to eat her lunch, reveling in the peace and quiet.

It didn't last long. Dean and Elizabeth arrived home, both glaring and sullen, and baby Robbie was crying.

"What happened?" Robin asked, reaching to take the baby from Elizabeth.

Elizabeth tightened, then surrendered the infant. If Elizabeth was upset or frightened, it upset Robbie. They'd found that Robin had a knack for soothing the infant, and the only time that didn't work was when the baby was hungry. And soothing the baby went a long way toward calming Elizabeth down.

But as Robbie slowly stopped wailing, Robin could see that Elizabeth would not calm down any too quickly.

Tall and blonde, Dean constantly reminded Robin of the perennial surfer dude. He had broad shoulders and an easy-going demeanor that was yet another reason Robin tended to be jealous of her brother.

Robin looked over at Elizabeth. The young woman was on the short side, and while not fat, she was significantly rounder than current fashion decreed was good. She had reddish-brown hair, pinned up and tucked under a ker-chief instead of a mob cap. In fact, Elizabeth was wear-ing considerably more clothes than fashion and the hot Southern California weather decreed she should, namely a long, flower-print skirt, tights, shoes, and a long-sleeved blouse with a matching jacket over it. Elizabeth hadn't quite gotten used to letting her shins show under her skirt.

"What's going on?" Robin asked.

Dean looked over at Elizabeth, whose lips were pressed into a thin, tight line. His shoulders sagged.

"Didn't Robbie get her vaccinations?" Robin asked.

Elizabeth snorted. "They pricked her heel!"

"We told you they'd want to test her blood," Robin said, wincing because she'd forgotten to tell Elizabeth how the nurse would probably get that blood.

"Roger didn't need to do that," Elizabeth said.

"And we also told you that Roger comes from even fur-ther in the future, and they've discovered things we haven't yet," Robin said, looking over at Dean.

Robin suspected Dean had already told Elizabeth all these things, which meant that they were not the source of

Elizabeth's unhappiness. Fortunately, the baby had fallen asleep.

"Looks like the baby's ready for her nap," Dean said suddenly. "Um, Robin, you want to help me put her down?"

"I—" Elizabeth started, but then stopped when she saw Dean's face. She flounced into the kitchen.

Robin followed Dean into the small bedroom at the back of the house. It was packed full with a bed and small crib and a bureau that had been Robin's when she was growing up. The carpet on the floor was old, gray, and spotted and the window blinds on the two windows were down, but several of the slats were broken. Robin had used the room for storage until Dean and Elizabeth had moved in.

"So, what happened?" Robin asked Dean as she got a fresh diaper from the pile on the bureau.

"It was the insurance," Dean said.

"I told you to put it on the debit card," Robin said. She laid down the changing mat on the bed and began changing the baby's diaper.

"I know. I did." Dean sagged down on the bed next to the baby. "It's just that they asked whether my wife was on my insurance or just the baby."

"And Elizabeth's not your wife yet."

"It's that stupid promise I made to her when we first landed in the Eighteenth Century," Dean sighed. "We're home now, so she figures I should make good on it."

"Well, you did say you would as soon as we got back home. And it's been almost six weeks now."

"You're the one who told us not to," Dean groaned.

"I told you two to wait until Elizabeth had recovered from having the baby," Robin said.

Dean sighed again. "I know." He put his head in his hands. "The worst of it is, she won't fight with me." He looked up at Robin. "You ever hear of family of origin issues? Elizabeth's got period of origin issues. All that training to be a virtuous, obedient wife. She just does whatever I tell her to, then sulks when she's mad at me."

Robin finished snapping up the baby's onesie and re-wrapped the receiving blanket around her.

"Alright," she said. "I'll talk to her about that. But it's hard training to overcome and there are plenty of women these days who pull the same nonsense. At least Elizabeth has an excuse."

"Yeah, but that's not much help right now," Dean said.

Robin laid the baby in the crib. "You know, Elizabeth has a point. You did promise, and if you're not going to follow through, you'd better have a really good reason."

"I'm not going to abandon her!"

"No, you won't." Robin sighed as she sat down next to her brother. "But it would have been bad enough for you to abandon her back in her own time. And I know she was scared you would because she told me so. You've got to figure it's even worse now, what with all this new magic and different expectations."

"She doesn't have anything to worry about. And I've told her that over and over."

"I know, and she believes you. But being married would help, especially since she hasn't figured out how easy divorce is now."

"It's not that easy," Dean grumbled. "Ralphie's was a mess, and they weren't married long enough to have anything in common to split."

Ralphie was their cousin. He and Dean were particularly close, even though Ralphie was closer to Robin in age. Ralphie's wedding had been completely over the top, which only underscored the ugly divorce eight months later.

"In Elizabeth's time, divorce was almost non-existent and involved the Pope," Robin said. "So, yeah. I think she'll feel a lot more secure if you two were married."

"Great." Dean sounded almost as if he was going to burst into tears.

"What's wrong, Dean?" Robin asked gently. "Don't you want to marry Elizabeth?"

"Yeah, I do." Dean popped up and began pacing. "It's not that."

Robin could see that it really wasn't. "Then what is it?"

"It's... Well..." Dean sighed deeply and sank back down onto the bed. "It's when I called Dad last month after we got back here."

Their father lived in Northern California and had since he and their mother divorced when Robin was thirteen. The split had been amicable, as the relationship had mostly just faded away. Her parents had remained friends with each other, and Dean and Robin were close to their father.

"Was Dad mad?" Robin asked.

Dean winced. "Sort of. Mostly worried, I think."

"Well, you can hardly blame him."

"I get that. He just..." Dean closed his eyes and shivered. "I told him that Elizabeth and I were probably just going to go to Las Vegas, keep it small and fast and private."

"I think the county courthouse would be better," Robin said.

"That's not it," Dean growled. "Dad just said that he didn't think that was such a good idea. I mean, he wasn't wild about the getting married part, but he wasn't saying I shouldn't. He just didn't think we should run off without... without inviting Mom, at least."

Robin nodded. "And you're scared to death of telling her."

Dean squeezed his eyes shut. "Wouldn't you be?"

"Well, yeah. But I'm not her fair-haired treasure. You are."

"Not so much at the moment." Dean sighed. "She's been mad at me since I told her I wasn't going to be a medical doctor."

"What? That's been years."

"Yeah." Dean sighed again. "But last winter I told her I'm not so sure I'm going to get the PhD. I don't technically need it to do what I want to do. Unless I go in hard for the research. Which I might. And I didn't say I wasn't going to do it. But she hit the ceiling. Said I was wasting my talent, and that I was being completely immature and that I'd be leaning on her and you for the rest of my life."

"And then she talked us both into going to Europe together." Robin rolled her eyes and shook her head. "Didn't she get that was kind of setting you up for dependence?"

"I think that's what she wants," Dean grumbled. "That internship I had last year? I thought I was going to be able to move out, then she said that if I had that much money, I could pay for my school fees and books, too. Which killed moving out."

Robin thought it over. She'd had her own fights with their mother over how independent she was going to be. She sighed.

"Look, Dean, I can't rescue you on this one. With Elizabeth and with Mom. I mean, I can talk to Elizabeth about being more upfront about it when she's mad. But you have to fix the mad part."

"I don't want you to fix it," Dean snapped. "I can't spend the rest of my life letting you take care of me. I've got a kid, damn it. It's time I stepped up." He sank into himself. "I just didn't think it would be so hard."

"Dare I ask how the job interviews are going?"

He shrugged. "Not so bad. It's just that I don't think I'm going to be leaving here any too soon." He looked at her. "You don't mind, do you? I don't want to go back to Mom's. I'm scared enough she's going to stop paying my school fees as it is."

"I…" Robin groaned. "Look, I don't want to keep you dependent. Believe me, I don't. But I can take care of your tuition and anything you can't. Okay? And you can stay here, too. We just need an exit plan. Is that fair?"

Utterly relieved, Dean threw his arms around Robin. "Woh. That's the best!"

Robin gingerly hugged him back. "It will be alright, Dean. But I need a good faith exit plan, in writing, by the end of the week. And you need to call Mom and get things settled with Elizabeth. Okay?"

"More than okay. I'll have it. Honest."

Robin got up. She wasn't terribly sure she should be backing her brother by supporting him financially. But he had been acting a lot more responsibly of late. And it wasn't fair to throw him, Elizabeth, and the baby to the wolves, or worse yet, their mother until Dean had officially abused the privilege.

But thinking of their mother made Robin cringe inwardly. Marlene Westmore was a formidable woman. She'd had to have been to not only establish her career as a cardiology surgeon, but head up one of the larger and more prestigious practices in Orange County. She'd always told her two children that they should do what they wanted to do with their lives. But there was no escaping that she'd harbored dreams of them following in her footsteps in the medical field. She'd accepted Robin's decision to become an engineer, as that meant another woman in a largely male field.

Dean was another matter altogether. Robin could well imagine that their mother was hurt by Dean's decision not to pursue his doctorate. He'd always been her favorite, and as Robin thought about it, Dean's ability to just amiably go along with things may have been his way of getting along with his mother.

Still, that was now his problem, and as Robin made her way to the kitchen to talk to Elizabeth, she was a little surprised to see Dean pulling out his iPhone. Seconds later, she could hear Dean talking to their mother.

Chapter Two

Elizabeth sprinkled white flour on the mass of dough she was kneading. They didn't really need bread at that moment, but it was better than not doing anything. The flour was so lovely and fine and baked up so beautifully that Elizabeth could not understand why Robin preferred the coarser whole wheat flour. Although that flour was finer than anything she'd ever baked in her native home. She stopped and mentally corrected herself. In her native time.

It wasn't so much that the magic was frightening, because as she got used to it, it really wasn't. It was how alone she felt. Had she been home and with a new infant, she'd have a whole community of mothers, young and old, who could have helped her through some of the rougher parts. Every time the baby did something odd, Robin opened her laptop (which was a computer, which basically added lots of numbers very, very quickly, which was how it did what it did), and minutes later, there were answers. The answers helped, but there wasn't the understanding, the sharing. Elizabeth sighed again. If she were honest, there hadn't been that much understanding or sharing back in her home time, either. But she needed something, and understanding would be nice.

Robin came into the kitchen and looked at her.

"You're upset," she said gently.

Elizabeth shrugged. "It doesn't matter."

"Yeah, it does." Robin came over and laid her hand on Elizabeth's back. "You can be mad at Dean and tell him about it and still be a virtuous woman."

"Oh, so I have to give that up, too!" Elizabeth slammed the dough onto the table.

"What?" Robin stepped back. "What do you mean?"

"Is nothing I do here right? Is nothing I am right for this place?" Elizabeth blinked back still more tears, the fury roiling within her. "Why can't I be the virtuous woman I was brought up to be? Why can't I just be a good mother and wife?"

"This isn't about not being married, is it?" Robin looked at her quizzically.

"Yes, it is! It's about being what I should be, which is a very clear thing where I'm from, as you know."

"But it's different now."

"I know!" Elizabeth felt herself shriek and couldn't stop it. "I know! And I'm tired of it. I just want something I know. Something normal. Something that isn't different. I want to be with other mothers who know why my baby is crying and who know how I feel when she does."

"You want to be home." Robin touched Elizabeth on the shoulder.

"I don't know." Elizabeth flopped into a chair. "If I am honest, I did not get on all that well with the other women in the villages." She grimaced. "I didn't like the gossiping and everyone telling you how you were doing something wrong. Or worse yet, not telling you but telling everyone else. Still, I am very lonely here. I know you and Dean try to help, and you two know better than anyone what my life was like. But no one else does and I can't tell them. And sometimes, I just want something familiar, something I know."

"Damn," Robin sighed. "And, yeah, I do sort of know what you mean. When we were back in time with you, I'd get homesick, too. Especially in Bath, when I didn't think we'd be able to get back home."

"I wanted to leave," Elizabeth said. "This is a better place for me."

"But you're still going to miss where you came from," Robin said.

"I don't want to miss where I came from," Elizabeth snapped.

Robin sat down and leaned forward. "Look, Elizabeth, I know the big attitude in your time was to suck it up because you can't change things. And there is a place for that. But it also got you and me and Dean into trouble because no matter how much you suck it up and hold it in, the feelings and the differences come out, anyway. I think that's what's happening now. You've been trying so hard to adapt and change and get used to things that you haven't given yourself a chance to be sad about all the things you've lost. Things have massively changed for you. You've got a new baby and a reasonably new relationship with Dean, and you've moved to a new home, and that's not even counting moving to a new time."

Elizabeth shrugged. "I just wish there were some other mothers to talk to. You're good with answers, Robin, but it's different when it's your own baby. At the doctor's office today, when the nurse bled my baby, she looked at me and smiled and told me she'd felt the same way when she'd had her baby get his first blood test and vaccinations. That she knew it was good for him, but she couldn't help feeling awful when he cried at being hurt. She knew what I was thinking in a way that even Dean didn't."

Robin nodded sadly. "You're right."

"And that was after the problems with the insur-what-ever it is and us not being married yet." Elizabeth tried to blink back her tears, but they fell anyway.

"Do you want to try that mother's group from church again?"

Elizabeth shuddered. "Those fools! Imagine never putting your baby down."

"Ah. Right. The attachment parenting ladies." Robin couldn't quite repress her smile at the small group of women who insisted that in Olden Times, women never put their babies down, but kept them in slings on their bodies. It had taken Elizabeth a meeting or two before she realized that Olden Times meant in the past before the Twentieth Century, a past she knew far better than they did.

She snorted. "My stepmother left the babies in their cradle often enough. It doesn't even make sense that one always held the baby. How on earth would anybody get any work done? Or that one... What did they call her, a lactation coach? For goodness' sakes, it's not that hard to nurse a baby. She insisted that before they made baby formula, if you couldn't nurse, your baby starved. What utter nonsense! When a mother couldn't nurse because she was dead, we gave the baby to another mother who'd either just lost hers or didn't mind sharing a teat. The same as if a mother's milk wouldn't come." Elizabeth suddenly frowned. "Of course, in that case, they started looking for a witch. Either way, babies didn't starve because there was no one to feed them. There's always a way unless there's a famine and then everyone is starving."

"Okay. So that wasn't the right group," Robin said. "Maybe there's a mother's group around with women who aren't quite so..." Robin shrugged.

Elizabeth doubted that, but chose not to say anything. Robin's mobile phone pinged with the sound of an owl, the tone she used to alert her that she had a message from one of her work people.

"Go ahead," Elizabeth said.

Robin pulled the phone from her pocket and checked the screen. "It's not that important." She put the phone down on the table. "Alright. You need some friends. Is that safe to say?"

"I suppose so." Elizabeth tried not to sigh and failed. She had no idea what she needed. She thought Robin might be right about feeling sad about everything she left behind to live with Dean. Robin was usually right.

Robin fidgeted with her phone. "So, we'll just have to find someplace where you can meet other women with babies who aren't fools. In the meantime, you need to talk to Dean about these things. He's not going to be mad or hurt or think you don't want to be here simply because you miss your past life. That's a normal feeling. Okay?"

Elizabeth nodded, glad that Robin hadn't told her not to obey Dean. She knew Dean didn't expect it of her, but it still felt wrong not to. Dean chose that moment to wander into the kitchen.

"Good. You're both here," he announced.

"What's up?" asked Robin.

"Well." Dean swallowed, then went over to Elizabeth and picked up her hand. "Elizabeth, it's time for me to make good on my promise. We've got the Labor Day weekend coming up, so we can go to Las Vegas and get married."

Elizabeth's heart swelled. "We can?"

"If you want to," Dean said.

"I want to very much!" she gasped as the tears flowed again.

"Congratulations," said Robin with a smile. "I'll leave you two alone for a bit."

She left quickly. Dean kneeled beside Elizabeth and held her.

"Are you happy?" Dean asked as her sobs abated.

"It's better," Elizabeth said. "It's so hard. Robin says I should tell you what I'm thinking."

"Of course. That's what I'm here for."

"I just don't want to be complaining all the time," Elizabeth said. "Or thinking about how alone I am."

"Alone?" Dean asked, puzzled.

"Not with you!" Elizabeth said quickly, then hung her head. "It's just that the nurse was so kind and knew how I felt when the baby was bled, and there aren't other mothers like that."

"Oh. Duh. Of course, you'd want somebody like that to talk to." Dean sighed. "But you didn't like that mother's group we went to."

"The fools."

"I know. They were idiots."

"And... And I miss being home. I don't want to be there. But I do miss it, sometimes."

"Oh. You're homesick." Dean looked at her and smiled softly. "Did you think I was going to be mad because you miss your own time, especially when things are so different now?"

"I don't know."

"Okay." Dean got up and started pacing. "I'm trying to understand this from your perspective. You're not supposed to make me mad, because that's not what good wives do. And I get that you want to be a good wife. That's cool. But I don't want you holding everything in until you can't stand it anymore then have a meltdown, like you've been doing. That's not good for you or me or even Robbie."

Elizabeth nodded, then realized she was doing exactly what he did not want her to do.

"I like my old feisty, in-my-face Elizabeth," Dean said, kneeling next to her again. "The one who gave me hell for being lazy, even though she thought I was this super powerful sorcerer."

Elizabeth couldn't suppress a small giggle. "You always say the sweetest things."

"I want you to be a good wife, too," Dean said. "And what will make you a good wife to me is to let me have it when I need it, and to talk to me about what's upsetting you. Okay?"

Elizabeth nodded, then sighed. "I want to agree with you now because I do."

"Good." His ears perked up. "I think the baby's awake."

Elizabeth got up and wiped her hands on her apron. "I'll tend to her."

She hurried out. Robin was in the dining room, talking on her phone. Elizabeth went on to the bedroom. The baby was awake and just starting to cry. Elizabeth picked her up, then sank into the rocking chair wedged in next to the crib and the bureau. She quickly undid her blouse and put the infant to her breast.

Robin wandered in, her phone in her hand. "You okay if we have someone over for dinner tonight?"

"I was going to roast a chicken. Would that be appropriate?" Elizabeth smiled.

"That's not what I asked," said Robin with a sigh. "Would it bother you if we have someone over for dinner? I know you're feeling pretty raw today, and I don't want to make it worse."

It was only fair, Elizabeth realized. She thought for a moment as she reached for a fresh diaper from the pile next to the crib, then sucked on the corner.

"I think it would be good," she said, wiping the baby's face with the wet corner of the diaper. "I won't be thinking about myself so much."

"Great." Robin pressed something on the phone's glass face, then put it to her ear as she wandered out of the room, talking to the person who'd called. "Looks like we're on. Six okay with you?"

As Robin finished her call, Dean came into the dining room.

"Everything okay with Elizabeth?" he asked.

"Well enough," Robin said. She tried not to glare at her brother. "Vegas? Dean, what are you thinking?"

"That's what Mom wants to do and..." he sighed. "After the way she reamed my ass, I didn't have the heart to say no."

"But don't you think that's going to be a little overwhelming for Elizabeth?"

"I don't know. The magic stuff isn't getting to her as much. We just have to show her Vegas shows over the next couple of weeks. She does pretty good when she knows what's coming."

"You've got a point." Robin looked at him again. "I'm guessing Mom was not happy."

Dean rolled his eyes. "No shit."

"I'm surprised she hasn't called to blame everything on me," Robin said as her phone played the Imperial March from Star Wars. "And there she is."

She briefly debated sending the call to voice mail but knew that would not deter her mother.

"Hey, Mom," Robin said, once she swiped the call on. "I know why you're calling."

"Why, in Heaven's name, are you encouraging this?" Marlene demanded.

Robin winced. "Aside from the fact that I've gotten to know Elizabeth and you haven't, I'm also aware that Dean is an adult and capable of making his own decisions."

She hoped she sounded as confident as when she'd rehearsed that response.

Marlene paused. "This is going to ruin his life."

"How? Dean's happy. Elizabeth is happy. The baby is adorable. Yeah, it might make some things harder. But Dean's totally stepping up and, frankly, I'm proud of him."

Dean looked at her, surprised.

"Really?" he mouthed silently.

Robin nodded.

"But his education. This will completely disrupt that. He'll have to work and support a baby."

"So? He's still going back to school. If he can't go full time, he can't go full time. Mom, this isn't the end of the world. In many ways, it's a good thing. Like I said, you haven't met Elizabeth. You know nothing about her. You're just assuming the worst."

Marlene sounded hurt. "How can you say that? I would never do that to Dean."

"Then why did you call me?"

"Well, somebody has to talk some sense into him. For heaven's sakes, why didn't the silly girl get an abortion?"

"Let's not even go there. Seriously, Mom." Robin sighed. "Look, I get that it's not the optimal situation. But like I said, Dean's stepping up and making the best of it. The least we can do is be supportive."

"I'm always supportive, Robin," Marlene said huffily. "I don't know why you keep saying I'm not."

Robin decided not to give her mother a list, especially since Marlene could be supportive – if she was getting her way. The trick would be to make her think she was, which, as Robin thought about it, probably explained why Dean had agreed to the trip to Las Vegas. He'd always been better at managing their mother's more controlling tendencies.

"In any case," Marlene continued. "I'll make the reservations for all of us."

"Someplace quiet," Robin said.

"It will be perfectly acceptable," Marlene said. "Will you see to it that Dean gets the license?"

"Of course, Mom." Robin pressed her lips together.

"I'll get you tickets out of John Wayne Airport."

"We'll drive," Robin said quickly.

"Oh, don't be ridiculous."

"It's not. By the time we get to the airport, wait to go through the security checkpoint, then wait for the flight, we could be almost there. And we'll have a car with us, so we won't need to rent one."

"I suppose that makes sense. I'll let you know which hotel we'll be in. Do you mind sharing with this girl until after the wedding?"

"That sounds good. And her name is Elizabeth. The baby is Robbie." Robin debated calling her mother Grandma, but decided that would not go over well.

She hung up a minute later and looked at her brother.

"Okay. Points to you on Vegas," Robin sighed.

"What do you mean?"

Robin shrugged. "Typical Mom. She can't have what she wants, so she's taking over as much as she can. At least, I talked her out of flying us there. She even wanted us to fly out of Orange County when I'm way closer to Burbank."

"Flying?" asked Elizabeth, who had wandered in. She'd strapped Robbie into the baby's carry cradle.

"In an airplane," Dean said. "We've showed you those."

Elizabeth shuddered. "I suppose, but…" She took a deep breath. "Oh, dear. You keep telling me to say what I'm thinking and I'm thinking I'm not ready for that."

Dean pulled her into his arms. "I'm glad you said so. And we won't do that to you."

"No way," said Robin. "And it's good you spoke up. It really is. But where we're going for the wedding isn't going to be easy for you to handle. It's very noisy and crowded. We'll stay with you, and you'll be fine."

Elizabeth nodded. Dean took Elizabeth into the kitchen to help with dinner. Robin went back to her email and then chose to get some work done on a project before her guest arrived.

Yvonne Trask was a generously proportioned African American woman of medium height, blonde hair, and medium-brown skin. She was technically one of Robin's employees, but the two had been friendly for several years. Yvonne mostly worked from home since she was the mother of a three-year-old boy and newly pregnant.

"Now, you're sure you're okay with me working at home for another four years," Yvonne asked Robin as Robin admitted her into the living room.

"I'm working from home, and I don't even have a kid," Robin said. She looked back at the dining room. "I'm just glad you could come over. It's been really hard for Elizabeth, coming from that super-sheltered background."

"Some sort of cult, was it?"

"Something like that. She doesn't really like talking about it and you can hardly blame her."

"Sounds like a pretty tough lady to me." Yvonne smiled.

"Yeah."

Dinner passed pleasantly. Dean took over the last-minute preparations so Elizabeth could show Robbie off to Yvonne. Elizabeth and Yvonne bonded quickly over baby talk and showing photos of their infants to each other on their respective phones. Robin couldn't help being thankful that Elizabeth had gotten over her belief that video images were elves and had embraced her mobile phone and texting, and especially the camera.

The next day, Dean left early and returned before noon, jubilant. He pulled Robin from her little desk in the dining room alcove and took her into the kitchen, where Elizabeth was sweeping the floor.

"I've got a job!" he announced.

"Congratulations!" Robin said.

"Oh, good!" Elizabeth said, then giggled as Dean swept her up and spun her.

"It's an internship at one of the local drug abuse clinics," Dean said. "I can work around my school schedule. And it's not a lot of money, but I can pay my school fees and books and most of my bills." He stopped and sighed. "Rent's going to be a problem, though." He suddenly brightened. "But I can kick in for food and maybe a little rent here."

Robin smiled. He had written up the requested exit plan, and she'd thought it was a good one. But it was still going to take some time.

"How about you save that money for the time being?" she suggested. "At least, the rent part of it." She found herself blinking back tears. "Looks like you're on your way."

"I guess I am." Dean squeezed Elizabeth once more.

Robin left the kitchen quickly, her emotions clashing within her. There was a bit of mistiness in seeing Dean grow up so fast. As much as his immaturity had annoyed her, she'd also felt a sense of purpose in taking care of him and Elizabeth. But the more settled he and Elizabeth were, the sooner Robin could leave for Roger's time, and that she wanted to do more than anything else. He'd told her things would be bad when she got there, and she couldn't help but wonder how bad they were. Still, the allure of a future time held her imagination in thrall.

But first, Robin had promised Roger that she would see to it that Dean and Elizabeth were well settled in before she left. What that meant, Roger apparently had expected her to know. So, Robin went over to her desk, pulled out her journal, and flipped to the page where she'd written out her own private list of figurative milestone markers.

Dean needed to be in school and employed. While Robin was fairly sure she'd be back and back soon enough that she wouldn't have to worry about Dean's finances, she didn't want to leave it to chance. She'd set up a joint bank account with Dean and Elizabeth and had already arranged for monthly automatic deposits to it for all the household expenses and then some and set up as many bills as she could on auto pay. Between her interests in her business and some other investments she'd made, she was confident Dean and Elizabeth could manage for a year or two if she didn't come back. And now that Dean had a job, she was even more confident they'd be okay money-wise.

But there was also getting Elizabeth acclimated enough to their time so that she wasn't dependent on Robin to smooth the way for her. Dean could deal with her fears. Robin had taken charge of her education. Fortunately, Elizabeth started out being able to read a little and do some math. In addition, she learned quickly. But there were four hundred years of culture and history that she'd missed out on.

Robin looked at all the home-schooling materials she'd bought. Elizabeth was reading at a fourth-grade level and doing fifth-grade math. Robin figured if she could get Elizabeth through the sixth grade, then she could manage most things she'd encounter. Given that when they'd started, Elizabeth could barely manage second grade work, they'd come a long way in a very short time. If Robin could keep Elizabeth curious, then she picked things up quite naturally. The problem was the drilling necessary to make reading, math and other subjects stick in her memory.

The next morning, Elizabeth frowned at the sheet of word problems that Robin had given her to solve.

"These are stupid," Elizabeth grumbled. "Why should I care how many miles some boy can pedal his bicycle?"

"It's not so much that, Elizabeth, as being able to look at a problem and figure out what math formulas will solve it," Robin explained. "That's partly what you have to do when you want to figure how many potatoes you need for dinner. And it takes a lot of practice to do word problems well. So that when you need to figure something out, it comes easily."

Elizabeth sniffed. "This is boring."

"I know. I'd let you skip ahead, but the last time we did that, you were stumped by the test."

Elizabeth sighed and went to work. She kept at it long enough to finish the page of problems, but when Robin handed her a geography sheet to work on, she balked.

"Why do I need to know the capitals of the states?" she asked.

Robin saw the tension behind Elizabeth's petulance.

"Because these are things everyone knows," Robin said.

"And how many of these can you name?"

Robin suddenly realized she couldn't. "Yes, I look these things up more than I memorize them nowadays. But I learned them at one point. It's like I explained with the addition. Yes, a calculator is faster, but you get a better sense of how the numbers go together if you do some of the adding in your head. If you were in school in England, they'd expect you to memorize all the different shires, even if there was no chance in hell you would leave yours. There are certain things that everyone knows, that we assume everyone knows, so that when we talk to each other, we're all talking about the same things."

Elizabeth snorted, then took a deep breath. "You keep saying I should say what I'm thinking. And I think I don't really need to know this nonsense. I can run this household better than you can and I don't know any state capitals. I don't need to know that chlorophyll makes plants green to take care of my baby."

"But you need to get through the sixth grade," Robin groaned, her heart sinking into her belly. She couldn't tell Elizabeth that she needed the young woman to be that far along in her education so that Robin could leave again.

"Elizabeth has a point, you know," said Dean, coming into the dining room where the two had been working.

Robin sank back, defeated. "I know, Dean." She looked at Elizabeth and sighed. "I don't want people to think something's wrong with you because you don't know things that most people have, at least, been taught. Even if they've forgotten that Carson City is the capital of Nevada, at some point they learned that. And who knows, Elizabeth? You're really smart. You may decide you want to do something besides caring for the house and Robbie. You may decide you want to become a midwife or a historian or something else, and while knowing chlorophyll is what makes plants green doesn't make all that much difference when you're studying computer science, it is the start of understanding how science works."

Elizabeth sighed. "But it's all so much. And some of it's so boring and repetitive."

"I know," Robin grumbled. "I had the same problem when I was a kid. But doing the work helped me in the long run. We just need to get you through sixth grade by Labor Day."

"Why sixth grade and why Labor Day?" Dean asked.

Robin suddenly thought of a very good reason. "Mom."

Elizabeth looked at the two of them, then shook her head and focused on the geography worksheet.

"What? You think Mom's going to quiz Elizabeth to see how much education she has?" Dean snorted.

Robin rolled her eyes. "No. But she's got enough issues with you two getting married so young and the baby and all. A sixth-grade education will put Elizabeth on a par with most people in our culture."

"That's assuming most people in our culture remember what they learned in sixth-grade," Dean said. "Wasn't there a TV show making fun of that?"

"Are you saying she doesn't need to learn this stuff?"

Dean glared at his sister. "Of course, she probably needs to learn it. I'm just saying you don't need to be pushing her so hard. You're talking two years of elementary school in two weeks. That's asking a lot, Robin."

"She knows a lot already," Robin grumbled.

"Then you don't need to push so hard."

Robin debated asking Elizabeth whether she thought she was being pushed, but already knew the answer to that one. Worse yet, Dean had a point. It really wasn't fair to push Elizabeth so hard just because Robin wanted to be elsewhere. Or elsewhen. Especially since Robin knew it wasn't going to change anything for Roger. It didn't matter when she left her time. She would land more or less when Roger wanted her to.

Chapter Three

Elizabeth giggled and then pressed a button on her mobile phone.

"Here, Robin, look," she said, swiping, then showing the phone to Robin.

Robin chuckled at yet another video of baby Robbie cooing and gurgling. Because Elizabeth had been pregnant the last time she'd traveled through time, Robbie had developed faster physically, and most people believed the baby was three months old, as her parents and aunt claimed. But in terms of other developmental standards, Robbie was more like the two-month-old she was, even if she was catching up. She was focusing on objects and swatting at them but couldn't quite lift her head yet. In the video, the baby had a firm grip on her mother's finger.

"That's sweet," Robin said.

"I know it's perfectly normal," Elizabeth put the phone down on the dresser in her bedroom and picked up a brush. "But I still find it so amazing that we can have pictures and moving pictures of ourselves. My father would have been so happy to have a picture of my mother."

The young woman began brushing her hair with vigor.

"I know." Robin gazed thoughtfully at Elizabeth. "Do you miss your family?"

Elizabeth shrugged. "I never knew my mother. She died in childbirth with me, and I sometimes think my father resented me for it. He loved my mother very much. My stepmother and my brothers and sisters were kind enough but thought me odd." She put down her brush and tied on a bandana over her hair. "That's what I do like about being here. At home, when people thought me odd, they became afraid of me. I suspect I would have ended up hung as a witch. Here, I'm just odd and no one thinks anything of it. Do I look alright?"

Elizabeth twirled, thankful that she'd let Yvonne take her out shopping. The two had found some clothes that were closer to modern styles than what Elizabeth had been wearing and still modest enough. Elizabeth now wore a dress that was gaily patterned, and while the hem still hovered near her calves and she still wore tights, the sleeves bared all but her upper arms. She still wore a bandana, but her long, curly hair hung loose down her back. Elizabeth was getting used to more and more of her body showing than she would ever have shown in the past. In addition, fewer layers of clothes were a lot more comfortable.

Robin grinned. "You look great."

"Good." Elizabeth grabbed a fresh diaper from the pile and sucked on the corner before wiping off the baby's face. "You be good for Aunt Robin, now. I'll only be gone a few hours."

That evening was part of Dean's plan to help her get herself together enough for Las Vegas. Elizabeth couldn't help wondering how bad it could be if the noisy bars that Dean had dragged her to were still not the same. Dean and his buddy Alex were taking Elizabeth and Alex's girlfriend, Diane, on a double date to see the latest superhero movie that everyone was talking about.

The two couples met at a restaurant near the movie theater. The room was noisy, but not so bad that Dean and Alex couldn't talk. Alex was just shorter than Dean, with bleached brown hair, tan skin, and broad shoulders. Diane, his girlfriend, was so exceedingly thin Elizabeth had to stop herself from asking after the girl's health. Diane had glossy, thick black hair in a braid she wore over one shoulder. She smiled easily enough when either Dean or Alex spoke to her, but her pretty face turned sullen whenever the guys weren't paying attention to her.

"Do you go to school?" Elizabeth asked her as Dean and Alex talked about something called football.

"I'm done," Diane said shortly, then pulled out her phone.

The waiter brought their food, placing a small salad in front of Diane and chicken strips and fries in front of Elizabeth. Alex was tucking into a veggie burger and trying to look happy, while Dean had opted for a real hamburger.

"If you've ever seen a chicken killed, you would not want to eat those," Diane said.

"I've killed and dressed many chickens," Elizabeth said, then glanced at Dean.

Dean nodded, smiling. "It's that rural background of hers."

Alex laughed, but Diane rolled her eyes. Elizabeth watched as Diane picked at her salad. The naked lettuce leaves did not look at all appetizing. Elizabeth had been reading enough to know that vegetables were considered healthy, and Robin had given her several science worksheets recently that explained why and why Elizabeth had been gaining so much weight since she'd come to the Twenty-First Century.

Elizabeth ran through all the questions Robin had coached her on so that she could start a conversation.

"What do you do?" Elizabeth asked Diane.

"I'm a receptionist now," Diane said. "But I'm actually a model. I'm between agencies right now."

"That sounds very interesting," said Elizabeth, who had no idea what Diane was talking about and was hoping she'd say more.

Diane shrugged, then looked down as her phone chimed. She immediately began texting a reply, then continued focusing on the phone.

Elizabeth glanced over at Dean. Dean quickly looked at her, then at Diane.

"So, Diane, who are you listening to these days?" Dean asked.

Elizabeth didn't hear Diane's answer, but Diane began smiling as she described how gorgeous this person was.

Later, after the two had returned home, Dean offered a glowing report on Elizabeth's performance.

"Honestly, Robin, she was more on top of it than Alex's girlfriend," Dean chortled.

Elizabeth looked a little bewildered. "I only asked was what the music was like. All she talked about was how the musician looked."

"Exactly," said Dean. "That's all she cared about."

"Which I still do not understand," said Elizabeth with a sniff. "She texted all through dinner. Didn't you tell me, Robin, that was terribly rude?"

"I most certainly did, and it is rude." Robin sighed. "But you're going to find, Elizabeth, that a lot of people are terribly rude."

Dean laughed. "But the best part was that Diane was going to go into her big lecture on how gross it is to eat animals, but Elizabeth totally shut her down."

"What do you mean?" Elizabeth asked Dean. "Why wouldn't people eat animals? Food is food."

"Diane is a vegetarian," Robin explained.

"She's a vegan," Dean said. "She's even got poor Alex eating vegan around her."

"Vegan?" asked Elizabeth.

"No animal products whatsoever," Robin explained. "Even things like eggs, milk, and cheese."

Elizabeth frowned. "But, Dean, didn't she say something about her handbag being real leather?"

That really set Dean off laughing. "Yeah, I know. Telling us how animals are our friends and don't deserve to be enslaved, then bragging that her purse is real leather, not the evil petroleum-based vinyl."

Elizabeth laughed, too. "Oh, dear. I thought I had misunderstood something. I'm so glad to know she really wasn't making sense."

"See, Robin?" Dean said. "Elizabeth totally has this down."

"She does," Robin said, smiling.

Elizabeth spotted the longing in Robin's eyes. She'd seen it several times during the past six weeks, usually when Robin was pushing Elizabeth to learn something, and Elizabeth wanted to know why. There was something Robin wasn't telling them, but Elizabeth strongly suspected it had to do with the time machine that Robin still had. Robin had hidden the machine, but Elizabeth had found it in Robin's bedroom while cleaning and had told Dean the machine was still there.

Neither of them wanted to say anything to Robin, but Elizabeth couldn't help being both worried that Robin would leave soon and wishing that she'd simply go ahead and go when she wanted to be. It was clear Robin was only staying for Elizabeth's and Dean's sakes.

"Anyway," Dean continued. "I think we're ready for Vegas."

"Nobody's ready for Vegas," Robin said, chuckling. "But we're as ready as we can get. How about we leave on Thursday? That will give us an extra day to get acclimated and find out what we need regarding getting the marriage license and any other paperwork."

"Sounds good," said Dean. His phone buzzed with a text message. He sighed. "Mom wants to know what colors the bridal party are wearing."

Robin frowned. Their mother was texting Dean because the week before Robin had told their mother that she would not answer any wedding-related questions. It was not her wedding and Robin had given Marlene Elizabeth's phone number. So far, Marlene had refused to text Elizabeth.

"Bridal party?" Elizabeth asked. "I have no maids to attend me. And why would it matter what colors they wore, even if I had them?"

Robin snorted. "An ill-used custom of our time that is finally starting to fall apart. Usually, you have your women friends and closest relatives stand up with you, and they all dress in identical poofy, ugly dresses. We're not doing that."

Elizabeth sighed in relief. Given that the wedding was rapidly turning into a much larger event than any of the three had envisioned, Elizabeth had invited Yvonne and her family. But they couldn't make it and Elizabeth was secretly glad.

"So, we put our foot down?" Dean asked.

"Yep. Oh, wait," Robin said. "I know what she's really asking. She wants to know what to wear."

Elizabeth perked up. Picking out what to wear was something else that was very new to her and often overwhelming. In her time, she'd only had two dresses, one for work and one for Sundays and holidays. Only royalty had as many clothes as Elizabeth had in Robin and Dean's time, and both Robin and Dean had repeatedly reminded her they were not even that wealthy, let alone royal. The worst part of all the clothes, though, was deciding what to wear each day. At least, even Robin's mother had the same problem.

"Why should we care?" Dean asked.

"Tell her it's going to be very casual, and she should wear what she likes," Robin said.

Dean texted, and a minute later the phone buzzed again. "She says we can't go casual at the wedding chapel."

Robin rolled her eyes. They'd let it go when their mother had somehow booked a Saturday afternoon wedding at one of the fanciest wedding chapels in the city. But they'd also had to hold firm against inviting a host of friends and acquaintances, hiring a band for the dinner after, and various other wedding traditions. Apparently, their mother still wasn't happy about there not being a full wedding party.

"Dressy casual then," said Robin. "And we can always go to the county courthouse."

Dean chuckled evilly. "That always gets her."

"Just us and the preacher," said Robin.

Dean looked up guiltily. "I did invite Alex and Diane. Before we went out to dinner. They said they were coming."

Robin shrugged. "Can't be helped."

Like Elizabeth, Robin was feeling somewhat apprehensive about the trip as she finished packing that Thursday morning. It wasn't so much the getting married part of the adventure. Robin knew Dean and Elizabeth were perfectly happy about getting married. But Elizabeth was, understandably, nervous about meeting her almost mother-in-law and Robin was wondering how she was going to keep her mother in check.

Dean seemed committed to letting it all roll off his back, and as they put the bags into the trunk of Robin's small, black BMW sedan, Robin decided to try to emulate her brother's attitude.

Elizabeth sat in the back seat with Robbie in her car seat. Dean sat in the passenger seat. He'd offered to drive, but Robin overruled him. As they got on the freeway, Robin checked the rear-view mirror and tried not to sigh. Elizabeth was a lot better about riding in the car, but she still did not like the high speeds of the freeways. The young woman smiled, but Robin saw her shoulders hunched and the squint of fear in her eyes. It was going to be a long five hours.

It was a long six hours, as they had to stop every two hours or so because the baby demanded to be fed and Robin would not let Elizabeth take her out of the car seat while the car was moving. Still, they made it into Las Vegas by late afternoon, as Robin had planned.

Elizabeth did not seem phased by all the architecture. But then it occurred to Robin that since Elizabeth had never seen either Paris or New York or Egypt or even a fairy-tale castle, it wouldn't occur to her that the hotels based on such things were in any way unusual. In short, the Las Vegas strip, at least by day, was no stranger to Elizabeth than anything else in the Twenty-First Century.

They checked in at the premium hotel where Marlene had made reservations. Robin had already called the hotel and arranged for the three to check into Robin's room a day early. Elizabeth had seemed somewhat more relaxed as the trip had gone on and was visibly curious and interested as they pulled up at the hotel.

The casino undid everything.

"It's so dark and noisy," Elizabeth sighed as they got settled in the room. "And it smells very bad."

"It's the cigarette smoke," Dean said. He looked at Robin.

"It used to be worse," Robin said. "But, yeah, this is one of the few places left in the country where people can pretty much light up when they want."

Elizabeth shook her head. "It's even worse than some of the salons in Bath."

Robin looked at her. Back in Eighteenth Century Bath, England, women did not go where men smoked.

"How would you know?" Dean asked.

"We'd visit during the day after the men had been smoking in there the night before," Elizabeth said. "I still do not understand the attraction of tobacco."

"Neither do we," Robin said. She checked her watch. "Why don't we walk around for a while?"

They made it out to the street without lingering in the casinos. Robin was a little tempted to do some gambling. However, Elizabeth was not quite old enough and didn't seem interested, anyway. Besides, gambling with a baby strapped to her chest was not going to happen.

The weather outside was very warm and dry, and the streets were filled with people. Dean kept a tight grip on Elizabeth as they wandered down the strip. Robin walked behind the little family, painfully aware of every time Elizabeth winced at something. The periodic blasts of music from open doorways were bad enough. But the hucksters were out in force, pushing coupons on everyone within reach. Dean kept pushing the bits of paper away. But Robin could see Elizabeth holding Robbie close and edging away each time.

"It's coming on for dinner time," Dean called back to Robin. "Any idea where you want to eat?"

"The first buffet that looks good," Robin said. "Maybe one where we can get some good beer."

The buffet almost flummoxed Elizabeth, but she was also quite pleased.

"Remember to pace yourself," Robin warned.

Elizabeth filled her plate with roast beef, turkey, pork chop, and chicken. Unfortunately, she could not have any beer because she'd gotten carded as they entered the buffet.

"It's a ridiculous law," she sniffed, as they settled down at a table. "I've been drinking ale since I was a child."

"We know, Elizabeth," Dean said. "But too many kids in our time were getting into trouble. So, they made the law. You'll be officially twenty-one soon enough."

It was a pleasant meal, although the three left the table feeling very over-stuffed. As they left the buffet, a man in a tuxedo stopped Elizabeth. He must have had a hidden microphone on him, Robin decided, because his voice was amplified by some sort of cheap speaker nearby.

"And looky what we have here," the tinny voice called out over the beeping and ringing of the slot machines. "A little mother! Hello, little mother. Now, watch the birdie." He held up a small yellow plush bird and a second later, it had disappeared.

Elizabeth gasped in terror.

"But look, here it is," said the man, reaching behind Elizabeth's ear. "Hiding right there."

Elizabeth tried to draw back, but the man whipped out a fistful of playing cards and demanded that she pick one.

"No!" she snapped and edged backward into the crowd that had gathered.

Dean saw her move off, but he and Robin were blocked by the people.

"Which way did she go?" Robin asked, over the shriek of a slot machine signaling a major pay-off.

"There!" Dean ran off.

Robin was able to follow only because she could see the top of his head over the crowd. Frantic to keep one eye on her brother as she searched for Elizabeth, and unable to use voice commands in the noise, Robin decided not to pull out her phone. Her watch hadn't vibrated, so Robin was fairly sure she hadn't gotten a call.

Then Dean suddenly stopped, and Robin almost ran into him. He had pulled out his phone and was listening, then shook his head.

"It went straight to voice mail," he said. "She probably forgot to charge it again."

"Oh, crap," Robin said. "And I forgot to remind her to hook it up while we were in the car."

"I still can't believe she took to it so easily," Dean said. He looked around. "Now what?"

"Go back to the buffet and keep looking, I guess."

As Elizabeth ran through the crowd, she decided she did not like Las Vegas even one little bit. The buffet, with its vast array of different foods, had been wondrous. But so many people had tried to talk to her and pushed bits of paper at her. And the noise and smell of tobacco smoke were most unpleasant. Then that horrible magician. Robin swore there was no such thing as magic, but Robin had been wrong. And that horrible box that had shrieked so loudly when she backed into it. The old woman sitting in front of the box had screamed also, first cursing Elizabeth, then screaming something else.

Her heart pounding with fear, Elizabeth ran through the dimly lit cavern of a room. With all the lovely bright bulbs this time had, why would anybody keep everything so dark? It was impossible to find one's way, either. Every time Elizabeth spotted what she thought was a landmark, it turned out to be something that looked like the buffet line, or a stand of trees, or something else, but wasn't quite right. She had slowed to a walk, but was completely lost, and Dean and Robin weren't anywhere to be found.

Robbie, sensing her mother's fears, had started crying, too. Elizabeth pulled her phone from her dress pocket and almost burst into tears. She'd forgotten to feed it again, and the screen was dark.

Suddenly, through a gap in the rows of lit-up boxes, Elizabeth spied daylight. She hurried through, hoping that she'd recognize the street outside. It was the first bit of good fortune she'd had. She looked around. Still no Dean or Robin. But she had the card that opened the door in the inn. And there was a wire there that would feed her phone. And the street was the same they'd taken to get to the casino.

The sky was growing dark, but lights of all colors were turned on everywhere. Why would they light up the outside and not light up the insides of the buildings? Fortunately, it didn't take long to hurry back up the street to the huge inn where they were staying. Robbie settled and fell asleep, too, which helped.

Elizabeth found their room, glad she'd thought to memorize the path there when they'd arrived that afternoon. She'd gotten lost at the nearby farmer's market not long after she'd come to this new time and had made a practice of memorizing any landmarks so that it would not happen again. It hadn't helped in the casino, where everything looked alike. She shuddered at the memory and inserted the card in the door as she'd seen Robin do. The tiny light flashed green, and Elizabeth opened the door.

The silence felt like grace as it enveloped her. The room was empty. Elizabeth found the wire for her phone and plugged it into a socket next to a lamp. A few minutes later, the phone was alive enough that she could call Dean. But the phone only rang and went to voice mail. Elizabeth left a message. She tried calling Robin, but that went straight to voice mail, which meant that Robin's phone was turned off or not working.

She tried calling Dean again, but he didn't answer his phone. If Robin's phone wasn't working, then there was no point in calling her. She paced the room for several minutes, trying to get a grip on her fear. Robbie squawked, so Elizabeth settled onto a chair and began nursing. Hoping to find something to distract her so she could stay calm, she turned on the television and put the sound on low.

There was a magician talking about how he did his tricks. Elizabeth watched, fascinated. So, it was all about fooling the eyes rather than demonic power. Elizabeth tried calling Dean again and was not happy when he still didn't answer. She tried Robin's phone and, finally, got an answer.

"Where are you?" Robin asked.

"At the inn. In our room," Elizabeth said. "Why didn't Dean answer his phone?"

"He probably didn't hear it ringing," Robin said, then mumbled something to someone.

"Elizabeth, are you okay?" Dean's voice cracked with fear.

"I'm here in the inn. Why didn't you answer your phone?"

"Yours was dead. Why didn't you call Robin?"

"I did. It went straight to voice mail, so I knew it wasn't working."

"Shit." Dean groaned. "Look, we're on our way there now."

They arrived in the room quickly. But it had taken long enough for Elizabeth's anger to grow and ferment.

"Why didn't you answer your phone?" she demanded of Dean as he got into the room.

"Because yours was dead! Same reason you didn't keep calling Robin," Dean groaned.

"But I did try Robin again and you could have kept checking. You tell me to."

"Then why didn't you?"

"I did! I was calling you! I left messages!"

"Hold on!" Robin yelled.

Elizabeth glared at her. "No! I was left alone, and it was terrible!"

"And you got through it," said Dean calmly.

Elizabeth made a face at him, not feeling entirely mollified. However, he was right. She had gotten through it. And had learned something.

"Maybe we ought to go home," Robin said, with a worried frown on her face. "Clearly, this is all a bit much for Elizabeth."

"I can handle it," Elizabeth said staunchly. "I will not be ruled by my fears!"

Robin backed away. "Okay."

Dean chuckled and slipped his arm around her. "That's my brave darling."

"Well, maybe we can do this in short chunks of time," Robin said. "Go out, then come back for a bit. Go out, then come back for a bit." She looked at Elizabeth. "Would that help?"

She nodded. "It also helped to know that magic isn't really magic."

"I thought we covered that," Robin said with a frown.

"Nope. We focused on Elvises," Dean said.

Elizabeth couldn't help chuckling. She had found nothing that strange about all the people dressed up as some long-dead bard. The problem was that even though she'd seen any number of programs on Robin's television, real life was so different when you couldn't turn the sound up or down and real people were trying to talk to you. She shuddered a little, then smiled as she gathered what she'd need to go out again.

Dean was feeling somewhat more relaxed that next morning. They'd done three more walk-arounds the night before, each one lasting a little longer, until Elizabeth was even eager to see a midnight show. Robin had stayed behind in the room with the baby for that one. That morning, as they went to breakfast, Dean got an idea as he passed the sports book section of the casino and came out with a big grin and a newspaper.

"It's the only way Elizabeth can gamble," he explained, holding up the racing form newspaper, as they waited in line at the marriage license bureau. "And Ralphie took me to the horse track for my twenty-first birthday last spring and showed me how to pick horses."

Robin rolled her eyes as Dean chuckled. Cousin Ralphie was a notorious party animal and while he and Robin generally got along, largely based on their interest in technology, the two had little in common philosophically. Dean braced himself for another protest from his sister, but she dutifully pulled up a website on how to read a racing form on her phone.

Robin was getting better about trusting him, he'd noticed. It was probably hard for her to give up playing the caretaker since she'd been doing it all her life. Inwardly, Dean winced, wondering if their mother ever would. He turned to the racing form, happy to see that Elizabeth had grasped the concept of looking for the signs that a horse would do well.

"Bet you want your time machine now," Dean teased Robin under his breath as Elizabeth considered first one horse, then the other.

Robin rolled her eyes again, looked like she was about to snarl, then suddenly laughed.

"I suppose it would be fun," she said. "But that's not what I'd use it for. Besides. It would take all the excitement out of gambling."

Marriage license finally gotten and sworn to, the three headed back to the hotel and returned to their room to put the license away safely. With another couple hours before they had to meet their mother for lunch, Dean decided to get their bets placed. Leaving Robin and Elizabeth to stroll the hotel's mall, Dean went back to the sports book section. It was off to the side of the casino and surrounded by a rail. In the middle, rows of narrow tables were lined up in front of plush chairs that rotated and reclined to make it easier to watch the array of large screen televisions on the walls above a row of teller windows. As Dean made for one of the windows, he saw a man with reddish-brown hair at the next window over. The man looked oddly familiar, but very out of place.

Dean placed the bets trying to watch the man next to him as the man first collected a significant pile of hundred-dollar bills, then spent several of them on some new bets. The man looked around and saw Dean looking at him. The man glared at Dean and Dean knew for certain that he'd seen the mysterious person before.

"Here are your tickets," the clerk behind Dean's window said, handing him the small slips of paper.

"Uh, thanks," Dean grabbed the tickets and turned.

But as he turned, the man at the next window turned also and the two collided.

"Sorry," grumbled the man as he turned and left.

"But—"

Dean's chest tightened as he finally realized that the last time he'd seen the mysterious man, they'd been in Bath, England, the man's hair had been powdered and curled, he'd been wearing a cutaway coat with very wide buttoned lapels and knee breeches, and he'd been holding a flintlock pistol on Elizabeth.

Chapter Four

"His name is Donald Long," Robin said, yet again.

She, Dean and Elizabeth were headed to the restaurant where they were going to meet Marlene. Elizabeth had Robbie strapped in her sling.

"And there's no reason not to believe he couldn't have tracked us here," Robin continued. "You guys just got a marriage license. That's a public record. I could have tracked it down on Google. You have to figure Donald has even better search capability."

"But it still doesn't explain why he didn't recognize me," said Dean.

"And in Bath, Elizabeth was still pregnant, and he referred to her daughter," Robin said. She watched as Elizabeth pulled the baby closer to her. "I didn't think anything of it then, but he knew what gender the baby was, and we certainly didn't."

"That's true," said Elizabeth. "But what does it mean?"

Robin sighed as she saw her mother glaring at her iPhone near the entrance to the restaurant.

"I have no idea," Robin said, then pointed. "In the meantime, let's get through lunch."

Marlene Westmore was a medium-tall woman with dark blonde hair cut short and tousled artfully. Her figure was very slender and of the sort that meant desperate privation to Elizabeth. However, to the rest of the Twenty-First Century, everything about Marlene screamed confidence and money, from her natural look make-up to her very tasteful combination of cotton knit dress and elegant flat sandals. For jewelry, she had limited herself to diamond ear studs and a fine gold chain necklace with a tiny pendant that dangled between where her collar bones poked up through the lightly tanned skin above her sternum.

She looked up and smiled as she saw the three of them approach. Robin took a deep breath and held back as Dean presented Elizabeth.

"Nice to meet you, Elizabeth," Marlene said with a cool smile, which grew significantly warmer when she addressed Dean. "And how are you, darling?"

She reached over and gave Dean a kiss on the cheek.

"Fine, Mom," Dean said jovially. "Excited about getting married."

Robin choked back a laugh. For all Dean was sincere, he hadn't resisted tweaking their mother. Marlene glared at Elizabeth briefly, then turned her attention on Robin.

"And how are you, dear?" she asked, kissing Robin's cheek.

"Pretty good," said Robin. "How are you?"

Robin was not surprised when her mother ignored the baby. So, Marlene was not quite ready to embrace being a grandmother.

"Quite well," said Marlene. She smiled again. "Apart from all the chaos, of course. And I have news of my own. But let's get seated first."

She signaled the restaurant hostess, and in a few minutes, they were settled at a table and perusing the menu. As they ordered, Robin could see Marlene sizing up Elizabeth. The older woman lifted her eyebrows a touch when Elizabeth ordered a steak for lunch. Marlene had ordered a small salad for herself, along with a glass of the house chardonnay.

After they had ordered, Robin noticed Dean looking meaningfully at their mother.

Marlene cleared her throat. "So, Elizabeth, you've chosen to use a sling to carry your baby. Does this mean you're practicing attachment parenting?"

Elizabeth looked over at Dean.

"Those ladies at church," Dean said.

Elizabeth gasped. "No! It's utterly ridiculous. You must put the baby down sometime. How can you get any work done otherwise?"

Robin smiled as Marlene's eyebrows rose in surprise.

Lunch arrived shortly after, and Marlene kept the discussion focused on people Dean knew, apparently hoping to remind him of all the fun times he'd miss by being tied down so soon. Robin smiled to herself. Over the past two weeks, Dean had been complaining about how shallow his friends were and had even confessed two days before that he'd known it all along and was trying to cultivate other friends and simply hadn't yet.

"You said you had news," Robin said as they finished.

Marlene's smile became broad and genuine. "Yes. I hope you two find this as happy as I do, but there's a man in my life. We met in Costa Rica."

"Speaking of, weren't you supposed to still be there?" Robin asked.

Marlene had left for a working vacation right around the time Robin and Dean had left for their aborted trip to Europe.

"And miss the wedding?" Marlene asked. "How could I? And my guy was perfectly sweet about cutting short his trip to join us."

"Why isn't he here now?" Robin said.

"We thought it would be easier if I broke the news to you two first, then let him meet you," Marlene said. "He's so thoughtful."

Robin looked at Dean. He didn't seem terribly shook by the news, nor should he have been. Their mother had always dated, even though she'd seldom introduced her male friends to her children. Elizabeth looked bemused. She knew that Dean and Robin's parents were divorced, and that divorce was a lot more common than in her time. But what that meant hadn't really sunk in for her. Or, at least, Robin was mostly certain it hadn't.

"I said we'd meet him at the sports book." Marlene looked at her phone. "And he just texted that he's there." She chuckled. "He says he likes the odds there better."

Fear suddenly tickled Robin's throat. It didn't seem likely. Her mother had said she'd met her new boyfriend in Costa Rica. But Dean had run into Donald Long at the sports book, and suddenly Dean's joke that morning about wanting her time machine became very unfunny. Worse yet, Robin could see that Dean and Elizabeth were thinking roughly the same thing.

Fortunately, Marlene wanted to use the restroom, so Robin, Dean and Elizabeth huddled quickly together.

"It can't be," Dean groaned. "Didn't Roger say we'd be safe from him?"

Robin thought. "No. He said we wouldn't be running from Donald for the rest of our lives and that we'd be safe in Pasadena. We're not in Pasadena. And we don't know that he's Mom's new boyfriend."

"He did try to marry Miss Deborah to get to us when we were in Bath," Elizabeth said.

"But it doesn't make sense," Dean said. "Why would he go all the way to Costa Rica to get a date with Mom when he wants us?"

"Dean, when you can go anywhere by just thinking about it, all the way to Costa Rica is no big deal," Robin said. "But you're right. Why go through Mom? I can see him tracking us here. And you're sure it was him that you saw?"

"Oh, yeah," Dean said. "It was definitely Neddrick, I mean, Farqhar, I mean, whatever his name is."

"Donald Long and that still doesn't mean he's Mom's new boyfriend," Robin said, trying to convince herself as much as the others. "It's probably just a coincidence. Lots of people like betting on sports."

"Especially if you've got a time machine," Dean grumbled as their mother approached.

Marlene smiled as she joined her children. "Well, are you ready to meet Donald?"

The three looked at each other, but Marlene didn't seem to notice. Sure enough, at the sports book, the man who looked up and smiled at them was Donald Long, looking much cleaner and dressed in an expensive Hawaiian shirt and cargo pants.

He gazed warmly at Marlene, then his eyes fell on Elizabeth, and he nodded. Marlene took his arm and turned to her children.

"Darlings, this is my new beau, Donald Long," she announced. "And, Donald, this is my son Dean, his sister Robin, and Elizabeth."

"Nice to meet you." Donald stepped forward and shook Dean's hand, then took Robin's hand. "So, you're Robin Parker."

"That's me," said Robin coolly.

Donald turned to Elizabeth and nodded. "Good to see you, Elizabeth."

Robin watched the interchanges, trying to make sense of what she was seeing. Donald clearly did not recognize Dean, but he seemed to recognize Elizabeth. Nor did he attempt to shake Elizabeth's hand, which would make sense if he'd known her back in the Seventeenth Century. And he'd acted as if Robin was the person he most wanted to meet.

"Why don't we go up to our room?" Marlene said. "We've got a lot of planning and organizing to do, and it will be quieter there. Dean, have you checked into your room yet?"

"It's too early, isn't it?" Dean asked.

Marlene checked her phone. "It's almost two."

"All right," said Dean. "Come on, Elizabeth. We'll go get our stuff."

"Just one minute, young man," Marlene said. "You're not married yet."

"Mom, let it go," said Robin, and she nodded at Dean, who grabbed Elizabeth's hand and left.

Marlene glanced at Donald, then glared at Robin. "Why don't we talk this over upstairs? Donald, darling, do you mind if Robin and I have a little heart-to-heart privately?"

"Not in the least," Donald said. "I'll be hanging around down here."

Robin debated skipping the heart-to-heart, but decided it would only delay the inevitable. So, she followed her mother upstairs.

Once in her mother's room, Marlene turned on her.

"What the hell is going on here?" Marlene demanded.

Robin almost quailed. "Dean and Elizabeth are getting married."

"And why are you supporting this? He's going to ruin his life!"

"And what makes you so damned sure of that?" Robin's anger filled her.

"He's only twenty-one!"

"And legally an adult for three years," Robin said. "Besides, he grew up a lot this summer. I was there. I know."

"And I'm his mother and I've been around him a lot longer than you. He doesn't know how to cook, how to keep a job."

"He does now, Mom, a job he went out and got on his own." Robin started pacing. "You know, you keep treating him like a baby, doing everything for him, telling him what to do, and then you complain that he's immature. And the worst of it is, you have no idea how he stepped up for Elizabeth this summer."

"How's he going to take care of a baby?"

"He and Elizabeth are doing just fine. She helped raise her siblings, so you might want to give her some credit, too."

Marlene snorted.

Robin's eyebrows rose. "Oh, I get it now. This isn't about Dean getting married too young. This is about Dean making his own choices without letting you in on it."

"I am not that controlling."

"Bullshit!" Robin laughed. "Mom, you are the most controlling person I have ever met. And now that I think about it, you pulled just this sort of temper tantrum when I told you I was going to MIT instead of med school."

"You would have made a great doctor."

"I didn't want to be a doctor! And I still don't."

"Robin, you have got to accept the reality that sometimes Mother really does know best."

"And sometimes you don't. And sometimes you do. But what you don't get, Mom, is that we get to decide. Not you. And if we screw up, we screw up."

"I'm only trying to protect you."

"We get that, Mom. But if you gave us a chance, maybe you'd discover we do pretty damn well on our own."

"I'm a doctor. My job is to assume the worst."

"But not about us. I could use a little optimism. Good lord, Mom, I own and run a growing technology provider that is not only maturing, it's survived a recession. You might give me some credit for what I've achieved instead of complaining that I would have been better off as a doctor."

"I don't do that. I've always been very proud of you."

"You never actually say so. Oh, yeah, once a year in my birthday card, you do. But when I put out that new circuit card last year, did you post about it on Facebook?"

"Nobody would have understood it."

"Aunt Jane didn't, and she still posted about it and shared it with all her friends."

"That's not the issue, Robin. I didn't bring you here so that you can point out all my failings as a parent."

"Well, I'm not here to listen to you point out mine. Or Dean's, for that matter." Robin sighed. "Can't you give him some credit, Mom? Elizabeth is a wonderful person, and she loves Dean dearly. Are they too young? Maybe, maybe not. But they are together, and they are working things out in their own way. You might even like her."

Marlene suddenly sniffed. "I don't want to."

"Why? Because she's stealing your baby boy away?"

"No." Marlene blinked back tears. "I don't want to fall in love with another of Dean's girlfriends only to have him dump her."

"What?" Robin caught herself shrieking and pulled her voice back. "Dean's not going to dump Elizabeth."

"You don't know that." Marlene pressed her lips together.

"And you don't know anything about her."

"I know Dean's track record."

Robin rolled her eyes. "Elizabeth is nothing like those empty-headed ding-a-lings he's dated before."

Marlene winced. "She is and she isn't. She doesn't have much to say."

Robin laughed despite herself. "Wait 'til you get to know her. Trust me, she's got plenty to say. She's probably just deferring to you as her mother-in-law."

"Oh, dear." Marlene sank into a chair. "That's almost worse."

"No!" Robin shook her head and sat down on the bed across from her mother. It was time to tell the story they'd planned. "It's not like that. She was raised in this super-conservative enclave."

"Like a religious cult?"

"Something like that. Anyway, she left them. Voluntarily, and she is very committed to bringing her world view up to date. But you know. It's what Dean calls primary socialization. She sometimes thinks in her old ways. And while she wants to be more modern, I suspect that she's not going to throw all her values out the window just because. She may not have a lot of education yet, but she's got a good head on her shoulders."

"And she left for Dean?"

Robin frowned. "She hadn't left permanently when she met Dean and he was behind her deciding to stay here. They were dating all last summer, and just about a year ago, Elizabeth suddenly broke up with Dean, which really messed him up. Turns out, she'd discovered she was pregnant and went back to her relatives. Then that didn't work out, so she contacted Dean and they got back together. He wasn't sure what he wanted to do about the baby, so he agreed to go to Europe with me. Then Elizabeth had the baby a little early, we came home, and that's pretty much it."

"So, she was the one," Marlene grumbled.

Dean had gone through a nasty break-up the year before, which made the Elizabeth tale more realistic.

"She was confused and didn't know what to do," Robin said.

"And why didn't Dean tell me about this?" Marlene sniffed again.

"He didn't tell me until we got to Europe." Robin looked away, then sighed. "Look, Mom, I know there's no way of knowing for sure whether Dean and Elizabeth will stay together, but they do feel good together, and they both seem very committed for the long haul. And there's Robbie, too. She's a sweet little baby."

Marlene all but groaned. "I can't believe I'm a grandmother." She shuddered. "I'm too young to be a grandma. Do I even look like one?"

Robin smiled. "No. But you will to Robbie, and that's what counts."

"I suppose." Marlene winced.

"If you ask nicely, I'm sure Elizabeth will let you hold her."

"Which is exactly what I'm most afraid of. I almost went into obstetrics, you know."

Robin reached over and put her hand on her mother's. "Mom, it's going to be alright. It won't be easy, but it will be okay."

Marlene sighed, then got up. "There isn't much we can do about it now, anyway. Much though I loathe to admit it, you're right about that much." She went through the large black leather handbag on the room's dresser. "Time to make the best of it. Now, you've gotten the license, correct?"

"Yes, Mother." Robin sat back. "Dean and Elizabeth took care of it this morning. And she has a nice dress. Dean has his sport coat, a tie, and he even thought to bring a shirt that he can wear a tie with."

Marlene made a note on the tablet she'd pulled from the bag. "I'll have to check in with the chapel. I'm assuming non-religious for the ceremony?"

"You'd better ask them."

"I've also made reservations for dinner at the restaurant in the next hotel over. The food's better there, in my opinion."

"Fine." Robin's phone pinged. "That's Dean. Dad just texted him. He's here at the hotel."

"Good," Marlene said neutrally. "We'd better collect Donald and get all the introductions over with."

She put the tablet back in her bag and slung it over her shoulder. Robin got up and followed her mother out of the room.

"About Donald," Robin said as they waited for the elevator. "When did you two meet?"

Marlene smiled warmly. "He came into the clinic where I was helping last month. Claimed he was having heart palpitations. I got him to confess the next night that he'd seen me in the village and wanted to meet me but couldn't think how."

"Hmm. What's he do for a living?"

"International land sales. He was in Costa Rica to broker a deal with one of the coffee growers there. He'd just finished up when Dean called."

"What good timing," Robin said dryly.

Marlene didn't seem to notice, or, Robin suspected, did not want to get into another fight with her. They found Dean and Elizabeth sitting in the Keno Lounge with Robin and Dean's father, Levi Parker. While Dean got his coloring from his mother, he'd gotten his height and full shoulders from his father. Robin, on the other hand, had her father's brown eyes and hair and her mother's more slender frame.

Marlene peeled off to greet Donald, who was walking up from another part of the casino. She gave him a kiss on the cheek, then brought him over to where Robin was hugging her father around baby Robbie, whom Levi was holding. Dean had, apparently, told their father that their mother had a new boyfriend. Levi was more than cour-teous when he and Donald were introduced, but Robin could see the reservation in his eyes.

"We've all had lunch," Marlene announced. "I have to check in with the chapel, but what do we want to do after that?"

"Well, Ralphie just texted," Dean said. "He's all checked in. And Alex and Diane should be here any time now."

"Maybe we ought to find someplace a little quieter," said Robin. She couldn't help looking at Donald. "That way, we can all get to know one another."

"Sounds good to me," said Donald.

It took a bit of walking, but they finally found a small coffee bar tucked away on the far edge of a long walkway of shops and restaurants. Alex and Diana had texted the news of their arrival and Cousin Ralphie was on his way down from his room, as well.

As the group got settled, Levi asked Donald about his business in Costa Rica.

"Nothing special," Donald said. "I had a U.S. client interested in investing in a coffee plantation. So, I found one, and made the offer."

Marlene had sat down next to Elizabeth. "So, are you working anywhere, Elizabeth?"

Elizabeth looked puzzled for a second, then smiled. "No. I'm working at home right now. I take care of Robin and Dean. And the baby, of course."

Robbie chose that moment to squawk.

"May I hold her?" Marlene asked, her face still taut with apprehension.

Elizabeth smiled and liberated the baby from her sling. "Of course."

Robin smiled as Marlene accepted the infant with a practiced hand. Robbie cooed.

"Hey, Mom," said Dean with a proud grin. "She likes you. See? She's smiling."

"Darling, at this age, it's probably gas," Marlene said, obviously pleased nonetheless.

And just to prove it, Robbie promptly spit up. Elizabeth grabbed a diaper from the bottom of the sling. She was about to suck on it when Marlene took it from her and wiped the baby's mouth and chest, cooing over the infant all the while.

"Think somebody's getting to like this grandma thing," Robin whispered to Dean.

"Deano!' bellowed a male voice behind the group.

Ralphie Westmore had the same blonde hair that his Aunt Marlene and Cousin Dean had with Marlene's slighter figure. He'd made his fortune before he'd left college, designing enormously popular mobile phone apps, then selling them to the highest bidder.

Dean scrambled to his feet and welcomed his cousin with an enthusiastic handshake.

"Robin!" Ralphie next crushed her in an awkward hug, then he waved at Levi Parker. "Hey, Aunt Marlene. Levi. And this must be Elizabeth."

"How do you do?" Elizabeth said softly.

Ralphie grinned at then looked at Donald. "And who are you? Elizabeth's father?"

Donald choked. "Uh, no. No. I'm with Marlene."

Robin couldn't help chuckling at Donald's discomfort, but then she noticed that he and Elizabeth did have a similar cast to the shape of their faces and that the color of their hair was almost the same. Robin shook it off.

Ralphie made the requisite coo at the baby, then started chatting with Dean about what shows he wanted to see and where the best bars on The Strip were. Alex and Diane appeared a minute later and were introduced, and the conversation about bars and gambling and other such things continued loudly.

"Dean," said Marlene. "If you want to go off and play with your friends, why don't you leave Elizabeth here with me, and we'll go shopping."

Dean looked at Elizabeth, who glanced at Robin, then nodded.

"What time do you want to have dinner?" Dean asked his mother.

"Let's see. How many do we have?" Marlene did a quick head count. "And what time does Robbie need to be fed, Elizabeth?"

Robin felt her eyebrows rise at her mother's quick turn-around.

"She usually gets hungry around six," said Elizabeth. "And then again around nine."

"Perfect," said Marlene. "Why don't we meet here at the hotel restaurant at seven, and I'll get reservations for us."

Robin and Levi looked at each other and grinned.

Dean looked at Elizabeth, then at Robin. "Okay. Well, I'll see you then."

"Come on, Deano!" Ralphie said, bouncing up. "It's party time."

Robin just barely caught the slight look of panic on Dean's face as he trailed after the others.

"What a relief," Marlene sighed when Dean and company were gone. "He may be my brother's son, but Ralphie is quite a strain at times. He always was."

Robin and Levi exchanged looks again, then Donald bounced up as Marlene rose.

"They've got some lovely stores here, Elizabeth," Marlene said. "And I saw the sweetest baby boutique on the way over here. Maybe we should get something for Robbie."

Elizabeth smiled at Robin as she got up and shouldered the diaper bag. Robin followed, wondering how there was a baby boutique in a Las Vegas hotel mall. But it was, indeed, there. Robin debated staying outside with her father and Donald, who were standing slightly apart and smiling awkwardly at each other. Robin didn't doubt that her father was feeling cautious about Donald, who didn't look much older than Robin.

"Robin!" Marlene suddenly called from inside the store. "Come look at this adorable onesie."

Levi nodded at Robin, and she sighed and went to see what her mother was so excited about.

Marlene ended up purchasing several outfits for the baby, plus several educational toys and a new baby monitor, all of which were sent up to Dean and Elizabeth's room. The next stop was a dress shop, where Elizabeth somehow deflected most of Marlene's more generous impulses with, Robin had to admit, far more tact than Robin would have.

"She is very sweet," Marlene whispered to Robin as they moved onto the next shop, which carried menswear.

Marlene bought a Hawaiian shirt for Dean, then called Donald over. Elizabeth watched with an odd smile on her face.

Finally, alone with her father, Robin smiled.

"How are you doing?" she asked him.

"About Donald?" Levi asked, then shrugged. "I just keep thinking, here we go again."

"What do you mean?"

"Your mother is about to get her heart broken," Levi winced. "We're still friends, you know."

"I knew that." Robin shrugged.

"We didn't want to flaunt it in front of you kids, because we knew you wanted us to get back together." Levi sighed and looked over at his ex-wife. "But your mom tends to get swept off her feet, then it doesn't work out, and she ends up calling me and crying on my shoulder." He looked at Robin. "It's tough for your mom. She's always had to fight her way through to get respect and most of her colleagues are just as over-confident as she is. And you expect that. It takes that kind of personality to handle cutting people open and playing with their major organs. It's just that most men of our generation don't react well to that kind of personality in a woman."

"My generation doesn't much either," grumbled Robin.

Levi nodded. "It is getting better." He frowned. "Part of the problem for your mom is that deep down, she doesn't really want a man in her life. She loves the romance, but she loves her independence more."

"Fear of intimacy," Robin sighed.

"What?"

"That's what Dean called it." Robin made a face. "He was calling me on it, though."

"You're more like your mother than you think," Levi said with a chuckle. "Which is a good thing." He stopped and looked at Elizabeth, then at Robin. "But to change the subject, are you sure about Dean and Elizabeth? I know you've been with them longer, but it still seems pretty fast."

"As sure as we can get," Robin said. She shrugged. "They really do love each other. And Dean's gotten a lot more mature lately. He really surprised me, even though I shouldn't have been."

Levi nodded. "I can't help being concerned. This kind of thing is not usually a recipe for a successful relationship."

"But it's also not a gimme for failure, either." Robin looked at her dad. "I mean, some things are going to be harder for them. But things have been hard for the two of them since they met. They don't like talking about it, but they've been through some scary stuff. You know, what will usually mess up a relationship, and it just made them stronger. I think they're going to be okay."

He nodded and smiled, even though Robin could see he was only marginally reassured.

A few minutes later, they were ambling off to their respective rooms when Donald caught up with Robin.

"You've been avoiding me," Donald said. "Are you uncomfortable with your mother having a boyfriend?"

Robin glared at him. "I'm uncomfortable with you using her for your own ends."

Donald stepped back. "I do genuinely care for her."

"That's not your usual pattern."

"You don't know—" The light dawned in Donald's eyes, and he suddenly nodded, then chuckled. "Maybe you do know. In any case, one can change."

"You'd better," said Robin before stalking off.

She sighed. The day was not getting any easier. Even though Marlene and Elizabeth seemed to be getting along, a thin veil of tension seemed to hover over the group. Donald and Levi were cordial, but clearly not friends. Marlene was still annoyed with Robin and worried about Dean and Elizabeth. Elizabeth was dodging Donald every chance she got.

Things didn't get any better at dinner. Dean and the others not only showed up half an hour late, Ralphie and Alex were more than buzzed and Diane's eyes had gone glassy and even more vacant. Alex giggled at everything that was said. Ralphie was more in control, but loud and he kept pawing at Elizabeth, who deftly avoided him. Diane glared at Elizabeth and called her a murderer, although the words were so slurred and soft, Robin thought no one else had heard.

Marlene was clearly not pleased, but stayed pleasant. After they'd eaten, Dean sent Ralphie, Alex, and Diane off on their own, claiming he had to stay with the baby.

"Come on, Deano!" Ralphie yelled. "You're turning into a stiff. Last night of freedom, dude."

Alex giggled and shakily stood.

"I'm done," said Dean. "I've got a big day tomorrow."

"Well, somebody has to go after them," Marlene said. "Robin."

"Nope. Not doing it," Robin said. "They want to act like idiots, it's on them."

Donald stood. "Come on, Marlene. We'll keep them out of trouble."

Marlene got up and followed Donald as he slapped Ralphie on his back and turned him toward the restaurant exit.

"Assholes," Dean grumbled when the others were gone.

Levi smiled wanly. "That used to be you not too long ago."

"Not really, Dad," Dean said sadly. "Yeah, I partied a lot. That's what I was expected to do. That's what all the guys were doing in high school and stuff. And Mom wanted me to be popular, so I did the frat thing, too. It was fun and all. And some guys were good. But I didn't like being drunk or stoned." He winced slightly. "And I guess I saw the bad side of it my freshman year, when my friend Eddie OD'd. I was with him when he did it. I mean, he'd been getting all drunk and strung out for months, and then was almost flunking out because he was always too hung to go to class. And I just couldn't understand why he kept doing that to himself. Which kinda got explained in my freshman psych class. But that's why I did my internship in the detox unit."

"It also explains your psych major," Levi said.

"Yeah. Everyone thought I was slumming it," Dean sighed.

"I'm sorry about that, Dean," Robin said.

"It's not your fault," said Dean. "It's what everybody else expected and the way I was acting, you can't blame them." He reached over and tenderly picked up Elizabeth's hand. "Elizabeth was the first person I'd ever met who didn't care who I was supposed to be and just liked me as I was."

"I didn't know anything else," Elizabeth said, looking at him fondly.

Robin felt her eyes filling and looked over at her father, who was smiling warmly at the couple.

Robbie squawked suddenly.

"Oh. 'Tis time to feed her," Elizabeth said.

"We'd better get her upstairs," Dean said, getting up and grabbing the diaper bag. He looked at Robin. "Can we talk later?"

"Yeah, sure," said Robin.

"You guys okay if Robin keeps me company for a bit?" Levi asked. "It won't take too long."

Dean's eyes rolled, but he smiled and agreed.

Levi watched as Dean took Elizabeth's hand and they moved off.

"Okay, I'm a little reassured," he said.

"Good." Robin sighed.

"You okay?" Her father asked.

"Sort of. Worried about tomorrow. Worried about Donald."

Levi's eyes twinkled. "As you so forcefully pointed out to your mother earlier today, adults have the right to make their own decisions."

"She told you about that, huh?"

Levi shrugged. "We are still friends. She was trying to get me on board with getting Dean to cancel the wedding. And she has a point about that."

"I know. They're too young." Robin shook off her father's objection.

"It's okay, Robin." Her father smiled. "Like I said, I am somewhat reassured. And there's a difference between being appropriately concerned and being a pain in the ass."

Robin found herself grinning. "As in, you're appropriately concerned and I'm being a pain in the ass."

Levi laughed. "Maybe. So why has Donald got you so worried?"

Robin looked toward the front of the restaurant. "He's using her." She fought for a plausible explanation. "I, uh, don't think he remembers it, but I've run into him before. He uses people to get what he wants, and he's pretty nasty about it. He, uh, messed up somebody I know by running up some false accusations against her."

Levi frowned. "Huh. Is he after your mom's money?"

"No." Robin grasped frantically for what she could tell her father. "I don't know. All I know is that if he's hanging around Mom, it's not because he likes her. Heartache is one thing, but I wouldn't trust him not to get physical."

"That's pretty harsh, Robin, and with no actual evidence to support it," Levi said.

Robin hung her head. Her father had a point. The worst Donald had done was wave a pistol at them. Well, the worst besides getting her, Elizabeth, and Dean in gaol on charges of witchcraft and heresy. And send thugs after her. None of which was that easy to accomplish in the Twenty-First Century.

"You've got reason to be concerned," Levi said. "But you also know you could be wrong. Why don't you try making friends with the guy? If he's using your mother, you'll find out and have some decent evidence to present her with. And even if he is, well, how are you going to convince your mother of that?"

Robin winced. "Good point."

"I've been dealing with her a lot longer than you have," Levi said with a smile. "And, uh, I'll keep an eye on Donald, too."

"Thanks, Dad," Robin said and got up. "I'd better go talk to Dean and Elizabeth."

She left, suspicious that Dean and Elizabeth were just as concerned about Donald as she was, which was confirmed the second Dean let her into the hotel room.

"I just don't get it," Dean groaned as he paced the floor. "I tell you, he did not recognize me in the sports book, and he saw me. He wasn't just faking it when Mom introduced us. He didn't know who I was."

"He knew who I was," said Elizabeth, taking the corner of the diaper out of her mouth and scrubbing Robbie's face. "But you're right. He didn't recognize you and he didn't recognize Robin, but he knew of her, which is odd."

"It's like he'd never met us before," Dean said.

Robin sighed, then frowned. "Maybe he hadn't."

Dean turned on her. "Huh?"

"Well, it's time travel, Dean." It was Robin's turn to pace. "There are, technically, two possibilities. One is that Donald is one of those sociopathic types that lie so easily they can fool lie detector tests."

"That's closer to a psychopath," Dean grumbled. He frowned. "That could be him, though."

"Psychopath?" asked Elizabeth, curiously.

"Basically, someone without a conscience," Dean explained.

Elizabeth's eyes widened in wonder.

"But it doesn't entirely make sense that he didn't recognize you," Robin said. "I suppose he could have been playing mind games with you, letting you see him while he pretended not to recognize you. But if he were truly a psychopath, he'd be more likely to let you see him and then gloat over it, especially with Mom not around."

"So, what's the other possibility?"

"Maybe he really didn't recognize because he hadn't seen you yet," Robin said slowly.

Dean and Elizabeth looked at each other, completely confused.

"He's a time traveler. Maybe he came here to our time before he met us in the Sixteenth Century," Robin said.

"It would make sense to look for Elizabeth here first. How he got our names— Wait. He knew my name. He didn't seem to know you at all." Robin shook her head to clear it. "Look. What's more important is what are we going to do about Mom? And keeping Elizabeth safe?"

"Well, one of us has to stay with Elizabeth at all times," Dean said.

"None of us should be alone," Elizabeth said. "He could attack any of us."

"Wait," Dean said suddenly. "Robin, if he really hasn't gone back to when we were, could it be that maybe we could change things?"

Robin frowned. "What?"

"I dunno." Dean frowned. "Maybe if we're nice to him here, he won't be such a bastard when he goes back."

"But, Dean, that would mean we'd leave Elizabeth in Downleigh. We wouldn't have to flee."

Dean laughed. "Well, we wouldn't. But I am convinced that I'd fall in love with Elizabeth no matter what."

"Dean, you're so dear," Elizabeth said, smiling.

Robin smiled, then sighed. "Look, we just have to keep an eye on him. Dad suggested we try being nice to him, too."

"Sounds good to me," said Dean. "Can you think of a better way to keep tabs on him?"

Robin couldn't. But she hardly felt reassured.

Chapter Five

Dean knew from the moment he saw her the next morning that his mother was going to yell at him. She was cordial as the family met outside the hotel's buffet for breakfast. Nor was Dean surprised when Ralphie, Alex, and Diane failed to show. But Dean knew he was in for a tongue lashing and only debated whether it was better to get it over with or try to eat breakfast first.

If he settled for getting it over with, it was only because Marlene didn't give him much of an option.

"Why, in Heaven's name, did you invite those idiots?" she snarled at him, having pulled him from the line waiting to get in.

"You told me to," Dean said. "You said I should invite a friend and maybe one of the cousins."

"You didn't have to choose Ralphie!"

"He's the one I know the best." Dean shrugged. "My cousins on Dad's side of the family all know me as the party boy and wouldn't have come. And Alex and I have been friends since, what, middle school?"

Marlene pursed her lips. "They made fools of themselves last night. I'm surprised they made it back to the hotel in one piece. Thank God they weren't driving. And I'm worried about Diane. I was certain I'd be treating her for an opioid overdose. I wouldn't be surprised if she's using fentanyl."

"Mom, I can't do anything about Diane. She and Alex are a package deal."

Marlene snorted. "Well, this does not reassure me in any way regarding your judgment, young man."

Dean glared. "Low blow, Mom."

He stalked back to the rest of the group. Marlene followed, then cooed at Robbie, who promptly spit up. Elizabeth grabbed a diaper but glanced at Marlene before using the corner to wipe the baby's face. Dean watched Donald as he smiled warmly at the little scene.

It was not the most auspicious beginning to a day that should have been filled with joy, Dean thought. He knew he loved Elizabeth and marrying her certainly seemed to be the right thing to do. But suddenly the doubts filled him. Maybe he and Elizabeth were too young. Maybe Dean needed to get more comfortable with his new self before making a life-time commitment. Although, as he looked at his daughter, he had to concede he'd already made a life-time commitment when he'd chosen to do the right thing by Elizabeth. It would have been so much easier to abandon her in London. But it wouldn't have been the right thing to do at all. And as he looked at Elizabeth playing with the baby, he was glad he hadn't.

The tension didn't entirely abate as the morning wore on. Dean went with Donald to place bets at the sports book and noted that Donald took care not to let Dean know how he was betting. Marlene took Elizabeth shopping again. Robin stayed with Levi.

At lunch, Marlene took over. Ralphie, Alex, and Diane had somehow managed to show up and, fortunately, did not look too much worse for the wear.

"We have the wedding chapel reserved at five," Marlene announced. "We only have it for an hour, so everyone needs to be there by four-thirty." She glared at Ralphie. "Sober, please."

"Sure, Aunt Marlene," Ralphie laughed.

Dean decided he wouldn't put any money on Ralphie doing what his aunt had said.

"Now, Elizabeth has her spa appointment at two," said Marlene, checking her tablet. "Levi, I want you to make sure Dean is dressed by four so that you have plenty of time to get to the chapel. Donald, you can follow me and Elizabeth."

Dean looked over at Robin, feeling a little panicked. "Mom, why don't I just hang with you guys?"

Marlene looked disgusted. "Dean, can't you at least play along with some of the conventions? It will only be for a couple hours."

"Yes, Dean," said Elizabeth. "It should be all right."

"I'll stay with you guys," Robin said quickly.

"Robin, I'll need you to stay with the others," Marlene said firmly. Her glare implied that Robin's job was to keep Ralphie, Alex, and Diane in line.

Robin shook her head. "I'll stay with Elizabeth, maybe get my hair cut or something."

Marlene paused. Getting Robin to spruce up her appearance had been a longtime project that Robin had solidly resisted. Dean hoped he could find a way to thank his sister for her sacrifice.

"Very well then." Marlene made a note on her tablet.

"I can take care of Robbie this afternoon," Dean said.

"I'll take care of her," Marlene said. "We'll need to keep her close in case she gets hungry. Now, let's see. I've picked the music for the ceremony. The flowers should arrive by four-thirty. You know what, Robin, I think it's better that you're with us. I may need someone to run errands."

"Looks like everything's in great shape, as always, Marlene," Levi said suddenly as he got up. "Come on, Dean. Let's have some bonding time."

Marlene glared briefly at her ex-husband as Dean followed his father from the restaurant, with Ralphie, Alex, and Diane on their heels.

Robin sighed as she watched her mother shake her head over her tablet.

"It's almost two now," Marlene said, as Robbie spit up.

Elizabeth fished a fresh cloth diaper from the bag, looked at Marlene, then simply wiped up the baby's mouth without sucking on the corner of the diaper.

Robin waited until the two were walking together toward the spa, behind Marlene and Donald.

"I noticed you're not sucking on the spit up rag," Robin said quietly.

"Your mother says it's unsanitary," said Elizabeth. She winced. "She may have a point, but it does make it harder to clean Robbie up."

"It's that doctor thing of hers," Robin said. "She's used to sterile because that's what's needed when you're doing surgery. She forgets that a few germs build immunity. And it's not like you're unclean."

Elizabeth frowned. "You don't seem to have a lot of respect for your mother."

"I have a lot of respect for her." Robin sighed as she watched her mother bend her head closer to Donald's. "She's an amazing woman and has done some pretty amazing things against some nasty odds. I just don't like it when she tries to tell me how to run my life."

"She is our elder," said Elizabeth. "And she has our best interests at heart."

"But she doesn't know what they are," Robin said. "She only sees things as she wants to see them without seeing how we really feel and think. There's a world of difference between really knowing your kids and knowing what's best for them and thinking you know what's best because you know what's right for you. Mom has a tough time seeing us as we are because she must be so sure of what she knows all the time. That's part of what makes her such a good doctor. It doesn't make her very easy to live with, though."

Elizabeth shrugged and didn't say anything more. That was, perhaps, more unsettling than had she continued to argue. Robin wasn't surprised, though. Elizabeth didn't have the history Robin did with her mother and was used to the idea that she should do as her mother-in-law said just because she said it. And it was possible that Elizabeth had a point. Perhaps if Robin were more willing to hear her mother out, maybe Marlene wouldn't feel such a strong need to control things so tightly.

As Marlene got Elizabeth settled at the spa, Robin found herself sitting next to Donald in the waiting room. They were alone, but Robin looked around anyway. She smiled tentatively at Donald. He smiled back.

"Your mother tells me you're quite the Renaissance woman," Donald said.

"What?" Robin suddenly laughed. "I guess. Why do you ask?"

Donald shrugged. "Just wanted to get to know you better."

"I see." She didn't entirely. "Well, I guess I like a lot of things."

"How about history?" Donald seemed to be thumbing through a magazine, but Robin doubted he was absorbing anything he was reading.

Robin shook her head. "So, that's what this is about."

Donald looked at her, frowning. "What do you mean?"

"Your experiment with Roger and Elizabeth."

"Ah." Donald took a deep breath and seemed to make a decision. "Look, I don't know what I've done to you. It hasn't happened for me yet."

"Nice to know I got that part right. Um..."

Donald held up his hand. "And I can't know. Do you understand why?"

"Yeah." Robin glanced around again. "Roger's fine with Elizabeth and Dean."

Donald snorted. "I'm not surprised. He never thought much of my idea."

"Oh," Robin swallowed. "I'm sorry."

"He's not the sweet fellow everyone thinks he is," Donald said with a smirk. "You might want to keep that in mind. He's got a lot of people fooled. They don't notice how manipulative he really is. How it's not a good idea unless it's his. How he expects you to do what he says and not think for yourself."

Robin shuddered slightly. For all she was wary of Donald and his motives, she had to concede that Roger was prone to giving orders. On the other hand, Donald hadn't exactly been straightforward in how he'd done things. In fact, he'd been very manipulative and even sneaky.

"Is that why you wanted to know if I was sure Dean was the baby's father?" Robin asked. "I know. You're not supposed to know."

Donald's eyebrows lifted in surprise.

"You're right. I'm not." He mulled some more. "That's an interesting thought, though." He paused, then looked at Robin. "Not that it matters."

Robin turned on him. "Look, whatever issues you have with Roger, I really don't care. I just want to protect my family. Especially my mother and Elizabeth."

"I suppose I can accept that," Donald said. "That doesn't alter reality. Just keep that in mind when you meet up with our good friend Roger."

"I might. But I wonder why I should take your word for it when every time I've come up against you, you're the one who's been manipulative and sneaky?" Robin held her hand up. "I'm not giving you any details."

Donald rolled his eyes. "You obviously haven't had any training in time travel yet. There's a reason we do things the way we do, as I'm sure your precious Roger will tell you."

"He's not my precious Roger," Robin said.

"Nonetheless," Donald said. "You know nothing about us. You know nothing about how we need to operate to keep ourselves safe. And yet, you feel free to make all manner of judgments against me."

There wasn't much Robin could say to that, and the spa receptionist entered to bring Robin to get her hair cut. Everyone was primped and ready by a little after four o'clock. They made their way over to the wedding chapel to find that everything was in order. Marlene was still operating like a field marshal in the middle of maneuvers and had not let go of baby Robbie for a moment. Until Robbie began to cry that she wanted to be fed. Marlene swept Elizabeth into a dressing room and forbade anyone to enter.

"They need quiet so Robbie can get a good feeding," Marlene insisted.

Robin was about to protest when she saw Elizabeth smiling at Marlene in approval.

Marlene again took the baby for the wedding itself. Robin had to concede that Marlene had arranged a genuinely nice little ceremony. Even better was the sweet and clear affection between Elizabeth and Dean. Robin felt her eyes grow misty as the two took their vows, then kissed. Even Ralphie's rude joke did not spoil the moment.

But as the group made its way to the restaurant where they were going to have dinner, Robin felt a lingering sadness that she couldn't quite place. True, she was worried about Donald, and that had caused her to snipe at him periodically. And the way he'd referred to Roger still nettled her more than she wanted to admit. But as she watched Dean and Elizabeth cooing at each other, she knew it wasn't about Donald or her mother or anyone else. It was that she was lonely.

She thought of the timetron, buried deep in her suitcase. She didn't know why she'd packed such a precious item. Only that it had called to her as she'd gathered her clothes together for the trip.

At the restaurant, the group had to wait while their table was made ready. Ralphie, Alex, and Diane wandered off and Marlene sent Donald after them. Levi finally convinced Marlene to give up Robbie, although Marlene hovered as he played with the infant.

Levi laughed as the baby spit up. "Doesn't she remind you of Robin when she was a baby?"

"Oh, yes, she does," Marlene replied, getting weepy-eyed.

Elizabeth had grabbed a diaper and was sucking on the cloth when she spotted Marlene looking at her. Elizabeth dropped the cloth and Marlene used a baby wipe to clean Robbie up. Donald sauntered up.

What Robin did not see was Donald picking up the diaper that Elizabeth had sucked on. Nor did she see him pull a hand-held screen from his pocket and place the wet corner on it. What she saw was him smiling at the hand-held screen. He put it in his pants pocket and returned the diaper to the bag.

"What are you doing?" Robin asked him, her voice surlier than she'd intended.

"The diaper fell," he said. "I was putting it back."

Robin watched him warily as he moved away. Dean slid up to her.

"Hey, can you lay off him?" Dean nodded at Donald.

"There's something wrong, Dean."

"I know. But you don't have to act like it." Dean sighed. "It's kind of bringing everyone down. You know?"

Robin took a deep breath. "I'm sorry."

Dean moved away.

The table was ready, and Robin held it together enough to smile through it and even enjoy herself a little. There were lots of photos taken, although Robin suddenly noticed that it was Donald taking all the pictures. Marlene had even arranged for a small wedding cake for dessert.

Donald took one last photo, checked something in his pocket that didn't quite look like a smartphone, then looked curiously at Elizabeth.

Elizabeth saw his stare and drew away uncomfortably. Donald laughed, then stood.

"Marlene, I'm leaving now," he announced.

"I'll see you in the room," she said with a warm smile.

"No. You won't. I'm leaving." He grinned maliciously at Dean. "And Deano-boy, I'd check your baby's DNA if I were you."

He turned and left as Marlene gasped in horror.

Robin stood and turned to go after him. "Donald!"

"What did you say to him?" Marlene grabbed her arm and held her back.

"I didn't say anything!" Robin yelled, tears rushing to her eyes. "You guys don't understand. I've met him before! He did just the same thing to someone else. He was using you, Mom. And he obviously got what he wanted, which is why he left."

"You could have been nicer to him," Marlene sank into her chair, blinking back tears. "Robin, you have been nothing but obtuse all summer."

"Why are you blaming me?" Robin cried. "I didn't do anything. Okay, I called him out on some past stuff, but he knew why I was worried and agreed it was fair."

"That obviously helped," Marlene snapped. "And what did he mean about Dean checking Robbie's DNA?"

"He apparently thinks Dean's not the father of Elizabeth's baby," Robin said.

"I swear—" Elizabeth gasped in horror.

"I'm not accusing you of anything." Robin turned to her. "Honest, Elizabeth, I'm not. But it's not the first time he's said it."

"Robin, could you possibly be any more hurtful?" Marlene growled.

"I don't have to take this." Robin grabbed her purse and stomped off.

"Robin!" Dean hurried after her.

He caught her outside the restaurant.

"I didn't say anything, Dean," Robin said. "I only caught him near the diaper bag."

"Look, you did what you thought was right," Dean said. He shrugged. "It just wasn't right this time."

"Dean!" Robin turned to leave.

"You're not perfect, Robin," Dean said, pulling her back. "And do you really think Robbie isn't mine?"

"No!" Robin blinked hard. "I don't know what to think. I know Elizabeth is one-hundred percent blameless. Whatever happened, if it happened, she knows nothing about it. It's just that they must have some way to play with her brain or something. I don't know! It doesn't make sense."

Dean shuffled his feet. "Robbie's mine."

"Of course she is."

"I know she is." Dean took a deep breath. "I sent away for the test when we got home last summer."

"What?"

Dean sighed. "Back when we were in Bath when he broke in on us that morning we left. He made this weird comment about giving Elizabeth his daughter. I'm not sure what exactly he said, because that's when you came in. But it got under my skin, so rather than stress out over it and what he might have done when we were in London, I got the DNA test done. It came back last week. Robbie's mine."

"Why didn't you tell me?"

"Because I didn't want to get you and Elizabeth upset, especially since it was going to be pretty easy to find out one way or another. If only you'd kept your mouth shut, Elizabeth wouldn't be freaking out now."

"I didn't say anything. Donald did."

"You didn't have to pile on. And maybe if you'd been nicer to him, he wouldn't have been so mean when he took off."

"You've seen what the man can do. What, in heaven's name, do you think would have changed anything?"

Dean snorted. "You don't know that!"

"That's it. I'm out of here." Robin pulled her arm away. "And don't try to come after me."

"Robin!"

She stomped off. When she got to the elevators, she hit the call button so hard it hurt her hand. She kept from sobbing until she got into her room. Roger had made her promise that she not leave her time for the future until Dean and Elizabeth were well settled in. But what constituted well settled in? Robin sniffed. Of course, the two could always ask Marlene for help if they needed it. It certainly seemed as though Elizabeth preferred the older woman's advice over Robin's.

The thought was unworthy, and Robin knew it, but it didn't matter. It was time to go and let Dean and Elizabeth manage for themselves. Robin opened her suitcase and got out the timetron and the bag of bits and pieces from the past. There was the hand-cranked coffee grinder that she'd wired to Dean's old iPhone. A towel. A few coins. A tankard and a candle mold.

Never mind that in her conscious mind, she'd planned on returning to Pasadena with Dean and Elizabeth. Something deep inside her must have known she wasn't going to leave Las Vegas the conventional way. It made sense. Dean and Elizabeth could use some time alone together to build their little family.

Robin opened her laptop and made a list of the household accounts with notes on which ones got paid automatically and which ones needed to be paid by hand. After putting the list in an email, she also verified that the automatic deposits to the joint household account would be enough for all the bills and other necessities, plus a few extras. She powered down the laptop and winced. She had every reason to think she'd come back to her world, but there would be enough money for Dean and Elizabeth to manage on with school fees and the rest until Dean could graduate and get a better-paying job.

She wrote a short note on some hotel paper, then took her suitcase down to the hotel concierge and checked it. She put her car key, the note, and the claim tag for her suitcase in an envelope and asked the desk clerk to hold it for her brother and sister-in-law and gave the clerk their room number. Then she went back upstairs, checked to be sure nothing would be left behind, left the room key on the dresser, then picked up the timetron and closed her eyes.

The next morning, Dean got the message from the front desk that someone had left an envelope for him and his wife. He returned to his and Elizabeth's room with a heavy heart.

"Robin left," he said to Elizabeth, handing her the note.

"I'm not surprised," Elizabeth said, reading the note.

"I shouldn't have been so hard on her," Dean sighed. He looked at Elizabeth. "Do you think she's coming back?"

Elizabeth looked over the note again. "She says that she expects to find her car in pristine condition, so I guess that means she does. She just doesn't say when."

Dean shook his head. "I was such a jerk last night."

"You didn't drive her away, Dean," Elizabeth said, putting her hand on his arm. "She wanted to go. She's been wanting to go for weeks now. She's finally gone where she really wants to be."

Chapter Six

The crushing, sucking sensation as Robin whisked through time and space left her winded. Gasping, she opened her eyes. The room was bright but small, with intricate designs painted in an explosion of colors painted on the walls.

"I cannot tell you how glad I am to see you," said a familiar voice.

Robin turned. Roger was there, smiling. He swept a lock of his soft brown hair away from his brown eyes. Slightly taller than Robin and slender, he wore a green robe with an ornately quilted and embroidered collar.

"Quick. Think what I'm thinking." Roger placed his forehead against Robin's and his hands on the timetron.

Robin got a brief image of a forest before the two suddenly landed there.

"Whew!" Roger's laugh was just a touch manic as he backed away from her and looked around.

"What did you do that for?" Robin asked, blinking.

"So sorry. I had to get you out of there before you registered."

"Oh." Robin looked around, then slid the time machine into the sack more out of habit than anything else. "Where are we?"

Roger smiled in approval. "Somewhere south of St. Louis." His gaze swept the sky.

Robin realized he was checking the position of the sun. He looked at her apologetically.

"I suspect I may have violated some of your free will," he said with a sigh. "But I couldn't think of anything else and some part of it must have worked because you're here."

"All you said was that things would be really bad," Robin said.

"Oh, they are," Roger sighed. He looked around again. "Do you mind if we do some hiking? They won't put the bloodhounds on us, but they might find a way to trace your timetron."

Robin shrugged. "I'm fine. You don't look as though you're dressed for roughing it."

If anything, he was dressed for lounging at home. The robe he wore had short sleeves and barely covered his knees. His legs were bare and Robin, at first, thought he was barefoot, but after a second look, she saw that he had sandals on, sandals with very thin soles and even finer straps.

Roger chuckled. "I've managed snow with not much more than this. How about you?"

Robin sniffed. Based on the sun's position, it was sometime in the mid-morning, and the air had the slight chill of spring. She was wearing jeans, a light sweater, and running shoes, as classic and timeless an outfit as she could think of, knowing full well it would not be right for Roger's time.

"I'm fine for hiking," she said. "I just hope I don't stick out too much clothes-wise."

Roger smiled. "We should be able to make it work. Of course, you could just go naked."

Robin gulped. "I think I know how Elizabeth feels about wearing short skirts."

Roger laughed. "And it's not nearly as comfortable as people tried to make it sound way back when."

They hiked in silence for several minutes. Robin let Roger lead the way along a wide path through a forest of relatively slender trees of all kinds. The path itself was overgrown with vines and dotted with huge, old trees. Every so often, Robin thought she saw a wall peeking through the growth on either side of the path.

"At what point do I get to find out what trouble you're in?" Robin asked.

"I'm under arrest for the experiment with Elizabeth," Roger said. He looked at her with a worried frown.

"Oh," said Robin. Her heart stopped as she heard Donald complaining about Roger yet again.

Roger stopped and sighed. "If you want to go back to your time, I understand. I shouldn't have brought you here this way. I must have known it was going to be okay somehow. Or maybe not. How did you get here? To my holding room?"

"You programmed the timetron for me," Robin said. "Don't you remember?"

"The fun of time travel." Roger started walking again. "It hasn't happened for me yet. It will, sometime further ahead on my personal time continuum. But that you're here means that I programmed your timetron to bring you here." He shook his head. "And I can't imagine what I was thinking that it would be okay to do that. I just know that before you arrived, I was thinking how great it would be to have you come get me."

"Why did you need me?"

"I'm caught in a perfect catch twenty-two."

"They're still using that expression?"

"It's a classic metaphor for a situation in which—"

"I know what it means," Robin cut in. "They invented it in my time. Or just before it."

"That's right. They did." Roger smiled. "Anyway, someone complained to the Intelligentsia Board about the attempt to bring Elizabeth forward to our time as a way to bring in new genes and re-establish some fertility. I told you that we're facing the potential extinction of humans, right?"

"Yes, you told me that much. But what's the Intelligentsia Board?"

"It's the board that oversees all the creative and science boards, basically, the thinkers and such."

"In the United States?"

"Oh, no. That's been gone for a hundred years. When Amazon became a total monopoly and everything collapsed."

Robin gasped. "That's horrible!"

"I'm told it was pretty ugly. And the reactor disaster in China didn't help, either. But land-based allegiances were already starting to fall by the wayside even by your natal time. Think about it, how many of your close friends are the people who live next to you?"

"None of them. I barely know who my neighbors are."

"And yet, prior to the late Twentieth Century, that's how most friendships occurred. And where you lived depended on where you worked, and often the reverse was true. As all that became more fluid and less dependent on where you physically were, governance got messier. Not to mention the global economy. So, what came out of the Amazon collapse was a corporatocracy based on competition. Amazon had already created the corporatocracy based on consumer culture. What it needed was just enough competition to prop it up and keep everyone employed. So instead of countries, we have environments now."

"You mean like Google and Microsoft?"

"Similar. Except that those two companies no longer exist. Your environment determines who supplies your power and all the stuff governments used to and usually your goods. And people are free to change environments. That's where the competition comes in. If someone gets too greedy, people leave. And apart from those environments are various affiliations. The Intelligentsia Board, for example. Some churches. The Factories Board. These handle most of the justice issues, although the environments usually provide policing and deal with criminal offenses. And within the larger affiliations, there are smaller interest groups, such as The Time Travel Board, which works under the Intelligentsia Board."

"And that's in what environment?"

"Affiliations are cross-environment."

"Sheez." Robin rolled her eyes. "Sounds like a perfect little dystopian mess."

"It's not any better or worse than any other system." Roger shrugged. "You could make an argument that monarchy works, and yet that's been effectively non-functional since before your natal time. In a sense, we have a true democracy because every person votes with each purchase. But there are problems and hitches because it's a human-made system, with all the problems that come with humans. And, as you've no doubt noticed, ideas and attitudes change, but people don't, really."

"True. But what about your arrest?"

Roger winced. "That. Well, the Intelligentsia Board is willing to let me prove that the experiment was appropriately carried out. But they're not willing to let me collect the evidence to do so. Or that the person who complained may have had other reasons for the complaint than concerns about out-of-control time travelers."

"What? That makes no sense."

"It does if you don't like the fact that time travelers are almost impossible to control but you can't really come out against them because then you'll alienate all sorts of other scientists and creatives that you can't afford to alienate. In short, they need a really, really good excuse to shut us down and the experiment with Elizabeth could be that excuse."

"And you going rogue wouldn't be another good excuse." Robin couldn't help glaring at him.

"It could." Roger looked ahead at the path, then at a smaller one leading east. "But I can't find the evidence to clear the mission stuck in a holding room, so I've got nothing to lose by taking off."

"So where are we going?"

"We're going to visit Cricklan. She should be able to help us, especially if the person who complained is who I think he is." Roger beckoned her to follow him along the narrower path.

It was uneven with rocks and what looked like the remnants of concrete. Whereas on the wider path, the trees in the forested sections had been mostly the same size with much larger trees following the path, here, the trees were mixed. Robin suddenly realized that many of the trees were the same variety, even if she couldn't say which one, and that the difference in the sizes meant that the bigger trees were significantly older. It was as if all the smaller trees had started growing at the same time and much later than the larger trees had.

It took most of the afternoon to get through the rough growth. As the sun sank below the treetops, they came into a clearing that ended with a cliff overlooking a wide, rushing river. Over the treetops, a rocky bluff rose, with a row of glass panes built onto its side. Robin assumed it was a house. All she could see was the row of glass and it didn't seem large enough for some sort of business and it was certainly remote. The sun lit up the side of the hill just enough for Robin to see pathways running up to house and down to the river.

Roger gazed up at the house, then exhaled. "Damn." He looked over at Robin. "Can I look at your timetron, please? I need to check for life forms."

"Sure." Robin dug into the sack and got out the small black box.

Roger traced something on the top. Robin held her breath as he briefly closed his eyes. He didn't disappear, but the frown on his face wasn't very reassuring.

"She's not there," he grumbled, glaring at the house on the bluff.

"How can you tell?" Robin asked.

Roger gave her back the machine. "The machine registers life forms. That's how it avoids landing us in front of people who might be freaked out by someone appearing out of mid-air."

"Then how did I land right back in front of Dean and Elizabeth the first time I tried it? And landed right in front of you?"

"It reads intent," Roger said, looking around the clearing again. "If you don't care about someone seeing you, it overrides the lifeform sensor."

Robin looked up at that house on the bluff. "Is that this Cricklan's house?"

"Yes."

"And the machine says it's empty."

"Yes." Roger paced the edge of the clearing.

"So, am I correct in guessing that with night coming on, we need a place to sleep? Maybe figure out food?"

"Fortunately, we have plenty of edibles here," Roger said. "We'll just have to forage for them. And we should be able to find a ruin that still has a roof on it."

"So, you're assuming your friend's house is being watched."

Roger looked up at the house. "Tracked, yes. You wouldn't happen to have a flashlight with you, would you?"

"No. I didn't bring anything with me except for some of the stuff from the Sixteenth and Seventeenth Centuries." Robin frowned. "I thought that stuff would be safer and easier to explain here than at home." She put her hand in her pocket. "Wait. I don't believe this. I brought my phone."

"Your version of mobile technology?" Roger frowned. "We might be able to pick up a signal."

Robin shook her head. "That's not why I brought it. It's just always in my pocket and I forgot to take it out when I left. But more important, it has a flashlight on it."

Roger grinned. "That's right. They did."

"It can really drain a battery, though." Robin said, turning the tiny beam on.

"We'll find a way to recharge it." Roger took the phone and swept the light across the brush on the edge of the clearing. "There are still quite a few old-style electrical batteries and generators floating around, although it's mostly hobbyists and time travelers who use them. We may even be able to signal another traveler, but we'll have to be careful. I don't expect the I. B. to be watching those channels. They don't usually see older technologies as something useful. But it could occur to someone that we time travelers do and that we know how to use them."

Robin suddenly shivered. "You said something about bloodhounds earlier."

"They won't send them after us unless they track us from Cricklan's house. I'm sure someone's figured out that would be the first place I'd go." Roger apparently saw something he liked because he suddenly headed down an almost obscured path. "But we're off-grid out here, with no real resources. In short, we're nowhere that we can cause any trouble or contact anyone, so what's the point?"

Robin followed him through the brush. "Except that you could call someone next month or something and have them meet us here with food and other stuff."

Roger stopped walking and sighed. "I suppose. We try not to do it too often because it can make yourself pretty nuts trying to figure out when and how. And we don't want the I.B. to know how often we do it because that just makes us harder to control, which is what makes them crazy." He suddenly sniffed. "Wait. Maybe I did set up a meeting."

Robin sniffed, too. The faint smell of wood smoke wafted through the trees. Roger immediately signaled for quiet and shut off the beam of the phone flashlight.

"We don't know that I did," he whispered in her ear. "It could be we've found a few off-gridders and they can be pretty tetchy if they don't know you."

"Oh, joy," Robin grumbled as she followed Roger through the gloom.

He paused in front of what looked like a white stucco wall overgrown with ivy. After listening, he motioned for Robin to hand him her sack, which she did. Roger pulled the timetron out, traced it with his finger, then closed his eyes.

"Only one lifeform," he whispered in her ear. "Keep the sack, but hide the timetron under your sweater, next to your skin."

Robin nodded and did as he asked, then followed him as he made his way along the wall. The smell of a wood fire grew stronger, and a tall male human emerged from a veil of ivy leaves. The man was almost blonde with strong, muscular shoulders and a slim build. He wore a dark robe similar to Roger's, but had on full, dark pants underneath, which were tucked into boots. As the man looked around through the gloom, Roger straightened.

"Beeman!" Roger called softly. "What brings you out here?"

"Cricklan sent me," Beeman said. Instead of trying to see where Roger was, he backed up a touch. "She was worried about your hairless backside."

Roger suddenly chuckled and moved forward. "I'm glad she doesn't think I'm out to get her."

Beeman shook his head as the two men grasped each other's forearms, then hugged. Robin stayed back in the shadows.

"So, where is she?" Roger asked.

"The New York holding center," Beeman said. "I got access because the I.B. thinks I'm on their side."

Roger stiffened. "Are you?"

Beeman snorted. "Of course I am. Everybody supports those candy-assed weenies. Didn't you know?"

"Everybody except the Intelligentsia, that is," Roger said, laughing. He turned and beckoned Robin forward.

Beeman's jaw dropped. "A woman?"

"And an anomaly," Roger said with a grin.

"So that's how…" Beeman shook his head, then turned and held back the veil of ivy. "Well, come on in and let's get settled."

Robin held Roger back. "Are you sure you can trust this guy?"

"Mostly." Roger shrugged. "Just make sure we're touching if we have to leave suddenly."

The ivied archway led into a large, empty room. The walls were covered with molds and plant growth, while small shrubs poked up here and there through the floor. Along one wall, a stairway led to a gap in the ceiling, but on the opposite wall, a fire burned in a fireplace. There was a grill over the flames and a small table had been set up with what looked like a cooler next to it.

Robin swallowed. "This was someone's house."

"Late Twentieth Century," Beeman said. He looked at Roger.

"Oh. Forgive me," Roger said. "Robin Parker, this is Beeman, a fellow time traveler."

"Hi," said Robin quietly.

"Do we have a Robin Parker in the system?" Beeman asked, looking a little worried.

Roger smiled. "If we don't, we will. The timetrons recognize her."

Beeman shrugged, then gestured at a row of logs set up around the fireplace.

"I'll get some food on the fire," he said. "I've got two sleeping kits, figuring I was going to stay here with you, Roger. And I was able to get some fresh clothes for you."

"Terrific. Thanks." Roger settled onto a log.

"Well, I could only bring one outfit," Beeman said with a grin. "On the pretext of getting you something fresh to wear."

There seemed to be some shared joke that Robin didn't get. Roger noticed and smiled at her.

"It's something you'll get used to," he explained as Beeman set about putting what looked like meat and vegetables into a cast-iron pot. "People change clothes a lot, even more often than they did in your time. Not having fresh clothes is considered almost inhumane. But because we travelers spend so much time in the past, when people wore the same clothes all the time, not having fresh clothes doesn't bother us."

The light suddenly dawned on Beeman, and he grinned at Robin. "You're the one that busted up the Wynford project."

"Well, technically, my brother did," Robin said. She shifted on her log. "He's the one who found Elizabeth. I'm the one who found the time machines. It was an accident that I was holding the hand unit when we saw the lights flashing and ran."

Beeman looked at Roger. "Was it really working?"

"Sort of," said Roger. He looked at Robin. "How well was Elizabeth adjusting when you left your time?"

Robin couldn't help wincing. "Well, things had gotten pretty tense, but that had more to do with Donald turning up."

Both Roger and Beeman looked alarmed.

"What was the date?" Roger asked.

Beeman grabbed for a hand-held screen about the same size as Robin's phone.

"I don't see anything for the early Twenty-First except a trip to Costa Rica," Beeman said before Robin could answer. "Looks like he left Las Vegas, came home, then left for Bath, 1776."

"Well, that finally makes sense," Robin said. "We met him in Las Vegas, and he didn't recognize either me or Dean. He recognized Elizabeth, but not from when we met him in the Seventeenth Century. She swore she'd never seen him before."

"So can you tell when he set us up with the Intelligentsia Board?" Roger asked.

Beeman's eyebrows rose. "It looks like he must have since he came back from Charing Vale, 1642. His trip line reads Bath, 1776, home for a couple hours, London, 1642, then Downleigh, some months before, then return from Charing Vale. And that's when the dates line up."

"So, you mean he was traveling backwards along our timeline the entire time?" Robin asked, gaping despite herself. "Why would he do that? Wait. He challenged us about Elizabeth's baby in Bath, and then right before he left in Las Vegas. Asked if we were sure Dean was the father."

"Wynford had a baby?" Beeman asked. He looked down at the pot he'd abandoned and suddenly put it in the fire.

Robin flushed. "That's the part of this venture that did work. Dean got Elizabeth pregnant."

"The stronger claim," Roger groaned. "Which is what Donald meant when he asked if you were sure that Dean was the father. So, was Elizabeth pregnant when you went through the drop?"

"Um. Yeah," said Robin sheepishly. "We already talked about that when you met up with us right after—"

Roger held up his hand. "Don't tell me. It hasn't happened for me yet."

"But she went through pregnant," Beeman said. He stirred the pot thoughtfully. "Did it affect the baby?"

"She grew faster," Robin said. "But she's been fine otherwise. The baby, I mean. Elizabeth has been good, too."

"But that's what we need to know," Roger said. "How has Elizabeth been adjusting to the time change?"

Robin shrugged. "A lot better than I would have thought. She's gotten past thinking everything is magic. Or if it is, it's not something evil and terrible. She really likes the camera on the mobile phone we got her. But things can still frighten her. A street magician freaked her out when we were in Vegas. It's the little things that get to her. And sometimes she tries too hard to not freak, which just makes things worse."

Roger sighed. "But she didn't recognize anything from your time period or maybe understood concepts that would have been foreign in her time."

"No," Robin said, thinking. "When we first left the castle, everything seemed to terrify her. It wasn't until we were in her time that I was able to explain more about how she'd been put to sleep like the Sleeping Beauty for a few hundred years. After that, things made a little more sense to her."

Roger shook his head. "She was only sleeping a few years at a time. We set it up that way so we could try some sleep learning. We were hoping that when we landed in our time, she would have some frame of reference and wouldn't be so frightened."

"And that part certainly didn't work," said Beeman. "Maybe Alayo was right. We should have tried with abandoned babies."

"But taking children through the Drop...." Roger shook his head.

"It didn't hurt Elizabeth's baby," said Robin. "But that could have been because she was pregnant, and the baby was protected from the crushing sensation."

Beeman and Roger looked at each other and Beeman quickly shook his head.

"That's one of the issues," Roger said.

"And speaking of issues," Beeman interrupted. "There is some good news. The I.B. has been getting a lot of heat about not letting you out of the holding center to gather your evidence. The bad news is that you getting out gave them exactly the argument they needed to keep you there."

Roger shrugged. "I was afraid it might."

"No other option," Beeman said, waving his objection away. "At least, not given what you knew. They'd made sure of that. And that part seems to be getting out. Which is why the I.B. made the big announcement that they will not be actively trying to recapture you. Now, if you stumble into them, then they must. You are officially out of control."

Roger snorted. "And I suppose the larger public is buying it."

"Yes and no. It's the usual mix. Most of the Intelligentsia community has figured out the double-talk. But there's no reward or any incentive for the larger public to be looking for you or turn you in, so that should help. And in their great generosity, they've given you until May 15 to find your evidence."

"So, about six weeks." Roger sighed again and looked over at Robin. "I'm sorry I dragged you into this. Or will drag you into this." He shuddered. "I have to think things turned out alright because you're here."

"It depends on when you went back to get her," said Beeman. "That trip hasn't shown up on your timeline, so you probably haven't made it yet."

"You still have access to everything?" Roger asked.

Beeman nodded. "Anything the Time Board has, as long as the I.B. thinks I'm being a good little boy."

"That's not very reassuring," Robin grumbled.

Beeman sat back for a moment and gazed at her.

"No. You wouldn't have reason to trust me," he said, then stirred the pot. "But the truth is, it doesn't serve me or anyone else to let those I.B. toadies get too powerful. And they know it. They don't trust me any more than you do, and they hate not being in control. But they also must keep up appearances or they will lose what little control they have. So, they're using me as their good faith pledge that they're treating the travelers justly. Which, while I can only do so much, gives me the chance to help you. What the I.B. doesn't understand is just how addicting time travel is. There's the Drop Effect, which I'm sure Roger will explain to you any time now, even though it is our biggest secret." He glared at Roger briefly. "But even without it, there isn't a traveler who would give up the chance to see the world as it was. Most people, including the I.B., they couldn't care less. Time travel is insanely uncomfortable and disorienting and you can't do the one thing most folks would love to do, which is change history. If I don't help you, the travelers get shut down. So, it doesn't serve me to turn you in." He suddenly smiled and nudged Roger. "Besides, I kind of like this guy, even if he gets too full of himself at times."

Roger laughed. It surprised Robin that she felt somewhat less worried.

"All right," Roger said, suddenly sobering. "Beeman, how do they think I got out?"

Beeman winced. "The I.B. is assuming another traveler helped you, but without any real evidence of who, they can't just demand that we turn our machine data over to them. The rest of us kind of figured you'd gotten a hold of an unregistered machine somehow. It's not as though most of us don't know where to find one."

"True enough." Roger pressed his lips together. "So, they know I can transport."

"But the I.B. doesn't. The Time Board certified that all registered machines are accounted for. That's one of the reasons why the I.B. was able to make such a big deal of releasing you. You're off the grid, which is a major plus as far as they're concerned. They've probably figured out you're getting help from us, but they can't pin down from whom. And since they've got the ultimate high hand with the trial, it's a waste of resources to look too hard for you, not to mention all the ill-will it would generate."

"Well, it sounds good enough," Roger said. "And we know for certain that it was Donald who complained to the I.B.? It's not just convenient timing?"

"Yes," Beeman said, handing Roger his handheld device.

Roger looked at it. "I would have to concur. Which means the next question is how do we prove to the I.B. that Donald had ulterior motives behind his complaint, or at least enough that they have no justification to shut us down?"

"But would busting Donald's complaint be enough to stop them from shutting everything down?" Robin asked. "If I'm hearing you two right, it sounds like your I.B. is looking for any excuse to dump on you."

Beeman rolled his eyes skyward. "Yes, but what you're missing is that they can't just shut us down without a really good reason."

"It's part of the delicate balance that makes things work in our time," Roger explained. "No matter how much the I.B. wants to shut us down, if it gets out that they're being less than just - and it will get out - they are in trouble. The executives who oversee the five primary environments need the Intelligentsia because they need the innovation and creativity that comes out of the arts and sciences. But the Executive Council really hates the Intelligentsia because they're so independent. So, the Council hand picks the members of the Intelligentsia's governing board. It's the only affiliation board that is run that way. The rest choose their leaders. And the Intelligentsia go along with it because they need the patronage of the Executive Council to fund their projects."

"And the current council didn't do themselves any favors by appointing this current crop of toadies," Beeman said.

Roger sighed. "It doesn't make them any less powerful. It just makes them harder to deal with. But we can show that the project was appropriately vetted, and it was the Council that tasked the Intelligentsia to take on the population problem."

"Then they should know about Donald's condition," Beeman said, stirring the pot again.

A tantalizing smell wafted out and Robin's mouth began to water, and her stomach gurgled.

"They probably don't," Roger said. "The Board deliberation on that part was sealed to protect Donald's privacy."

"So that's what Cricklan meant," Beeman groaned. "She didn't want me to find you. She wanted me to find the Board documentation."

"What?" Roger asked.

"It's not like we weren't being observed," Beeman said. "She asked me how your hairless backside was, and I took it to mean she wanted me to look for you. But then she said something about making sure the I.B. saw the full report on the Time Board's vetting of the Wynford project."

"She's got it hidden somewhere and my hairless backside is the pass image," Roger said. He glanced toward the hill. "Which means we have to get inside her house."

"That's not going to be easy," said Beeman. He glared at the pot. "Looks like this is done. You two eat. I was going to sleep here tonight, but I'll head out and get my own food at home." He sighed and looked at Roger. "I won't be able to get in there. The I.B. is going to assume that anybody who goes in is the one who helped you, and the last thing either of us needs is to give the tracking dogs something to track."

"What about the fresh clothes excuse?" Robin asked.

Beeman rolled his eyes. "Woman Privilege. They made sure she had a full wardrobe. At least, I can still visit. Anything you want her to know?"

Roger looked over at Robin. "Let's keep Robin a secret for the time being."

"I wasn't going to acknowledge you, let alone her. I'm not supposed to have seen either of you."

"If you can find a way to let her know I'm okay, that would be good. I'm sure she's worried."

Beeman chuckled as he got up. "Not that she'd say so, but, yeah, she is."

Roger got up with him, and Robin struggled to her feet. Beeman grasped both their forearms, then took out his handheld unit and looked at it.

"Looks like we're clear," he said.

"Aren't you afraid you can be traced through that?" Robin asked.

"It's a traveler handheld," Beeman explained. "It's useless for communication and tracking because you can't do those things in the past. But great for research on the fly and some other basic functions. The only thing that can be tracked is when I update it, and I always do that from home." He looked at Roger. "I included one in your clothes, but updating it is going to be a problem."

"We'll make it work," Roger said.

Beeman nodded and slipped through the vine-covered opening. Roger got the pot out of the fire and looked at Robin.

"I'm sure you've got a million questions," he said, looking a little abashed.

"I don't even know where to begin," Robin said.

She watched as Roger scooped meat and vegetables onto a pair of metal plates. He made a face as he handed her one.

"The worst of time travel is that you occasionally can't help finding out about something you did in the past that hasn't happened to you yet," he said, fumbling for the forks that had been laid out next to the plates and other cooking paraphernalia. He handed her one. "And the more you try to draw conclusions on how things turned out based on whatever, the more confusing it gets."

"You keep saying that you have to believe it will be alright," Robin said, after taking a bite of her food. "This is very good, by the way."

"Beeman's a hell of a cook," Roger began eating. "Unfortunately, it's not just this situation. We may be able to get out of this problem - and there's no guarantee we will, depending on when I went back to get you. But even then, I may have messed up something else that will have just as dire consequences. The result is that you keep second-guessing yourself and second-guessing yourself and sometimes second-guessing yourself right into the very thing you were trying to avoid."

Robin nodded. She knew there were questions she wanted to ask, but as the food and the warmth of the fire worked on her, she suddenly yawned.

"It's been a long day for both of us," Roger said. "Why don't we turn in? Maybe after some sleep we'll be able to plan better."

Chapter Seven

R obin woke first. The first glimmer of dawn slid into the old house through the gap in the ceiling next to the stairway that no longer led anywhere. She shifted and got up. Roger had put the remains of their meal into a cooling box. Looking around in the pale light, she saw an old stove top percolator coffee pot. A water jug was nearby and there was a round of ground coffee sealed into a fabric filter. The grounds smelled delicious. At least, that hadn't changed.

Robin stirred up the fire, then filled the pot with water and added the round of coffee to the pot's basket. She set the pot on the fire, then looked around to see if there was anything else she could make for breakfast. In addition to the cooling box, there was another metal box containing all sort of breads and vegetables. Whatever Beeman's motives had been, he'd left them well-stocked for an extended stay.

She took a deep breath. It was hard to know just how different things were in Roger's time. The good thing about camping out is that it would give Robin a chance to adjust to it all.

"Is that coffee I smell?" Roger asked in a sleepy voice.

"Yeah. I found an old percolator." Robin found a padded rag and pulled the pot from the fire. She found what looked like plastic mugs missing their handles. The surfaces were decorated with ornate scrollwork, but they also appeared to be insulated. She poured the coffee into them.

"How do you like yours?" she asked Roger, and suddenly remembered she'd already asked him that some time before.

"Any way I can get it." Roger sat up and stretched. He looked at Robin. "Side effect of being too many whens where I can't get it at all."

Robin looked in the cooling box. "I don't see any milk or creamer. But there's some sugar here."

She adjusted her mug and handed him his and the sugar.

Roger looked up at the hole in the ceiling. "Dawn?"

"Looks like."

Shaking the last of the sleep from him, Roger wandered about the room, taking everything in. He opened the food safe and the cooling box and nodded.

"Looks like the travelers pulled together a collection," he said.

"What do you mean?"

"Purchases are tracked, mostly for convenience's sake," Roger said. "You don't have to worry about running out of things that way. It's not unusual to do some extra buying for a gathering of some sort. But if you have a known fugitive among your acquaintance and suddenly start buying more than usual, then the provider might think it worth their while to report it. Either Beeman or someone else pulled a bit here and a bit there to cover us. It's not enough to last six weeks, but we'll find a way to get around that.

We should be able to do some hunting and gathering to fill things out."

"You think it's safe staying in one place like this?" Robin asked. "And so close to someone else that's being held?"

Roger shrugged. "I don't know. Will you excuse me while I change clothes?"

"Sure."

Robin slipped out of the old house into the forest. The sky above the trees was turning a deep blue. She took a deep breath. The air was even cleaner than it had been in the Sixteenth Century. She couldn't help but wonder what had changed. All Roger had said was that the population was decreasing to an alarming rate, that there had been an economic meltdown. And he had mentioned one disaster, but he hadn't made it sound as though there had been some sort of apocalypse in terms of governments blowing each other up. If anything, it all seemed as though everything had naturally evolved. Robin sighed. It probably had. If the population were decreasing as he'd suggested, that would account for the cleaner atmosphere.

Roger came outside and took a deep breath. The last time she'd seen him, his behavior had been overly familiar - the easy intimacy of an established relationship - and an event in his future, but in her past. Now, he seemed a little distant. Robin wondered what would happen between them, then realized Roger was right about second-guessing.

"Would you like some toasted bread?" he asked suddenly. He was wearing a dark brown robe, intricately embroidered, with long sleeves and a hem that reached his calves, which were covered by dark brown boots.

"Um, I can eat it untoasted," Robin said. "I mean, it looked fresh enough to."

"For today, it is," Roger said.

There was another awkward pause.

"Should I be asking more questions?" Robin asked.

Roger suddenly laughed. "Only if you want to. I guess I'm trying to give you room to deal with everything." He looked at her curiously. "I guess I'm also trying to figure out why you came. And why you're still here. If I were you, I'd probably have blipped back home after letting out a blood-curdling scream."

"Probably because you're asking questions like that," said Robin, haplessly. "I suppose I don't have any solid evidence that you're some evil genius out to use me. What I have is evidence that Donald is a hard case. And people can be accused innocently. I've seen enough of that in my own time, let alone what happened to Dean, Elizabeth, and me."

"I'm still a fugitive," said Roger, his face drooping.

"So?" Robin said, laughing a little. "You warned me, and I still came. And... Okay, it's not just that. It's what Beeman said last night. Time travel is incredibly addicting. I can't imagine why more people don't want to. Dean and Elizabeth both said they'd had enough and definitely do not want to do any more, and all I can think is, are they out of their freaking minds?"

Roger laughed loudly and hard. "Okay. For a lot of reasons, there is no question that you are one of us. Travelers, I mean. But if I didn't know that, if you were just applying to join us, what you just said right now, that would immediately qualify you for the exam."

Robin paled. "There's an exam?"

"That frightens you?" Roger cocked his head. "You don't strike me as the type who has problems with tests."

"Not normally. But this time, I'm missing almost two hundred years of science, technology, and history."

"Yeah, that is a significant gap." Roger shrugged.

"And it doesn't worry you?"

"Why?" He nodded as if he suddenly understood, then smiled at her. "Robin, the timetrons recognize you. Which means you'll be in our system at some point or another. The machines have to be set up that way since some of them get left in secret places to rescue those of us who lose ours."

"But how?"

"That we're not entirely sure about. There's a lot about time travel that we don't know. We know it works. We know a lot about what doesn't work, which helps. We know you can't change history."

"But how do you know you can't?"

"Presumably, a returning traveler would remember a different history or world." Roger's face scrunched up as he thought. "I suppose it's possible that a memory could be altered, but there would have to have been some inconsistency among our collective experiences or blackouts or something. None of that has ever happened, that we know of."

Robin's stomach gurgled, and she sighed. "I guess we'd better get something to eat."

"Hey." Roger's voice was soft and gentle. "You don't have to worry about the exam. What I was trying to say is that you have obviously passed it. Or it's obvious that you will."

Robin smiled, then turned to the house shelter. "So I guess all we have to worry about is finding evidence and getting you out of trouble and teaching me all about this time while we're doing it."

"Oh, is that all?" Roger said, with a chuckle as he followed her into the house.

They had just finished breakfast when Beeman arrived outside the house.

"I didn't think we'd see you again so soon," Roger said as he held back the ivy for Beeman to enter.

Beeman dropped the large fabric sack he was carrying next to the cooling box. "I didn't think you'd have an anomaly with you. I've got clothes for her, plus some more food." He focused on Roger. "A bunch of us met last night."

"Uh oh," said Robin, trying not to take a defensive stance.

Beeman smiled at her. "No one even knows you exist. I kept that quiet. They think you're a kindly off-gridder who deserves our protection. But you being here does add a layer of complexity to the equation, especially since you know little to nothing about us." He held up a hand as Robin began to protest. "No one expects you to. According to Cricklan's notes, you were born in the late Twentieth Century, and this would have to be your first trip forward. And Roger, here, had minimal contact with you, based on his notes. So how much could you know?" He looked at her, his gaze a touch on the sad side. "Time travel is disorienting enough when you know what you're doing. That you did as well as you did in the past with no training whatsoever tells me that you're good and strong.

You should be fine here once you get used to things. But it also means you've got a lot to learn in a very short time."

"I'm not worried about that," said Roger brusquely. "We need to get a plan together."

"We've got six weeks," Robin said.

"Six weeks of dodging the I.B. police," corrected Beeman. "They weren't being generous. They were giving themselves more time to catch Roger."

"But I thought they weren't going to do that," Robin said.

"Not publicly," Roger said. "And not having an incentive hanging over me makes things a little easier. But Beeman's right. Just because they aren't publicly looking for me doesn't mean they haven't set a few traps or that they aren't looking."

"Which is going to make getting into Cricklan's house pretty difficult," Beeman said, settling onto a log seat. "Wassman took a meeting with Sylvesteri on the pretext of trying to hunt you down."

"Wassman is the Time Board chair," Roger explained to Robin. "Sylvesteri is a member of the Intelligentsia Board but tends to be a lot more sympathetic to the Intelligentsia, which makes her not very popular with the others."

Beeman snorted. "She's a Doctor of Literature. They needed a pure academic. Anyway, both Wassman and Sylvesteri seem to be using this opportunity to score some points with the rest of the I.B. But at the same time, they're also letting out little bits of news. According to Wassman, they've figured out some traveler came from the future to help you, even if there wasn't enough of an aura left to track."

Roger looked at Robin. "That's why I got you out of there so fast. I didn't want any of your aura dispersing."

"My aura?" Robin asked.

"All the microscopic bits of ourselves that we leave behind everywhere we go," Roger explained while Beeman waited impatiently. "It's basically what dogs smell and track."

"In any case," Beeman said, wrenching the conversation back to his news. "The I.B. wants to make coming back to help somebody illegal retroactively. How they're going to pull that off is anyone's guess. But I'm pretty sure Wassman doesn't want that to happen. He was fishing me hard. The trouble is, he knows he's too close to the I.B. for anyone to trust him. He's figuring you had some help and none of the timetrons are showing the trip, so it had to have been somebody whose trip hasn't registered yet. But something should have registered the arrival, and it hasn't."

Roger looked guilty. "I may have used an unregistered timetron to get to Bath to rescue Robin to prevent Donald from finding out I was there. And I may just happened to have given her the timetron, again to escape Donald, knowing that I could find another and that he wouldn't be able to track her."

"You're not making things any easier on yourself." Beeman glared at him.

Roger shrugged. "Cricklan knew what was going on and I filed a trip plan."

Beeman sighed. "You're just lucky that they're assuming that the timetron hasn't been built yet, which is why it's not registered and won't show up in the logs until it's been built."

"We have to do that to keep the logs from giving away too much about our futures," Roger said to Robin.

"I kind of figured that much out," Robin said.

Beeman made a face at her.

"Alright," Roger said, getting up and pacing. "Let's look at our current reality. Being stuck out here means that I am just as effectively imprisoned as if I were in my holding room. The advantage is that I can move freely and receive bits and pieces of aid from my colleagues."

"Assuming they can find you," Beeman said.

"That's right." Roger glared at him suddenly. "How did you find me?"

"I didn't," Beeman said. "I just went somewhere near where we figured you'd go, and you found me. But I imagine you're not going to want to stay in one place."

"Of course not," Roger said. "We may want to find some way of communicating. We do have a working mobile telephone on us."

"That might help if we don't use it too often," Beeman said. "But that forces me into the designated contact position, at least for the time being. You're not going to want to cast around for receivers."

Robin looked at Roger, not wanting to say anything.

Roger stopped pacing. "The trackers on Cricklan's house. Are they set to record anyone or just the travelers?"

Beeman's eyebrows rose. "Actually, Sylvesteri was probably in there yesterday. Wassman told me he'd messaged her to look for the full Board hearing report and she'd told him last night that she couldn't find it." He pulled out his hand-held unit and tapped it.

"Isn't Wassman on the Board that vetted the project?" Robin asked. "Why can't he testify that there was a problem with Donald?"

"People lie," Beeman said. "Documentation usually doesn't. Even when a report has been sealed, or a part of it has, there are time notes embedded into it that can be traced. We just have to find the file. And it looks like the trackers didn't pick up Sylvesteri."

"And how do you have access to the trackers at Cricklan's house?" Robin asked.

"Everyone does," Beeman said. "Nobody minds being monitored if everyone has access to it."

Robin shuddered.

Roger looked at her thoughtfully. "You know, we also have a non-person with us."

"Excuse me?" Robin snarled.

"You essentially are," Roger said. "Even a non-gridder usually has some record somewhere. The last records on you, so far, are almost two-hundred years old."

"And if they search for her aura print and it doesn't come up, that only means she went off the grid before her print set," Beeman said. "We have established that there's a kindly off-gridder helping us, at least among the travelers. Still, if an off-gridder wanders into Cricklan's place, the I.B. can't prove that it was on our behalf."

"Isn't there some sort of video that will show me doing it?" Robin asked.

"Video has been considered too intrusive since your time and it's too easily altered," Roger said. "Sniffers are far more accurate and are considerably harder to defeat."

"But Beeman just said that no one cares about being monitored if everyone has access to it." Robin looked pained.

"It doesn't entirely make sense," Roger said. "Things don't sometimes. But there seems to be a world of difference between being watched and mindless data bots tracking you."

Robin sighed. "So, how do I get in, and what am I looking for?"

Beeman winced. "Getting in should be easy. She left the place open."

"What?" yelped Roger.

"Maybe she wanted you or Donald to be able to get in," Beeman said. "And what's the worst that could happen? Some off-gridder comes in looking for some easy food and wrecks the place? All her artifacts are at the Time Center. We're going to have a bigger problem figuring out what we're looking for."

Roger shook his head. "That is not going to be easy. Knowing Cricklan, she probably hid it in plain sight. Which means it's probably a handheld of some sort that's slow and clunky but will suddenly respond to the pass image. But it could be just about anything. The only reason I think it's a handheld is that it would have to be sealed from the general system, but still certifiable for evidence."

"Okay," said Robin. "So, what do I do? Show this pass image around the house until something turns on?"

"You think about it," said Roger. "Think about me and the phrase hairless backside and that should do it."

"You think so?" asked Beeman. "That's a pretty specific image."

"I'm hoping for intent to carry it over," Roger said.

Beeman shrugged.

"Why don't we let Robin get changed into something more time-specific," Roger said, looking at Beeman and gesturing toward the ivy-covered opening.

Beeman opened the sack for Robin, then followed Roger outside. The dark-brown pants that Robin pulled from the sack were lightweight, with wild scrollwork woven into a fabric made of some fiber that Robin didn't recognize. They were very full and stopped mid-way down her calf, but the matching boots reached her knees, so Robin tucked the pant legs into the boot tops. She found a tan robe that wrapped around her like a kimono, with sleeves that were as form-fitting as a t-shirt and the collar draped around her neck in a plethora of softly pleated folds. Robin even found a wide variety of sturdy pockets sewn in among the folds of the pants and robe. Everything fit perfectly and felt perfectly comfortable and easy to move in. There was even a hidden pocket large enough to hold the timetron without it being visible, so Robin hid hers there.

Robin paused before parting the ivy curtain. Beeman and Roger were talking quietly together, or rather, Roger was telling Beeman something. Beeman didn't seem too happy with what he was hearing, but he handed Roger his handheld and Roger gave him one from the hidden pockets of his robe.

"I'm ready," Robin announced, pushing the ivy aside.

Roger smiled in approval as he saw her, but didn't say anything. Several minutes later, Robin followed Beeman through the forest and up a steep slope toward the house on the hill that she'd seen the day before. Beeman had insisted that Roger stay behind and break camp. Robin was glad that she'd made a point of working out at the gym those weeks she'd been at home from the past. Beeman started panting with the exertion long before she did. Beeman asked a couple of intelligent questions about her time, which she answered.

About halfway up the hill, however, Robin decided to ask the question that was weighing most heavily on her mind.

"Um, I get the politics driving what's going on with Roger," she said slowly. "But what I don't get is why bringing Elizabeth forward in time was such a terrible thing to do."

Beeman sighed. "It's because you just don't do it. Period."

Robin rolled her eyes skyward, and Beeman sighed again.

"I don't know how much Roger wants you to know," he finally said. "He's acting like you've already been accepted, which I guess you have since the machines recognize you. But you still must pass your exam, you know."

"I know. So?"

Beeman took a deep breath and stopped walking for a moment. "Well, I don't know how to say this, but there's a lot about time travel that we don't know."

"Yes. Roger's told me that." Robin waited for Beeman to start walking again.

"Oh, good. Anyway, we don't know what all the effects are on the human body and mind. Obviously, it's a lot easier going back into the past because you know that part from studying history. But bringing someone forward from their time, especially from a time when time travel was completely unheard of, that's chancy. Things get strange enough when we accidentally find out things about our own futures. Which is why we do not go past our natal times. Period. The only reason the Wynford project was approved was that things are getting desperate. That's why we had her on the sleep learning module. It didn't entirely work, but since she's adjusting to your time, it must have had some good effect."

"It seems so sad that Roger's in all this trouble for something that he didn't think was going to work."

Beeman gasped slightly. "Nobody thought it was going to work. That it sort of did is a good thing. And we'll have to find some way to document what you said about the effects on Elizabeth, because I don't think anybody wants to try this again with adults."

"You said something about trying with abandoned babies. But there's another problem with bringing children through? Roger said something about the drop stimulating cell growth."

Beeman nodded. "That's one of the problems. The other is the crushing sensation. The last thing we want to do is harm an infant. That's why, even though we ultimately failed with Wynford, we got enough data to make some significant corrections and may, in fact, be on the right track." Beeman gasped and stopped again. "Which is why it's a good thing you're here. It's just that convincing the I.B. is going to be, um, interesting."

"You mean challenging," Robin said with a sigh.

They walked a bit further in silence, then Beeman stopped again, this time on a flat round space.

"This is Cricklan's landing pad," he said and pointed to the front door of the house.

It almost looked as though live trees formed the frame, but then Robin saw the glint of gilt paint along the trunks. The rest of the house matched the rock face which rose over it. As she'd seen the day before, the only hint that there was a dwelling there was the row of glass panes overlooking the river. Assuming they were glass.

"Okay," said Robin, trying not to let on how nervous she felt. "Roger's hairless backside."

She went over to the door and slowly opened it, fully expecting to hear loud sirens and lights flashing. Instead, there was the deep silence of an unoccupied space.

The house looked almost the same inside as it did outside. Tree trunks with their natural ridges highlighted in gilt paint stood up against walls that looked like the hard granite they'd been built on. The ceilings mimicked the leafy boughs of the trees, with tiny, glistening elves painted among the leaves. Soft, white light filtered down from the ceiling, glowing brighter as Robin came into the front room. The glass panes ran along the side of the house from floor to ceiling, and Robin could see the wide river on the other side of the forest below. The water was a deep blue and tiny whitecaps splashed as the water rushed along.

The door opened near the edge of the rock wall and into a huge front room. The furnishings echoed the forest theme, with cushioned chairs and a sofa on three sides of a fire pit in the center. On the empty side, a large foot-pedaled loom was set up next to a spinning wheel. Bags of wool and huge spools of yarn lay scattered nearby, and a drawer poked out of the rock wall, overflowing with tools.

"Roger's hairless backside," Robin muttered. Images of what Roger possibly looked like naked flashed through her head, and she had to concede they were not entirely unwelcome.

She poked at the drawer, then slid several others open. They all contained weaving tools and yarns. Another closet was packed full of fabrics.

Beyond the front room was a dining room with what looked like kitchen appliances built into the rock face. A stove had been partially pulled out, but whatever sink there was remained hidden. Robin kept thinking about Roger's naked backside, but nothing flashed.

A door cut into the rock face led into a small toilet. Beyond the dining room was an office with a standing desk in the middle alongside a moveable reclining chair. The desk held a rack of brushes, fountain pens, and pencils. Several pots of different colored inks sat in a well on the side of the desk. Five small bits of paper were randomly scattered across the top. Each bit had a short phrase written on it. The phrases were in various states of embellishment, as if someone had played with one for a bit, then decorated another, then started another one, then went back to the first one.

They were pretty little bits of art, Robin thought, and they were in plain sight. Robin scooped them up just in case.

A door cut into the wall led into a tiny, bare room. The letters C, E, R, and D were painted on one wall, but the other walls were empty of any embellishment or decoration. Robin focused on the pass image, but nothing happened. She shut the door, then moved on to what was the bedroom.

It was the largest room in the house, with a bathroom, just as large, beyond it. The bed was huge and piled with all manner of cushions. The foot faced the glass wall, and the view was even more stunning. Robin looked for handhelds on the bedside table and found herself thinking all too easily of Roger naked. But there weren't any machines of any kind. The personal belongings in the drawers didn't look all that familiar, but there was an air of intimacy about them.

The bathroom held little more. If there were toiletries, they had taken a different form than what Robin was used to. The shower was huge, as was the tub, which was placed right next to the windows. There were no trees and rock faces on the walls, but they'd been just as carefully decorated as the small slips of paper Robin had found. There was something deeply intimate about the space that left Robin feeling as though she had crossed a line she shouldn't have.

She left and slid through the other three rooms and went back to the dining room to see if she could find anything.

The lights began flashing. Terrified, Robin backed into the corner between the dining room and the office. She heard the door in the office shut and a grunt. Slowly, she eased herself to the edge of the opening between the two rooms and looked into the office. Donald Long, wearing a ruffled shirt of Hawaiian print fabric over a coordinating skirt, stood with his back to her, stretching. With a satisfied grumble, he sniffed and went into the bedroom.

Her heart in her throat, Robin slid along the back wall of the dining room and then the front room and slipped through the door. She shut it as silently as she could, then ran for the cover of the trees and the path that she'd come up. Beeman was waiting for her and motioned her further along the path. They moved quickly and almost silently, pausing every so often to listen for pursuit.

Beeman, finally satisfied that they were not being followed or overheard, waved for a stop.

"What happened?" he gasped.

"Donald," Robin said between gulps of air. "There's some sort of transporter room. He came in that way. It looked like he was dressed for this time."

"Wonderful," Beeman grumbled. "Did you find anything?"

"Sort of." Robin got control of her breath, then pulled out the scraps of paper. "There weren't any handhelds or anything like that."

Beeman snorted when he saw the papers. "Those are just her hobby."

"But couldn't she have written a password or something like that on one of these?"

"Why?" Beeman shook his head. "It won't convince the I.B. of its authenticity. Besides, pass images are much more secure."

"Apparently," Robin grumbled.

They made it back to their camp a short while later. Robin, having felt Beeman's scorn for the papers, didn't mention them to Roger as they told him all that had happened.

"And you kept the pass image in your head?" Roger asked anxiously.

"I was thinking about your bare butt the whole time," Robin said, her face flushing.

"Wait," growled Beeman. "You were thinking about his butt as an adult, weren't you?"

"Well, yeah," Robin said, flushing even hotter.

Beeman turned on Roger. "See? This is why I said sending her was a bad idea. She doesn't know us well enough."

"What do you mean?" Robin said.

Roger sighed. "The pass image." He shrugged. "In our time, referring to a man's hairless backside is a mild insult. It's basically calling him a baby, since that's the only time his backside is hairless. But if your parent refers to your hairless backside, then it's a term of endearment because she or he is recalling your childhood."

"So, I was supposed to think about you as a baby," Robin said, feeling more annoyed than not.

"That wouldn't necessarily have done it," said Beeman a little snidely. "Remember, your backside is pretty specific to Cricklan."

"Cricklan is my mother," Roger told Robin, then turned to Beeman. "If she gave you that as a pass image, it couldn't have been that specific because she'd know I couldn't use it."

"Or the report isn't there," Beeman said. "But let's not forget who is."

Roger grimaced. "You said there was a loom set up."

"Yeah. A big one," said Robin.

"Donald's hobby." Beeman nodded.

"That's some good news," Roger said. "It does help regulate his behavior."

"But it also means that he's moved in there," Beeman said. "We'll never be able to get in and find that report."

"That is, as you pointed out, assuming it's there," said Roger. "And he has every right to be there." He glanced at Robin. "Donald is my brother."

"As well as the one person who stands to be hurt the most by that full report," Beeman said.

"Your brother," Robin said. "And I thought my family has issues."

"If it were a mere case of sibling rivalry, we would not be here now," Roger said. "Donald has emotive dysfunction syndrome. It's a genetic brain trait that usually makes it hard for an untreated person to feel empathy or shame."

"He's a psychopath," Robin said. "That actually makes sense."

"He'd been treated," Roger said. "There was no reason to believe that his syndrome had reactivated until you and your brother found Elizabeth. We were just getting a few hints that something was wrong when the project was first developed, which is why Cricklan made sure Donald couldn't be the one to run the project. She had that part sealed because at that time, we didn't know for sure and didn't want it to hurt Donald later. The treatment is technically permanent."

"Apparently not in travelers," Beeman grumbled. He glared at Roger. "But Donald is the least of your worries right now, old man. Right now, we've got an anomaly to bring to current understanding and find evidence that Donald's motives were less than pure and then convince the I.B. that they shouldn't shut us down."

"We have the evidence," Roger said. "Robin, here, can testify to that. As for the report, we know it exists. We just have to find it."

"But Robin is an anomaly. Why would they believe her?" Beeman said.

"We can bring her current."

"With enough time, yes," said Beeman.

Roger's eyes lit up. "That may just work. Beeman, if I can get Robin current, are you willing to help prep her for the exam?"

"Yes," Beeman said. "But how is that going to help your case?"

"Exactly," said Robin. "Beeman said people lie, documents don't."

"But a verbal testimony can add strength to a document," Roger said. "Plus, as a technical non-person, Robin can go places and do things we can't."

"That makes some sense," Beeman said with a very reluctant sigh. "So, what do I and the rest of the crew do in the meantime?"

"See if you can find that report," said Roger. "Robin and I will stay off the grid, then get in touch with you in maybe three weeks or so. Right now, the less contact we have with you, the better."

"But if you need something..." Beeman protested.

"Your cell network connection is on the handheld, right?"

"Yeah." Beeman sighed. "We just can't use it too much. The last thing we need to do is let those I.B. toadies find out these things still work. They're paranoid enough without finding out we can communicate off the normal channels."

Roger snorted. "The only thing that will stop their paranoia is having me safely locked up and the travelers shut down. You know that as well as I do."

Beeman looked utterly miserable. "I do very well."

"Beeman, we've been in worse spots." Roger pasted a hearty smile on his face that he clearly did not feel.

"Not with the I.B.," Beeman said.

"It doesn't matter," Roger said. "The final issue is that we travelers are more resourceful and creative than anyone on the I.B. That's how we function. That's how we identify potential travelers. Which means we can get this resolved."

Beeman did not look entirely convinced, but he had to concede there were few better options. Roger had Robin give Beeman her mobile phone so that Beeman could set it to work with his cell network. It took only a minute, then Beeman left. Roger watched his handheld.

"He's gone," Roger announced after a minute.

Robin looked at him. "So, you don't trust him."

"I trust that he won't intentionally give us away," Roger said. "But you may have noticed, he is a bit of a worrywart, and he does have to try and stay on the good side of the I.B. Frankly, I don't envy him or Wassman. They're in a tough position. Neither of them is naïve enough to believe that the I.B. wants to do anything but shut us down. But the best chance they have of helping me, well, us, is to act like they support what the I.B. is doing." Roger sighed. "Sadly, not everyone understands the value of history, never mind that we travelers have paved the way for some of the best of current technology and sociology simply by bringing ideas from the past."

Robin couldn't help rolling her eyes. "It would appear that some things never change." She looked around at the small camp. "What all do we need to pack?"

"Let's go ahead and bring all of it. We'll probably need it eventually." Roger looked up from his handheld. "Just make sure we can touch everything and each other. I've got to look something up." He grinned. "And here is what I thought. This will be perfect."

He pocketed the handheld and helped Robin gather up the camp items. Some minutes later, he had Robin bring out the timetron. They touched hands and the crushing sensation began.

The room they landed in looked like a refugee from the Star Trek set, Robin thought. White panels covered the walls. On an adjacent wall were inset panels that were light blue doors. Next to one of the doors was a tall, dark blue box-like structure that reminded Robin of an armoire. Up against the wall facing the other door was a dark blue table. Above that, simple white shelves displayed numerous antiques.

"I've been here before," Robin said. "It was 2199."

"Oh. It hasn't happened yet." Roger picked up her sack. "I think we can add these items to the collection for the time being."

Robin yelped despite herself as Roger put the coffee grinder that had been wired to an iPhone on the shelf.

"I remember seeing that," she said in a strangled voice.

"You do?" Roger swore silently. "Try not to think about it, then."

"This is your house, isn't it?"

"Yes. Why don't we move all the camp gear to that closet there?" He pointed at the dark blue armoire.

"It's funny," said Robin, picking up the food box. "This is more like what I expected the future to look like."

Roger looked around the room. "Sorry about that. But I can't help it. I've always loved antiques."

"These are antiques." Robin's eyes opened wide in shock.

"At least a hundred-odd years old," said Roger. "You may have noticed that things have gotten a lot more ornate these days."

"Yeah. I had," Robin frowned. "How long do you think it will take to bring me current?"

Roger mused. "It depends. You seem like a pretty fast learner. Maybe four months. Maybe six months."

Robin gasped. "Roger, you don't have that much time!"

Roger smiled. "Time is the one thing we've got."

Chapter Eight

R obin stretched out her legs on the soft sand, the sun wrapping its warmth around her and her body. Roger lounged propped up on his elbows, watching the waves rolling in and out. The two horses they'd been riding stood close by, occasionally nickering.

"It's hard to believe this was Santa Monica," Robin said.

"You've seen the pictures of it under water."

Robin grimaced. From the forest near St. Louis, they'd only gone back about eighteen months or so. They'd spent a fair amount of time at Roger's house, which was in Paris. Roger explained that there had been a massive nuclear meltdown about ninety years before in China, largely part of the economic collapse that had occurred ten years before that. Population rates had already been declining, but the disaster had had a devastating effect, with the Chinese suffering the immediate losses. But then radiation disease claimed a hefty chunk of the rest of the world's population in the years that had followed. So, while the Paris of Roger's time was still a bustling city with many of its oldest structures intact, it was nowhere nearly as crowded and most of the skyscrapers had been torn down and replaced by single dwellings.

They'd had to leave Paris periodically to prevent Roger from running into himself. This time, they'd gone to Southern California. Los Angeles, as a city, still existed, as did many of the older buildings. But most of the sky-scrapers and other large buildings were all gone, torn down by wreckage bots as the sick slowly died off and left them empty.

It had been an intense eight months. There was so much to learn, and Robin found it hard to see familiar landmarks razed or grown over. Worse yet was coming to terms with the fact that Dean and Elizabeth were long dead, having lived out their natural lives. Robin shuddered. It really was a good thing that time travel policy did not allow for traveling into the future. It was genuinely crazy making knowing what was coming and not being able to do anything about it.

"Still, it's amazing how the planet has bounced back from all the pollution my time created," Robin said, again watching the water.

"Mother Earth does have incredible regenerative power," Roger said. "Your time came close to killing it, though. There are still mining bots out in the Pacific, working on that plastic patch."

Robin watched him out of the corner of her eye. He had remained distant the entire time they'd been together, which was rather remarkable considering that they'd had no real social interaction with any of Roger's friends. Since they were out of sync with Roger's natal time, he didn't want to chance it even though he didn't have any memory of someone seeing him when he hadn't technically been there. Even lounging in the sand, Roger kept his eyes solid-ly fixed on the ocean rather than on her.

And yet, there had been moments. They often went out for entertainment purposes, popular culture being an excellent way to learn about an era. The night before, they'd eaten dinner at a nearby restaurant. They'd had some lovely wine and laughed over a holo-game they'd played earlier that afternoon. Roger had looked at her fondly, as if he'd wanted to do more, but couldn't.

Then, as they'd ridden along that morning, they'd come across a couple engaging in copulation - in a world that didn't seem to care about privacy, it was not unusual to see people having sex in public places. Robin had flushed deeply and looked away. Such things didn't bother Roger. He was used to it. But this time, he'd become even more gruff and distant.

Shifting in the sand, he cleared his throat. "Okay, time for a pop quiz."

Robin groaned exaggeratedly.

He chuckled despite himself. "What were the three primary effects of genetic selection in the mid-Twenty-First Century?"

"The problem with genetic selection was that parents continued to select for Caucasian heterosexual male traits, thanks to a lack of regulation in that industry," Robin recited. "This resulted in a - a significant imbalance in the male to female ratio; b - a major hit to the populations of people of color, which led to c - Caucasian male traits becoming so dominant that there is a lack of genetic diversity, which is contributing to falling fertility rates. These results now place the human species in danger of dying out. Hence the need to bring genetic diversity and females, specifically, back into the gene pool."

"Exactly," said Roger, his gaze rigidly fixed back on the waves.

"Who knew women would get equality by becoming only thirty-five percent of the population," Robin grumbled, and not for the first time. "At least people of color are also getting their due, just because they are rare."

"And the reason we can't use genetic selection to get ourselves out of the present dilemma?"

"Genetic selection often perpetuates problems with later fertility, let alone the justice issues of deciding what constitutes negative traits. Supposed defects are actually a sign that there is healthy genetic diversity in the population. Selecting out things like a tendency for cancer or cystic fibrosis or Down Syndrome puts the larger population at risk and is unnecessary, thanks to other medical advances."

Roger smiled at her. "I know you're bored with all of this, but you've really gotten it down."

"Maybe it's because the technology changes, mores sometimes change, but people really don't," said Robin.

"Or maybe you're a natural traveler," Roger said. He forced his gaze back to the water.

Robin frowned. For the most part, she couldn't help liking Roger. He was charming, considerate, supportive. And sweet. He could be a little on the moody side, but it wasn't about meanness. He was just comfortable being vulnerable, something that amazed Robin to her core. That the two shared the same sense of humor and love of history made them compatible. That they sometimes had differing opinions just added variety to the relationship.

Robin paused. It felt like things were progressing toward a relationship, except that Roger kept putting distance between them. Perhaps it was because she was still in training and Roger thought he shouldn't impose himself. While attitudes toward simple sexual liaisons had loosened quite a bit and marriage was more of an economic agreement, how actual love relationships were expected to go, that Robin had yet to find out. Whether or not she even wanted such a relationship, she wasn't sure if she did.

She looked at him. "You know. I just thought of something odd. You don't call Cricklan mom. Is it normal now for kids to call their parents by their first names?"

"Some do," Roger said. "I don't know why we did."

"You mean you and Donald."

"Uh, yeah." He looked away.

"I noticed you don't talk about him much," Robin said softly.

"What is there to say?" Roger looked at her and sighed. "I love him as anyone would love his brother. But our relationship has always been difficult for reasons that have nothing to do with either of us. The thing is, Cricklan and our dad, Eric, adopted both of us. When I was an infant, my birth father killed my birth mother and then himself. It was apparently pretty gruesome and spectacular."

"In other words, we're still dealing with domestic violence," sighed Robin.

"It's better, but it still happens. People get angry and then let it get into their souls and things happen, no matter how we try to prevent it." Roger waved that part away. "Anyway, Cricklan and Eric took me in, and I never knew any other parents. When I was about eight, Donald had been surrendered and his parental records sealed. He was around two at the time and almost immediately, my parents began to suspect they knew why he'd been surrendered. But we were able to get him treated, and he was fine.

Except that I continued to get a lot of attention because of my parents' deaths, which made Donald start acting competitive. Then our father was killed, and Donald thought that Cricklan and I blamed him. That's one of the reasons why we weren't all that sure that Donald's condition had reactivated. Or it may have been the remnants of Donald's condition driving the competitive behaviors. There's really no way of knowing. Which is why Cricklan didn't want Donald leading the project with Elizabeth and why she insisted that part of the record be sealed. What she didn't anticipate was the Time Board giving it to me. It was Donald's idea and not getting to lead it must have really hurt. And then to see me get it." Roger sighed. "It may be what reactivated his condition."

"I can't imagine it would have helped." Robin wanted to reach out and touch Roger's arm, but held back.

"Either way, as soon as I get this current mess settled, it looks like I'm going to have to go rescue Donald." Roger got up.

"Can you force him to get treatment?" Robin got up, also, and began wiping sand off her legs.

Roger made a face. "It is technically a violation of his free will. But the argument is usually made that the condition has knocked out the person's free will. That the patient would prefer to be treated if the condition hadn't knocked out the ability to make that choice. And in all but a very few cases, that remains true. Very occasionally someone decides they're better off with the condition and will sue for damages. But it's hard to prove. The person usually must have a solid history of exceptionally creative works that was clearly disrupted by the treatment. And people who have some sort of neuro-psycho condition but who are also doing exceptional work are not usually pressed to be treated, unless it's getting hard to control their suicidal impulses, and by then, you have to assume they want to be treated." Roger finished brushing himself off and smiled at Robin. "In any case, getting Donald treated is going to be pretty much moot until we get things squared away with the I.B. You're about as ready as you're going to get. Why don't we check out that place we saw near the stables and have dinner there?" Roger pulled a handheld out of his pocket. "Paris is clear for me as of this morning. So, we can head back to my place tonight, then get our gear and blip back early tomorrow."

Robin shrugged. "Blip where?"

"Back to my natal time continuum." Roger gathered the reins of the horses. "Tell you what. I'll ride sidesaddle back and let you ride astride."

One of the worst bits of Robin's training had been riding horses. She had never really liked horses, but conceded that one had to be able to ride them if one was going to inhabit the persona of a reasonably wealthy person while traveling.

"I can't imagine why you like riding sidesaddle," Robin grumbled, mounting the horse with the regular astride one.

"You only hate it because that's your only option," Roger said, wrapping his leg around the pommel on the other horse. "There are a few of us guys who have figured out that it's a lot more logical for us than astride."

Roger took the lead on the way back to the stable. He seemed cheerful enough, but Robin suspected he wasn't any more eager to return to being a fugitive than she was. But while the break had been as restful, in some ways, as it had been necessary to bring Robin current, it was no more than a respite. The real work lay ahead. Robin's heart clenched as she desperately hoped she'd be up to whatever would be required when they were going.

Roger purposefully refrained from any more pop quizzes and the evening was spent pleasantly chatting and relaxing.

The next morning, however, any relaxed feelings had fled. Roger's tension grew as they went over all the camping gear and added a few more items to their equipment. Robin debated combing out the intricate braids a hair bot had woven into her hair, but had to concede that the braids did keep her hair out of her face. Roger had insisted that she let it grow, since women were expected to wear their hair long pretty much throughout history, and even during the times when women did cut their hair, it was not unusual for some to keep it long.

Roger's face became grim as they got in physical contact with everything they were bringing, then touched each other's hands. The crushing, sucking sensation ripped through Robin's body, then was gone almost as suddenly. They landed in another forest, in a small clearing that opened out on one side to a river. An old bridge still crossed the waters to an almost familiar skyline. Robin gasped.

"Where are we?" she asked.

"The Garden State of New Jersey," Roger said with a grin.

"You realize that in my time, that can be a rather ironic statement," Robin said.

Roger nodded toward across the water. "That is the fair city of New York, one of the more densely populated cities on the planet, which is why you still see some of the more iconic skyscrapers."

"Isn't that where they're holding Cricklan?" Robin asked.

"According to the news on the handheld, yes." Roger shrugged. "Or at least, they were when Beeman last updated it. We're only about three weeks ahead of then, depending on when the timetron set us down."

Robin looked at the collection of boxes and bags. "So, now what?"

"Well, if I did this right, we should be near some abandoned row houses." Roger retreated briefly into the trees and came back quickly. "I just found one with a roof on it, even, and maybe even some working plumbing. Let's get all this stowed away. Then we'll find another spot where we can meet Beeman."

It didn't take long to build their camp. Robin was happy to see that the plumbing in the old house was working well enough to flush toilets and provide water, even if it wasn't hot. It didn't matter. There was the slight chill of a spring morning in the air, and both Robin and Roger were wearing the heavier robes and full pants considered outdoor wear. Even better, the fireplace flue was clear enough to draw the smoke from a fire. The stove didn't work, but Roger had said that natural gas stores had long been depleted. If one were to use a gas for burning, it was usually done with methane, which was not only renewable but also stored in tanks.

When sleeping kits and cooking utensils had been set up to Roger's satisfaction, the two left the abandoned row house and walked down the river's edge until they found a similar row house. Roger took out Robin's mobile phone, swiped the face, then pressed a few different spots. Then he looked at Robin and waited.

"So, how long do we wait?" Robin asked.

"I have no idea," Roger said.

They both felt a rush of energy as Beeman appeared in front of them. Roger had explained that the timetron technology had been built on human transporter technology, which was the common way of getting around.

"I thought you were going to stay away until closer to the trial," Beeman said, glowering at Roger as the two grasped forearms.

"I told you, I want to get Robin ready for the exam," Roger replied, completely unfazed. "If we can get her certified, that will add credibility to her testimony, if it's required. You agreed to do the final tutoring. Besides, this should give us some extra time to find that report. Unless you've found it since we've been gone."

"No," sighed Beeman. He took a long look at Robin. "How long were you two back?"

"About eight months," Roger said. "Robin's picked up quite a lot."

Beeman did not look terribly happy, but he didn't protest.

"Have you got an updated handheld for me?" Roger asked.

Beeman sighed, and the two exchanged units.

"And how is Cricklan doing?" Roger asked.

"She's been released. Sort of," Beeman said.

Roger groaned. "They put her on the streets, didn't they?"

"From what I can tell, she's just as happy to be there," Beeman said. "She isn't fully off the grid, for one thing. But she's not where they can monitor her that much, either."

Roger noted Robin's puzzled look and nodded. "Cricklan's basically been let loose, but with minimal resources. Which means she's going to have to surface occasionally, and they'll be able to reel her in, if they want. And I guess she went into hiding, probably somewhere in New York. Which means she's safe, but it will be pretty hard to get a hold of her." He looked at Beeman. "Unless you've found a way to make contact."

"Not quite," Beeman said. "There's a code we can activate. But there's no guarantee she'll see it, let alone respond."

Roger dismissed the response with a wave of his hand. "Then we can't count on her. It's probably just as well. Is Donald still at her place?"

"Yes," said Beeman with a roll of his eyes. "You will be shocked and pleased that Wassman pulled off a spectacular bit of brinkmanship with the I.B. He convinced them to let Donald stay at Cricklan's house to keep any potential off-gridders out. Which means we can monitor his movements. He also needs to stay around long enough to testify at the trial."

"Doesn't he have a place of his own?" Robin asked.

"That's the not so good news." Beeman looked guilty. "He relinquished his apartment."

"He what?" gasped Roger.

"Gave it up. He's planning to bolt." Beeman sighed. "He's going to shut us down and take off to somewhen he likes better than now."

"Which will mean he won't have to worry about us coming after him and getting him treated." Roger shook his head.

"More like he's punishing you," Beeman said. "Shutting everything down is simply an added value."

Robin thought Roger was about to start crying.

"His condition is escalating," he sighed. "He wasn't that bad before we left to get Elizabeth. Another time trip and he'll be a complete monster. He's probably got a stash somewhere."

A stash, Robin remembered, was a collection of gold and or other tangible goods that could be easily converted to any kind of money. Roger had explained that time travelers sometimes kept them to make it easier to go somewhen quickly. Pulling together a stash was usually a sign that a traveler was up to no good and possibly had intentions of hiding in the past to escape some wrongdoing.

"Most of us have gotten one together since the current I.B. was seated," said Beeman. "None of us want to get stranded here."

"Do you know where Donald's is?" Roger asked.

"No," Beeman said. "We can't risk violating his free will without permission from his family."

Roger smiled. "You have it. Go do what you must do. We'll have some hope of containing him if we can get his stash."

"I thought you wanted me to prepare Robin for the exam."

Robin tried not to smirk. Roger sighed and started pacing.

"We're going to need Robin's testimony," Roger said. "And we need that report."

"It's probably in the system, but that only means we're going to need Cricklan to unseal it," Beeman pointed out.

"But that's perfect," Roger said. "Robin and I are off the grid. I can look for Cricklan in the city. They restricted her to the city, didn't they?"

"What if they're using her as bait to trap you?" Robin asked.

"I wouldn't put it past them," Beeman said.

"Then we go in with our eyes wide open," Roger said. "Beeman, who can we trust?"

It was an odd thing to ask, Robin thought, given that Roger didn't perfectly trust Beeman, either.

"Not Wassman, for sure," Beeman said. "I mean, we can, but it would be safer for him not to let him in on too much. I've got a couple guys who can monitor Donald as he moves. Jim and Adam. Alayo can help me - he'd be spotted too easily following Donald."

"Good," Roger said. "Now, how do we set up a learning center for Robin?"

Beeman gazed across the river at the city on the other side. "We've got an empty we can use. Full power and access. Minimal monitoring. Of course, since only we know about Robin, no one will be looking for her."

"But will it register an unknown?" Roger asked.

"It doesn't seem likely," Beeman said. "After all, I have every right and business to be in the city, and there's no reason to monitor me. Most of the others are avoiding connecting too much, so it doesn't look like we're getting ready to stage something. It's all about looking like good little boys so we don't get shut down. If the toadies think we're afraid of them, then they're less likely to keep an eye on us."

"This is the Intelligentsia Board?" Robin asked. "They don't sound very smart."

"They're smart enough to know that if too many of us are being monitored, it will get out that the I.B. is getting pushy again and that will cause trouble with the other affiliations," Beeman said. "It's the balance. We can't push the limits too hard, or they have an excuse to intervene. They can't monitor us too closely or we cause trouble for them."

Roger was scrolling through his handheld. "Okay. I think I know how to do this. Where is your empty?"

"Midway down Central Park, on Park Avenue."

"Perfect," Roger said. "Send me the address on the mobile phone and I'll have Robin there tomorrow at 10 a.m."

Beeman did not look happy, but agreed.

Chapter Nine

The next morning, Roger left Robin outside a tallish building of tan brick. She didn't see it as she walked inside, but Roger swallowed back the terror in his chest. They were taking an enormous chance. Beeman seemed unlikely to give them up, but that didn't mean the I.B. couldn't or wouldn't use him to get to Roger. It was a delicate balance, indeed.

Roger spent that first day outside the building, making sure Robin was safe. When she emerged as they had planned, he felt better. She spent the evening complaining about sub-medical training. He sympathized as they cooked dinner over the fire in their New Jersey camp. But Beeman was better at teaching sub-med, and it was a required part of the test.

The next morning, he left Robin again, but this time, headed downtown. The city was a good place to hide, unless someone was actively searching for you, and Roger could not assume that the I.B. wasn't. So not only did he have to find Cricklan, he had to make sure he did so without either leading the I.B. to her or letting the I.B. catch him. The one advantage he had was that he knew Cricklan as only a son could know his mother.

He headed into the park. The green lawns of the previous centuries had long been replaced by natural growth, although Roger had always noted that the so-called "natural" growth was as meticulously designed and tended as the lawns had been. The paths wended through trees and glens, and Roger followed along until he came to an ancient bridge. He hid behind a tree until the man he was looking for sauntered over the bridge. Alayo was of African descent and from a group of families that had decided to keep those genetic traits active. His skin was very dark, but his body was as trim and muscular as every other male's, and he kept his curly hair closely cropped.

Roger had arranged the meeting the day before when Alayo found Roger watching for Robin. Alayo had said he might have something for Roger, but wouldn't say what it was. Being a relatively new traveler, Alayo was mostly beneath the I.B.'s notice. Still, Roger wasn't going to assume that Alayo hadn't been followed, or worse.

And it almost seemed worse when another man hurried over the bridge and greeted Alayo. The new arrival was a touch shorter than most and his blonde hair had red glints in it. His short-sleeved robe was dark blue and almost without embellishment. The two men clasped forearms, then Alayo looked around.

"I'm betting he's around here someplace," Roger heard Alayo tell the man. "He's pretty skittish."

"He ought to be." The man looked around as well. "The Exec Council is so excited about shutting down you travelers, they're practically drooling." The man shuddered. "They get you guys, it's only a matter of time before they try to dump us."

Roger suddenly recognized the man. Steven was an artist who had memberships in several art affiliations, including one overseen by the Intelligentsia Board, which was how Roger knew him. Arts were considered as necessary and more dangerous than most of the Intelligentsia. Steven's concern about the Executive Council was well-warranted. Roger slid out from behind the tree.

"Steven, good to see you," he said softly, staying near the trees in case a run would be necessary.

"Hey-ho, Roger," Steven said, a grin lighting up his face. "Alayo told me he'd found you."

"Why were you looking for me?" Roger asked, still keeping his distance.

"I heard about Cricklan being put on the streets and had some help for her," Steven said. "She asked if I'd share it with you. She's staying on the move, you know."

"Actually, I didn't." Roger glared at Alayo, who shook his head.

"I didn't know," Alayo said. "I thought she might be. All Steven told me was that he had a message from her and some help."

Roger nodded.

"So, what have you got?"

Steven grinned even wider. "A restricted access pass for you. Me and another digital artist had hacked a couple for the fun of it. We did it again and gave one to Cricklan and now we've got one for you. All I need to do is imprint your thumb, then we'll connect your wave pattern and override your identity."

"How did you get access to it?" Roger couldn't help asking.

"Easy," Steven said, laughing. "They gave it to us. We're doing the visuals re-design on the interface." He shrugged. "Admittedly, it can't get you anyplace the I.B. really gives a crap about. But do you really want to go to any of those places?"

"Nope." Roger debated asking for a second one, but didn't want to give away Robin's presence. Beeman should be able to get Robin into the Time Center with his access and Robin couldn't trip any alerts because she didn't technically exist in that time. "All right. Where's your imprinter?"

Steven looked at Alayo, who suddenly got very distracted by the bridge. Then both Steven's and Roger's eyes swept the sky above them.

Steve whipped out his handheld, thought for a second, then had Roger place his thumb on the screen.

"Give it about five minutes for it to be fully active," Steve said. He touched Roger's arms. "But, um, Cricklan specifically asked me to tell you not to look for her."

"What? Why not?"

"She's worried about Donald." Steve glanced around again. "She thinks he's found a way to watch her, and she's afraid that if you find her, it will lead him to you. That's why she's staying on the move."

Roger sighed. The only problem was that he didn't know if Cricklan knew that they still needed the full report on the Elizabeth project. The way Beeman had been talking, it seemed as though she thought they had it. And Beeman had said he hadn't seen her since he'd met up with Roger since they were in St. Louis. That she was continuing to stay in hiding likely meant that she expected Roger to have the report.

On the other hand, if she was that worried about Donald reaching him through her, then it would make sense to keep as much distance as possible.

Roger finally nodded and sent Steven on his way.

Alayo came up with a sad look on his face.

"I don't think either Cricklan or Donald are in the building you were watching yesterday," he said. "We've gotten some intelligence that Donald is mostly staying in Cricklan's house."

"I heard about Donald," Roger said. "And why don't you think Cricklan is there?"

Alayo shrugged. "I've been watching it off and on. A lot of people don't know it, but Wassman and Cricklan and some of the other Time Boarders formed a cooperative a few years ago and bought the building. They wanted it as a safe house."

Roger's eyebrows rose. "That's the building. I'd forgotten."

"You knew about it?"

"I'm also one of the owners." Roger frowned.

"Anyway, there are sniffers just inside the entrance, but as far as I can tell, they're only set to alert if you show up." Alayo shrugged. "And probably Cricklan."

"Maybe not Cricklan, but she's not going to take that chance."

"I know. What are you going to do now?" Alayo asked.

"Go back to hiding," Roger said.

He looked at Alayo rather pointedly, and Alayo nodded and disappeared.

Feeling at loose ends, Roger left the park on foot and melted into the crowd on 5th Avenue. A crowd that would seem incredibly sparse to Robin.

Several blocks later, he arrived at his destination. The building had started out as the New York Public Library, but it had evolved into a public learning center for advanced education. Roger looked fondly at the old lions on the sidewalk doors. Students rushed past him from the glide cars on the street and scurried up the stairs. Roger followed more slowly. The great reading room was filled with young adults earnestly poring over their books and holograms. More streamed out of one of the side rooms as class, apparently, ended.

Roger headed for the basement levels. He pressed his thumb to the entry on the floor he wanted and was immediately granted access. That was a good sign, which still didn't mean that he was in the clear. He looked at his handheld. There was no sign of a sniffer or that any alert had gone off. It wasn't a guarantee, but having gotten in meant that he could use the stairs and otherwise move around unnoticed.

The section he was looking for was only one level up from the very bottom of the basement. He cleansed his hands in the rapid cleaner, then strolled through the aisles of ancient books. The soft scent of old leather and parchment gently tweaked his nose. It was tempting to linger, but he needed to stay focused. There was a light patina of dust on the shelves and volumes. Few needed to see the actual volumes, as all the content was otherwise available. The volumes themselves were occasionally brought out for display. A few scholars wanted to see the pages, but that was more for the joy of touching something almost two thousand years old. The only others interested in seeing the actual volumes were generally time travelers doing research on some when they were planning to visit, along with acclimating to the older way of doing things.

After wandering through several aisles of shelves, Roger finally found the signs he was looking for. The dust under two volumes had been scraped away. Roger smiled. He recognized the books immediately. They were a pair of psalters that he'd brought his mother from a visit to Fourteenth Century England before he knew better. Cricklan had been furious, but had also appreciated the fine lettering and artwork.

Roger pulled the first volume off the shelf and gently opened it. He leafed carefully through the pages. They had been treated, as everything on this level had, but that still didn't mean one could be careless. A small slip of wood paper slid out and wafted its way to the floor. Roger picked it up. It was an image of himself and Donald together as very young boys, drawn in Cricklan's hand. Tears sprang to Roger's eyes. There was so much at stake.

There were no more slips of paper or parchment in the first psalter.

But as soon as Roger opened the second psalter, a hologram formed. Cricklan's squat figure and tightly curled, tousled hair suddenly stood in front of him.

"Am I to hope that you did not get my message to not look for me?" the hologram asked.

Roger could lie and the hologram would not know the difference, unlike the real Cricklan, but he decided that it wouldn't change anything.

"Yes, I got it," Roger said. "I wasn't necessarily looking for you. Besides, we need to find you before the trial."

"You don't need me. You need the report."

"We need you to unseal it."

Cricklan's form wavered in irritation. "I left the pass phrase out where you could find it. In plain sight."

"I couldn't use it," Roger said. "I didn't want to go into the house and give a sniffer something to track."

"Well, at least you showed some sense there," Cricklan's form said.

"So, how do we get the report?" Roger asked. "We've only got a few weeks before the trial."

"The I.B. is the least of your troubles," Cricklan said. "They're not actively looking for you. Why should they? If you don't show up at your trial, they'll have the perfect reason to shut the travelers down. And if we all escape into the past, why should they worry? On the other hand, Donald is actively looking for you. I don't think he knows the report exists, but he doesn't want you to get any other evidence to save your hairless backside. Can you transport?"

"I'm trying not to. I'd rather folks believed that I'm land bound."

Cricklan's form almost smiled. "You always were a bright boy. Go back to my house—"

A door opened at the far end of the cavernous room. Cricklan's form wavered.

"See what I mean about Donald?" she said, and the hologram abruptly disappeared.

Roger had no doubt the hologram had picked up Donald's brain waves. There was probably another message in the book that would only play when Donald opened it. Assuming he did. Roger silently replaced the book and wiped down the surrounding shelves. There was no point in drawing attention to the two volumes.

He could hear footsteps going down the aisle next to him, although he couldn't see for sure that it was Donald doing the walking. Roger slid down the aisle toward the door. As he peeked around the shelves, he could see the door on the side wall. There were no sniffers waiting. Roger checked his handheld. No additional life forms registered on at least three floors.

As Roger slipped past the aisle next to him, he glanced quickly down it. Donald was about two-thirds of the way along. He'd pulled a heavy volume down and was engrossed in what he was reading. His lips moved as he read, a sure sign that he was reading something in another language, and an ancient version of it at that. Just based on the location of the book, it was probably from somewhere in the Sixteenth Century.

Roger didn't wait for Donald to see him. He silently slipped through the room.

He paused as he came to the doors leading to 5th Avenue. Down next to the street, a small russet-colored dog was busily sniffing the sidewalk, the dog's handler ambling along behind. The dog was one of the smaller alert sniffers. It was highly accurate but couldn't run nearly as fast as the tracking dogs, from which there was no escape except transporting, and Roger did not want the I.B. to know he could transport. As long as the I.B. thought he was relatively contained by being off the grid, then he and, most importantly, Robin were safe.

The sniffer yipped and its handler suddenly perked up. Roger didn't wait. He hurried through the library to the back entrance. The little sniffers were very good at remembering a scent to alert on, but notorious for losing a trail, especially in the heavier traffic of the city. The tracking dogs could stay on a trail for weeks as long as they had the scent they were looking for in front of them. If not, they were not likely to remember it long enough to alert on.

It was worrying that the sniffer had been outside the library, assuming it had been there to find him. It wouldn't be the first time this particular Intelligentsia Board had played the benevolence game when, in fact, it had been doing exactly the opposite. Roger wondered if Cricklan knew.

It didn't really matter, except that Roger had to be even more careful not to be seen. That afternoon, he met Robin not far from the safe building and led her through the park on a winding track. They eventually made their way back to New Jersey through one of the many tunnels that had been maintained for the benefit of hikers and other outdoor enthusiasts.

Robin took over making the fire, as always. She was grumbling again, but this time Roger couldn't fault her.

"I didn't think anybody could be so dry," Robin complained as Roger assembled meat, vegetables, and some bread in their cooking pot. "I'm having a terrible time not nodding off. Then Beeman gets cranky because he thinks I'm not listening to him."

Roger smiled. He was growing fonder of her by the minute, but he didn't dare initiate anything. That was the worst of knowing pieces of your future.

Robin stared at the flames in the fireplace grate. "He said something pretty interesting today." She looked at him. "You were the first time traveler?"

"Uh, yeah." Roger ducked his head, his face growing hot. "Cricklan, Eric, Donald, and I were all part of the project. We were following up on the theoretical work by Dr. Aaron Frawley."

"I know. Turns out I worked with Dr. Frawley when I got my master's degree," Robin said. She chuckled. "Everyone then thought he was getting senile or something."

"Well, he did lay the theory out, but nobody could do anything with it until they developed transporter technology," Roger said. "It was kind of my idea to apply Dr. Frawley's theory to the technology." He grinned at the memory. "It was amazing to see all those power sources blazing and ready when I turned the machine on for the first time. I probably should have waited to make that first drop. Cricklan nearly skinned me alive."

Robin suddenly laughed. "I probably shouldn't have tried to play with that machine I found, but I couldn't help myself. It was almost like it was calling to me."

Roger's heart clenched. "Yeah. It's how we know you're a time traveler." He swallowed. I don't know why that pull is so strong with you, though."

"Okay," said Robin, her eyes twinkling mischievously.

Roger decided to let it go.

"The weird thing is that the dates don't really line up," Robin said. "If what Beeman says is true, then you'd have to be in your late seventies. I get that people don't age as fast in this time, but that is pushing it."

"Yeah. That's why the I.B. knows me as Xavier instead of Roger. My permanent I.D. is York, but only the Time Board can access that. It's that cell growth thing that happens in the Drop. It doesn't happen when you're transporting from place to place. Why, we don't know. But if you move across time, it stimulates cell growth. Not a lot, but if you time travel enough, you don't age perceptively."

"You mean, like eternal life?" Robin gaped.

"Not hardly," Roger said with a sigh. "You're still just as susceptible to disease as you ever were. And accidents or other disasters." He scrunched his face up at the memory. "That's what happened to Eric. Anyway, it's our greatest secret."

"No kidding," said Robin. "You don't want people time traveling for vanity's sake."

"And it's still very dangerous, as you know."

He noticed Robin staring at him.

"So, why didn't you say anything?" she asked. "I mean, you could have."

"Lots of reasons," Roger said. He allowed himself to watch her eyes as he debated what to tell her. "Some of it's stuff that hasn't happened to us yet. The rest, well, I really liked being around someone who didn't know. You treat me like anybody else. Being the great First Time Traveler gets pretty tiresome, especially since I got that way by acting like an idiot."

Robin laughed. "Tell that to Beeman. He thinks I don't treat you with enough respect."

"That's Beeman. He means well."

Robin poked at the fire. "I know. I'm just having a really hard time trusting him. One minute, he's by the rules. Do it this way, or else. The next minute, he's all excited about getting something past the I.B. It's really hard to read him."

Roger sighed. "That's because Beeman is... What's the term they used in your time? Conflicted? He really is a rule-bound sort, and he worries when things aren't going the way he thinks they should. The problem is, he tried to get a seat on the I.B. He would have been great, too. But he has his intellectual pride and the Exec Council tried to get him to compromise it."

"I can see that not going well," said Robin.

"Our dear Beeman is many things, but a politician is not one of them." Roger couldn't help chuckling. "But the upshot is that while he behaves himself and follows the rules, as is his nature to do, he deeply resents the current board and is perfectly happy sabotaging whatever they want."

"So, he's mostly trustworthy, but not completely."

"Exactly."

Chapter Ten

Robin's misgivings about Beeman were somewhat eased over the next few weeks. She also came to be impressed by the sheer breadth of his knowledge, no matter how dry his presentation was. He understood her mistrust, too, and even encouraged it at times.

She knew that while she studied, Roger was busy playing cat and mouse games with the Intelligentsia Board's enforcers and sniffers, trying desperately to find Cricklan and find Donald's stash. In the evenings, he'd tell her what he'd found (which wasn't much) and the two would rack their brains trying to put the few clues they had together. Roger remained distant, too, which didn't help.

As the date of his trial grew closer, Robin fretted. Beeman seemed no closer to letting her take the test.

"We've got ten days before the trial," Robin complained to Beeman as soon as she arrived at their learning center that morning. "What if something goes wrong?"

"But that's also ten days of you as a full person in our society and ten days for others to find you," Beeman said. "Plus, you're still a little weak on the Twentieth Century."

"Oh, come on!"

Beeman rolled his eyes. "It's not what you know about the era, it's what the test wants to hear about the era."

"It's my natal time. You've got to spot me something for that knowledge," Robin groaned.

Beeman sighed and looked away. "Very well, then. Let's go."

They transported to the Time Center, with Beeman using his usual sign in to enter. Given that nowhere on the planet was particularly remote, thanks to transporter technology, Robin thought it odd that the travelers had still hidden their center on the barren, icy plains of Siberia. Inside, the room was warm and perfectly comfortable. Robin still shivered as she settled into her testing pod.

Three hours later, her brain felt utterly wrung out, and the look on Beeman's face was not happy.

"I failed, didn't I?"

He shrugged. "It wasn't a bad fail. Your rote memory was perfect. That's the part most people fail, you know. But you missed the three key Twentieth Century questions."

"Oh." Robin's eyes filled with tears. "I've never failed a test in my life."

"Most people fail this one the first time through," Beeman said. "That's why I let you take it today."

Robin was grateful for Beeman's odd burst of sympathy, although she was a touch annoyed that he would not let her take the test again that day.

"You need to rest your brain," he explained, then transported her back to her learning center.

Roger, for his part, had not had a good morning. Thanks to a trail of holograms left behind by Cricklan, he was able to find out that she knew he didn't have access to the certified project report. She also confirmed that the I.B. was, in fact, actively looking for him.

"I ought to let them have you," her hologram told Roger.

They were hiding in the manuscripts section of the Museum of Ancient Art.

"But we need evidence," Roger said. "I might have one ace card, but knowing where Donald's stash is will help immensely."

"It's here in the city," the hologram said, crossly. "At least, he's given me reason to believe he has one here. I don't know where. But I want you to stay away from him. You can't help him, and it won't do either of you any good to get him upset."

"I'm not going to try to fix him," Roger grumbled.

"Roger, I know you. You've been trying to fix him since he came home to us. Now, let him alone."

"Believe me, I am doing everything in my power to avoid him."

Roger had to concede as he left the museum that he hadn't been able to even fool the hologram. Cricklan was right in that as long as Roger was a fugitive, he could do nothing to help his brother. Which made finding the evidence that Donald had lied to the I.B. about bringing Elizabeth forward all the more imperative. Beeman had hinted that Robin was almost ready to take her exam. Having her in the travelers' fold would help, especially since she'd be able to talk about her role in the project and what had happened with Elizabeth.

But finding Donald's stash would go a long way toward convincing the I.B. that Donald was the one out of control and that the travelers stood the best chance of helping him. Robin had asked about storage units, such as the ones popular in her time that provided extra storage for people who had more things than space. Even in Roger's consumerist culture, that didn't happen very often, largely because people had plenty of living space. But there was one space that used to be a transportation hub before glide cars and transporters.

The old Grand Central Station had been restored to much of its former glory and was now a food fair, filled with restaurants and entertainment centers. Still, at the back, Roger knew there was a series of lockers. They mostly existed as a novelty and Roger seriously doubted that there would be one large enough for the amount of money and valuables that Donald would probably need to stay afloat for an extended period of time in the past.

But Donald had apparently found just such a locker, for he had it open as Roger entered the small ell where the lockers were. The two men froze as they looked at each other. Then Donald laughed.

"Good to see you, Roger," he chuckled.

Roger didn't wait but ran full out. Any second, he expected to hear the baying of the tracking hounds behind him, but the worst was the yip of a sniffer. Roger tore down the steps of the building, nearly falling in the process. Fortunately, the free glide cars were pulling up and leaving as he got to the street. He slid into one, let it get a couple blocks away from the station, then took another car going in the cross traffic.

Several hours later, he had made it back to the camp in New Jersey. Robin was already there.

"We'd better pack," Roger said. "Donald spotted me today. The worst he was able to do was call was a sniffer, but that's bad enough."

"Sure," said Robin listlessly.

She got up and started pulling together the bits of food and clothes that had somehow gotten spread around the abandoned house.

Roger looked at her. "What's the matter?"

"I took the test today and failed."

"You what?" Roger's stomach tightened into a dozen knots. "How could you have possibly failed?"

"I choked, okay?" Robin snarled back, her voice almost breaking into tears. "I answered the Twentieth Century questions from my perspective. I knew I wasn't supposed to, but those were the only answers that made sense."

"But you had no reason to choke!" Roger yelled, even though he hadn't intended to. "You knew you were going to pass."

"No, I didn't! I had no way of knowing."

"Yes, you do. The timetrons respond to you. They don't do that unless someone is already in the system. Or will be, like you."

"Well, I'm sorry." Robin threw a boot at the nearest sack and stormed out the door.

"Damn!" Roger dropped the bag he was holding and ran after. "Robin! Robin!"

She was at the back of the house, crying.

"Robin," he said gently.

"I can't help feeling like I'm lousing everything up," she said, sniffing. "I probably abandoned Dean and Elizabeth before they were ready, after pissing everyone off in my family off because I challenged Donald and pissed him off. And now I can't do anything because I don't know enough about this time, and I can't learn fast enough. And you need me to pass that test so that I can testify at your trial, and I go and flunk it. Beeman said I was weak on the Twentieth Century, and he was right."

"Robin, it's okay," Roger said, pulling her to him. Even as her shoulders shook with her sobs, it felt nice to have her next to him. It was dangerous, but he couldn't help himself. "I'm sorry I yelled. Look, Beeman wouldn't have let you anywhere near that test if he didn't think you were ready. He hinted the other day that you were almost there."

"We've got less than ten days."

"I know. But you'll just have to take it again. That's all. You can do that. I know guys who've taken it five or six times before they passed, and they didn't have to catch up on almost two hundred years of history in one month." He pulled away and looked at her tenderly. "The important thing to remember is that you will pass the test." He sighed. "And I shouldn't have yelled. I guess the strain is getting to me, too. If anybody should apologize, it's me for getting you into this mess. If you want to go home, I wouldn't blame you."

Robin stepped back and shook her head. "It wouldn't do any good. Given what's going on, if I go home, then you guys get shut down and I don't get to travel anymore. I've always dreamed of time traveling. That's why I had so much fun working for Dr. Frawley." She took a deep breath. "I'm in this for the long haul."

"At least, you have a home to go to," Roger said, a little sourly. "This is my home, my natal time."

Robin's lips quirked in a slightly ironic smile. It looked as though she was about to say something, and Roger held his breath, hoping against hope that she would, at last, initiate something. But the moment passed.

The next morning, Roger had Robin pull Beeman from the learning center to the park so the three of them could talk. But Beeman's news was pretty bad.

"The I.B.'s enforcers questioned me last night," Beeman squeaked as he looked around nervously. "They wanted to know why I was at the Time Center yesterday. We're not supposed to be processing any new applications."

"You aren't," said Roger. "Robin's application is already in progress. They don't have to know it was started almost two hundred years ago."

"I don't think they want us finishing any new ones either," Beeman grumbled. "They were afraid I was going to take off."

"Well, aren't you?" asked Robin.

"If the trial goes badly, of course." He blinked and sniffed. "I'll have to. But until then, I can't have them thinking I'm the one helping you."

"Yeah, that would be pretty bad for us, too," Roger said, a little dryly.

Beeman caught the subtle dig and winced. "I'm not going to turn you in. It doesn't serve any good purpose, and besides, I'll get stuck staying in the Thirteen-Forties." He shuddered.

"You don't have to go then," Roger said.

Beeman drew himself up. "It's my specialty." He sighed. "But it is not a very pleasant time to live. Look, I'd better have as little contact with you as possible." He looked at

Robin. "You'll pass your test. You almost did. Just keep working on the Twentieth Century."

He scurried off.

"Now, what?" Robin asked.

"Back to looking for Cricklan, I guess," Roger said. "And find some way to get you into the Time Center to re-take that exam."

They spent the next week dodging sniffers and talking to Cricklan's hologram. Wherever it was that Cricklan was hiding, she was able to get around quite a bit, and usually had some news. However, it was a chance meeting with Alayo that brought the worst news.

"The I.B. gave Beeman his seat on the board," Alayo said, four days before the trial. "He doesn't have it yet, but they promised him the next one. He told them he'd seen you briefly and that someone, he didn't know who, had given you a transporter."

"At least we can get around that way and maybe avoid the trackers," Robin said.

"Yeah, but they'll be looking for me in more places," Roger grumbled.

"Steven may have something for you," Alayo said. "He and a couple of other guys have found a way to mask the robo trackers on places like the safe building, or your place, or even the Time Center. We just have to know ahead of time when you'll be where and who will be with you."

Alayo glanced over at Robin, who shrugged and tried to look like the kindly off-gridder she supposedly was.

"Except how are we going to be able to contact you?" Roger asked.

Alayo shrugged. "That is a bit of a problem, but I've heard you two have a mobile telephone."

"Which Beeman also knows about and has used," Roger said.

"Not anymore, he won't." Alayo grinned. "I scrambled the receiver on his handheld."

Roger let Alayo enter his contact number into Robin's phone. It still took until three days before the trial for Steven to confirm that the tracker mask was in place. He simply needed to know when they were going to be where. Roger got the call while he and Robin had separated to look for food. It was with no little sense of relief that he told Steven he'd find Robin and call him back. The only problem was that Roger wasn't sure where she was.

Robin was headed back to their camp, feeling very jittery and desperately trying not to let it show. They'd had to leave her phone on so that Steven could call them when they were safe, and the one battery they'd managed to get was running low. But the worst was that their food was almost gone. They had been foraging - fortunately, greens were plentiful. They'd both done a little hunting, but there'd been little time for it. Roger was off checking the few traps he'd set.

She had gathered some wild carrots and potatoes and was bringing them back to yet another abandoned house, this time north of Manhattan, when she heard voices.

"It's a camp, all right," said one male voice.

"Are you sure it's them?" answered a woman who sounded like she was in charge. "The dogs haven't alerted yet."

Robin stopped and stood stock still. How was she going to warn Roger when she didn't even know where he was?

What Robin did not know was that Roger had gotten the message. He couldn't tell what had frightened Robin, but the fear burst through his brain as her timetron called him. It startled him, and he tried to figure out how it was happening. But then he heard the baying of hounds. Trackers, and it sounded like they were on his trail. There was one trick that could sometimes confuse the hounds for a short time, although it seldom worked well enough to keep them completely off the trail. Roger circled around back toward the house, listening as the dogs bayed in glee. When he had reason to believe that he was behind the dogs and their handlers, he hurried to the trail he'd taken earlier, the one the dogs were presumably following, and hurried along it as closely as he could.

He could feel Robin wanting to run. He focused on her staying in one place and hoped she would. He ran as hard and as quietly as he could, letting his mind lead him through the trees and undergrowth. Finally, he left the trail toward the house and found Robin standing and breathing heavily.

"There you are," she gasped.

"We'll head down to the park," he said.

She nodded and a second later, they landed near the abandoned zoo. Roger got out the old phone and dialed Steven.

"Uh, yeah?" came Steven's voice, the sound crackling unevenly. "Why can't I see them?"

Someone near Steven mumbled something.

"How you folks manage in the past, I have no idea," Steven grumbled. "Who is this?"

"It's Roger," he gasped. "Me and one other person are heading to the Time Center."

"Okay. Give me five minutes to turn everything on."

A dog bayed in the distance.

"We don't have five minutes!" Roger yelped.

Robin looked around frantically, then ran for the zoo. Gasping, Roger followed.

"I'll do the best I can," Steven grumbled.

"Include the transporter portal."

"Of course." The dogs' baying got louder. "Sounds like you're on the run."

"No kidding," gasped Roger.

Robin pushed the rusty gate just open enough for the two of them to squeeze through, but it took both of them to get it shut again. Robin kicked some dirt into the gate's track as Roger scrambled into more undergrowth.

"There's a rumor there are still some wild animals that got loose and have been breeding," he whispered as Robin ran up.

A lion roared somewhere to the side of them.

"I'd say that was more than a rumor," Robin grumbled.

"Steven, are you still there? Can we transport yet?"

"Not yet."

Robin nodded at what looked like a rocky bluff in front of them. "Let's climb. It should give us more time."

As they crested the bluff, the lion roared again, and the dogs bayed even louder.

"Steven!" Roger yelled into the phone.

The next sound was static.

"Steven?"

Two brown bloodhounds came running up to the edge of the bluff.

"I said, go ahead."

Roger and Robin looked at each other, their eyes fixed on each other, and a minute later, they landed in the Time

Center portal. Roger signed in with his thumb and they were allowed entry.

"Didn't we just tell somebody we're here?" Robin asked.

"Steven reassigned my identity, sort of," Roger said.

Breathing heavily, Robin looked around the simple room. It had the clean lines of a past time, with a bank of tables along the circular wall overlooking the Siberian tundra.

"Well, if we can snag a caribou, we should be able to eat until the trial," Robin said.

"We've got all the comforts of home here," said Roger. "Including bathing facilities with hot water and fresh clothes. Steven insists that no one will notice us doing anything unless we communicate with the outside world."

Robin shivered. "What about my phone?"

"It is getting a little low on battery. But we're probably in the best place of all to recharge it."

Robin paced the room restlessly. "I'm sorry. I'm still pretty shook. How did you find me?"

"The machine called me. It's like you said about what happened when you found Elizabeth. It almost felt like the timetron was calling you. It was. It makes it easier to find one when you need one fast." Roger frowned slightly. "Although it doesn't usually call unless your brain waves are triggering on something you're afraid of." He blinked and shook the thought away. "But also, if you're within half a klick or so of another traveler, the machine can sometimes be used to communicate. It's not real accurate, but it worked this time."

Robin looked at Roger. He seemed to be thinking something over. At the same time, he did not want to discuss it, whatever it was.

"So, now what?" She paced again.

"We relax, get some food, get cleaned up, get some rest, then tomorrow morning, you take your test."

"As if that's going to make me feel better," Robin grumbled.

"Robin, you're going to pass it." Roger smiled at her.

"Yeah, but when?"

"Presumably when you need to. Now, come on. We'll just have fun tonight. I think some smart ass stashed some Cheval Blanc Forty-Seven around here. Brought it from when it was new, so it's only aged about twenty years."

Robin looked around the room once more. There was something about it that reminded her of some other spot, and that she should be seeing it as something important. Roger was going through cupboards and closets, pulling out clothes and towels for each of them. There was only one cleaning stall and Robin insisted that Roger use it first while she played Free Cell on one of the center's info portals.

That night, Robin tossed and turned. The beds in the center were as comfortable as any she'd ever slept on. But Robin couldn't shut her brain down. She finally got up and alternated games of Free Cell with other solitaire games and the required reading on the Twentieth Century. It had always worked before.

That didn't mean she felt any more ready to take the test as the light dawned in the center, somewhat behind the actual light outside. She could hear Roger moving around the Center, fixing breakfast. Grabbing a wrap, she made her way to the cleaning stall. Dressed and comfortable, she found a mug of coffee waiting for her, alongside a full breakfast. Robin ate as much as she could, but it wasn't very much.

"Now," Roger began.

Robin held her hand up. "I know. I'm going to pass it."

"Uh, actually, that might be the wrong way to go about this," Roger said. "I know. I thought it would be reassuring to you. But I have been known to be wrong occasionally."

"You think?"

"I just want you to concentrate on relaxing," Roger said. "Seriously. You were right last night. We don't know when you're going to pass it. Just that you are. We've got a couple of days. And even if we don't, we'll have to assume that the I.B. listened to you anyway. You don't have to pass it today. Consider this another practice test."

"Okay."

Robin still didn't feel entirely reassured. There was simply too much at stake. But, she reminded herself; she had always joked that she did best in high-pressure situations. She settled in and began.

The test wasn't any easier. If anything, it felt harder. But somehow, Robin felt a little more confident. Three hours later, she was exhausted, but not as worried. Until she saw Roger's face.

"Oh, dear," she said.

He suddenly grinned. "You passed."

Chapter Eleven

I t only took a couple of hours to get Robin fully entered into the system. She already had a permanent identification number, which Roger explained merely meant that someone researching his or her ancestry had identified her as a relative.

"You can't mean to tell me you're giving every human being who ever existed a number?" Robin asked.

"That is the basic idea, yeah," said Roger. "Since family names became extinct, there had to be some way to uniquely identify a person, especially since family names were not all that effective, anyway."

"I suppose," said Robin.

Roger continued entering her data, including her aura print and her biometrics. He had her choose an environment (she selected his) and added her to a couple affiliations, including the travelers. Finally, he leaned back in the console chair and smiled.

"You're officially a member of our society," he announced. "I'd say this calls for a celebration."

But before Robin could agree, the transporter portal thrummed with a new arrival.

"I thought Alayo said everyone was staying away from here," Robin gasped.

Roger grabbed her arm. "Bad information."

The door to the portal slid open and a rotund female with light brown skin, freckles and gray and black hair twisted into short dreadlocks walked into the room. She glared at Roger.

"We've got a new problem," she announced.

"Newer than Beeman selling us out?" Roger grumbled back.

"If he'd sold us out, you'd be in a holding room," the woman complained. "No. I've just gotten word that Donald moved his stash from that storage locker at the old Grand Central." She looked around and finally saw Robin. "Huh. Are you our friendly off-gridder?"

Robin looked at Roger. "Um, not quite."

"Meet RP170," Roger said. "Robin, this is Cricklan."

"How do you do, ma'am," Robin said.

Cricklan's eyebrows rose. "Robin Parker?"

"Yes, ma'am," Robin said.

Cricklan glared at Roger. "So that's how you did it. We couldn't figure out how you'd gotten out. No one would admit that they'd helped." She suddenly slapped Roger behind the head. "You know better than to do that kind of playing with your continuum!"

"I haven't done it yet!" Roger yelped. "I was just thinking about it and Robin appeared."

"I don't want to know any more," Cricklan grumbled, pacing the room. She suddenly pulled up a page from the info portal. "At least she's a registered traveler. That should help with the I.B."

"And you can unseal that full report on the bring for-ward project," Roger said.

"No, I can't. I told you, I wrote down the pass phrase and left it out where you could find it."

"We can't get into your house. Donald's living there." Roger threw up his hands. "And I don't want to leave anything for the trackers to get a hold of. You agreed that was a smart thing to do. Or at least, your hologram did."

"That was back then." Cricklan resumed pacing. She looked over at Robin. "Maybe Robin could…"

"I already did," Robin said. "I went all over the house, thinking about Roger's hairless backside and nothing popped."

"What?"

"That's what Beeman and I thought was the pass phrase," Roger said. "You asked about my hairless backside and we concluded that was the pass image."

"You idiots!" Cricklan groaned loudly. "It figures that pompous dope would infer more than I intended. I simply wrote it down and left it in the office area."

"On a slip of paper," Robin said suddenly. She began digging through her pockets. "I still have them. Here."

Cricklan looked at Robin with a hint of approval, then rifled through the pieces of paper.

"This is it," the older woman said, handing Roger one. "But keep those others just in case. If we can find and document Donald's stash, that ought to prove that you're not the one out of control."

"It'll be enough for public opinion," said Roger, smil-ing at Robin as he added the slips of paper to one of his pockets.

They spent the rest of the evening mulling over multiple potential locations for Donald's stash. As they opened the third bottle of wine, a bottle of Chateau Lafite from the early Nineteenth Century (which had been aged at least 40 years), Robin suddenly sat up.

"What?" asked Roger.

"The penny has finally dropped," Robin said.

"What?" asked Cricklan, who looked utterly puzzled.

"An expression from my time, meaning I finally get it," said Robin.

"And that is?" Roger asked.

"What this room reminds me of," said Robin, getting up and walking around, touching the simple cabinet doors along the wall. "Your place, Roger. Remember how I said it looked more like what I expected the future to look like, and you pointed out how all the furnishings were actually antiques?"

"Yes. So...?" Roger looked at her, puzzled.

"Well, this place reminds me of your place," Robin said. "And is suddenly occurs to me that if Donald wanted to hide something where nobody is going, why not hide it at your place? That way, he can hide where nobody is looking and if someone does, it makes you look guilty, not him."

"A mechanical sniffer would find his aura prints all over it," Roger said.

"And if somebody, like the I.B., manages to suppress that?" Robin said with a grin.

"She's got a point," said Cricklan.

Roger rolled his eyes but had to agree.

"Okay. But what do we do about it?" he asked.

"Is there any reason I can't go over there, find the stash, document it, then call the enforcers?" Robin asked.

Roger looked panicked, but Cricklan laughed.

"What a perfectly devious plan!" she chortled. "The enforcers aren't going to know her from anybody else and she'll be able to scoot before they realize that she's a traveler."

"You are leaping across chasms of conclusions," Roger countered. "I can't number all the ways this could go badly."

"But it could go right," Robin said. "And how much do we have to lose?"

Roger obviously thought there was a great deal to lose, but he was quickly over-ruled by both Cricklan and Robin.

The next day, Robin took one of the transporter units in the Time Center and thought about the transporter portal at Roger's home in Paris. Once she appeared there, it didn't take long to find what she was looking for. The dark blue armoire was filled with all manner of gold pieces. Robin used the handheld to log the aura print on the gold, hid it in one of her many pockets, then called the enforcers.

It was a little frightening how fast the two women appeared. Robin pointed out the stash, and that she thought it belonged to Donald. The two women didn't seem to care that much about what Robin thought. They registered the aura print on the stash, but before Robin could transport, they grabbed her arms and took the transporter.

They shuffled Robin from small windowless room to small windowless room while someone, apparently, tried to make up his or her mind about what to do with her. She thought it odd that she wasn't being questioned, but was grateful for that much. Eventually, the enforcers moved her to a medium-sized room without a visible door.

There was a cleaning stall behind a screen. She could move around comfortably and there were two beds, simply and neatly made, and two easy chairs. Robin found an info portal in one of the chair arms and looked up what to do if arrested.

"There's got to be something about what rights I have," she muttered.

"As an off-gridder, you won't have many," came Cricklan's voice.

Robin turned. Behind her, a hologram had materialized.

"This is a live projection, by the way," Cricklan said.

And no doubt monitored, Robin realized.

"You're only being held as a witness," Cricklan said. Her smile was pleasant, but there was nothing reassuring about it. "I'm here to help you prepare your testimony. The Intelligentsia Board wants to assure you that they have only your best interests at heart."

"They do?"

Cricklan nodded, then raised her hand with her forefinger touching her thumb and her other three fingers extended. If this had been Robin's own natal time, Robin would have guessed Cricklan was trying to say, "okay." Suddenly, Robin sensed a nudging in her brain. Cricklan wanted her to play along. Robin wondered how much the Intelligentsia could play with her brain.

"Not that much," whispered the nudge. "I have your timetron."

"I need you to promise that you'll testify tomorrow," Cricklan's hologram said out loud.

"Why should I do that?" Robin asked.

Cricklan turned her head to someone behind her that Robin couldn't see. "I told you she wouldn't buy it."

Cricklan turned back to Robin. "It's the best way to help your friend."

"Help him to what?" Robin snarled.

Cricklan turned away again. "I need to get in there. She's not going to trust a hologram and, really, do you blame her?"

The hologram winked out. Some minutes later, a wall panel opened and Cricklan stepped into the room. The panel slid shut and disappeared.

"Well, let's see what we can do," Cricklan said out loud, but put a finger to her lips. "Oh, so you're going to stay silent. All right. I can work with that."

So, they were being listened in on, but they couldn't be seen.

"I'll just settle in here," Cricklan said, easing into a chair. "We'll talk when you're ready."

But instead of leaning back and resting, Cricklan pulled out a pen and several sheets of paper. Robin's eyebrows lifted.

"We can write notes," Cricklan had scribbled when she handed Robin the sheet. "They can't see it, nor will they think of it. Handwriting for communication was already going away by your time."

Robin nodded and wrote, "Is Roger okay?"

Cricklan smiled. "Yes, he's fine. He turned himself in, voluntarily and in public. He has to for the trial, anyway."

"Why are they letting you prepare me?"

"It got out that the I.B. was holding a poor, innocent off-gridder who only wanted to help someone."

Robin pointed to herself and Cricklan nodded.

"No wonder they didn't question me," Robin wrote.

"Now, we have to come up with your actual testimony and your supposed testimony. Be sure not to agree with me too quickly."

They spent the next few hours writing and talking for the benefit of the monitors. Cricklan decided to stay the night.

Robin woke early only to find that Cricklan was already awake and working on her notes. The two dressed silently, the room filled with the weight of the upcoming trial. It wasn't just about setting Roger free. The Intelligentsia Board would most likely be deciding whether to even allow time travel, let alone how much control the travelers would work under.

The two enforcers showed up right before the trial was set to begin and transported Cricklan and Robin to the trial chamber. The room was decorated to look like a huge forest glen, surrounded by gilt-painted trees. The seven members of the Board sat in chairs along one edge of the round room, while tiered rows of more chairs filled the rest of the circle, forming an amphitheater of sorts.

Roger sat in the front row, flanked by two large women enforcers and a tracking hound. Robin and Cricklan sat in the next row back, behind Beeman and across the room from Roger. The rest of the seats were half-filled with spectators, most of them carrying signs that denounced out-of-control time travelers. A few of the signs read, "Keep us safe from anomalies!"

"I can see I'm going to be real popular here," Robin muttered to Cricklan.

"In a way, it's good for us," Cricklan whispered back. "It looks like they've stacked the house for the benefit of the larger public, which means they're not feeling too confident about their case."

"That's not going to matter much if the larger public buys this."

As Cricklan shrugged, there was a pounding on the outside door. Three enforcers tried to push the door closed, but it burst open on a tide of people, all bearing signs in support of the travelers.

"Can't stack the audience! Can't stack the audience!" that part of the crowd cheered as they filled the remaining seats.

By the time they were seated, the board member seated in the center rose. She was a tall woman, wearing a cape and full pants, all in a deep forest green with golden flecks.

"That's Rinalda," Cricklan whispered. She pointed out the other six, whose names Robin promptly forgot, except for a nervous woman on the end, who was Silvesteri, and a wizened man named Arnold, who sat next to Rinalda.

Rinalda announced that the board was met to decide whether Roger was out of control, or whether the whole Time Board was regarding the cultivation of an anomaly as part of the Wynford project, thanks to the complaint filed by DL1223.

"Is DL1223 present?" Rinalda intoned.

"Here!" came the answer from the back of the room.

Donald finished fighting his way through the crowd at the door and sat down near the back. Robin hoped he did not see her.

"Donald, is it your sworn statement that the project was conducted without care for the primary victim's safety and sanity and that it went ahead without proper vetting?" Rinalda asked.

"It is," Donald called back.

Half the crowd cheered, waving their signs, while the other half yelled that Donald was lying.

Rinalda waved the crowd quiet enough to begin the wrangling over the procedural rules. It took an inordinately long time, as each board member had to have his or her say on the issues at hand, and then each tried to bend the others to his or her way of thinking. The only thing they seemed to agree on was that anomalies were bad and very frightening.

Finally, they agreed they would start by letting Roger present his evidence, which set off a debate over whether the Time Board's report on the vetting process was acceptable evidence, especially as it had been sealed.

"Excuse me," Roger finally yelled over the crowd and the board. "If you will check the above info portal, you'll see that this is a certified full report covering the entire span of the deliberations, and it has not been tampered with in any way. It also includes the sealed part of the deliberations. Please note that despite the crisis we face, the deliberations were undertaken over an extended period of time, far longer than was required by the I.B. You'll also note that the sealed deliberations concern Donald's psycho-neuro condition."

The crowd roared, with everyone yelling over each other. Two enforcers sidled up to Donald, just in case.

"May I continue?" Roger hollered and paused. "In addition, a stash was found in my domicile, a stash that does not have my aura print on it, or anyone else's, except that of Donald, DL1223. With the stash, Donald could go to just about any when he pleases and be comfortable, meaning he's probably planning to do a bolt after this trial, and go someplace you cannot reach him. Between this stash and Donald's recent behavior, we believe his psycho-neuro condition has reactivated and is what is behind the complaint. Not concerns about travelers being out of control."

"That's not at issue!" Arnold screamed.

"Enough!" Rinalda waved everyone quiet. "Roger, it's established that the surgery for such conditions is permanent, and it does not reactivate."

"It mostly does not reactivate," called a heavy-set woman. "There are rare occasions in which it can."

The enforcers looked at Rinalda. She nodded. Somehow, Donald managed to stay calm.

"Donald's health is still not the issue," Arnold screamed. "The issue is and always will be, do we even need time travel?"

"Seriously?" Robin heard herself yelling. "Seriously? What do you mean, do we need time travel? You idiots clearly need time travel."

The crowd hushed as Robin scrambled to her feet and into the small half circle in front of the board.

"You've got to be shitting me," she continued, too enraged to worry about what she was saying. "I know you need time travel because you dopes are still playing the same old stupid power games that were tired in my time."

"And who are you?" sniffed Arnold.

"RP170," Robin answered coldly. "And I know more about the Wynford project than anybody here because I lived it and Elizabeth Wynford married my brother."

Rinalda gasped. "But that means..."

"Yep," said Robin. "I'm everything you're afraid of. I'm an anomaly. A living, breathing anomaly, born in the late Twentieth Century and here because one of your machines recognized me. No, it doesn't make a lot of sense. But that's too bad, because here I am, and I'm here to tell you, being an anomaly is not so bad. It's not the sort of thing for everyone, especially for that grump over there." She pointed at Arnold and received a loud laugh from most of the audience. "Now, I'm sorry my brother had to go and put his foot in your big project to regenerate the population with Elizabeth's genes. But you're forgetting something. The experiment was working. Elizabeth is doing just fine. So's her baby. She's just not doing it here. And the reason that happened was because an ion locked failed. Now, correct me if I'm wrong, but ion locks are considered pretty reliable and they're pretty common. So, the experiment didn't entirely fail. There's some good data that can still be retrieved. But most importantly, the part that went awry didn't happen because the project was not carefully vetted, with every concern for Elizabeth's well-being. It happened because of a lock that everyone here depends on every day." Robin turned and glared at Arnold again. "Oh, and, Mr. GrumpyPants? I'll repeat this slowly for you. You are making the same mistakes my ancestors did. If you really want to stop acting like a horse's ass, then you need time travel. Otherwise, you and your heirs are just going to keep making the same mistakes over and over and over again."

Shaking inside, Robin went back to her seat. She didn't dare look at Roger. Cricklan put her arms around Robin's shoulders. Rinalda signaled the board. They confirmed the information regarding the stash, then sidled together into a circle and began deliberating.

"Did I just fuck it up for everybody?" Robin asked softly.

Cricklan sighed. "I don't think so. If we get shut down, it will probably be because they had already planned to."

"I know it's not home, but you and Roger will always have a place with me back in my time."

"Thank you," Cricklan said with a chuckle.

The board continued to deliberate as the crowd grew restless. The occasional shouting match erupted in the audience, which the board largely ignored. Robin eventually got the courage to look at Roger, who smiled warmly back at her.

After another hour, Rinalda called for a vote, which ignited yet another debate on what was being voted on. Finally, it was decided that the board would vote on whether to allow time travel to continue.

"That's not good," Robin said.

"No, it's not, but it also means that's what they planned to vote on, anyway," sighed Cricklan.

Rinalda took her time calling for each member's vote. Predictably, Silvesteri voted to keep time travel and Arnold voted against it. In the end, the vote was tied with three members for and three against. The room grew silent as everyone watched Rinalda to see which way she would go.

She slowly stood and looked down at Roger.

"Roger, you and the other travelers have quite the reputation for renegade behavior," Rinalda said crossly. "And renegade behavior does not contribute to the smooth running of a society." She paused. "That being said, your little anomaly over there made one good point about repeating our mistakes. I vote to keep time travel under its current board and in its current functions."

The room erupted in cheers.

"Nooooooo!" Donald's scream rose above the cheers as he rushed toward the board.

He aimed a device at Robin, who was certain she was about to breathe her last. Sparks flew, but she was barely conscious of them. All she knew was that she was on the ground underneath Beeman, of all people.

Donald transported away.

"Robin!" Roger yelled.

Robin squeezed herself out from under Beeman.

"Thanks," she said softly to the prone man.

He smiled and gasped. "Trust me now?"

The life slipped out of him, and his eyes gaped open and unseeing.

Robin spent the next few days in the hospital being treated for her shock. Roger made a point of visiting each day, hoping she'd finally initiate their relationship. But she slid into herself, and by the time she could process what had happened, it was too late for romantic notions.

After that, both were too busy working on their next trip to think about anything else. They'd been elected to go find Donald whenever he'd gone and bring him back to be treated again.

"It's okay," Robin told Roger when he told her.

"We're the only ones who can," Roger said with a sigh. "He'll just hide from anyone else and there's a lot of time and world for him to hide in."

Robin nodded with a weak smile. The research was fun, and Robin tried to concentrate on that. In a few short weeks, everything was ready. Robin and Roger each held a horse, looked at each other, then closed their eyes and focused on the coordinates.

Chapter Twelve

Robin thought she would be used to the sucking, crushing sensation that meant she was passing through time, but once again, it caught her with its force. She looked over at Roger, who was also gasping. The horses nickered, but stayed calm. Roger had explained that the drop didn't seem to have as profound an effect on the larger animals.

Robin adjusted her velvet and jeweled hat. She wore a deep green velvet bodice over an emerald-green skirt that had been embroidered with gold-colored satin thread. The skirt parted in front to reveal a pretty print petticoat that had tiny pearls sewn onto it. This went over full petticoats, a hoop skirt called a farthingale, and a pad over her backside. Her brocade sleeves ballooned from her shoulders.

Roger wore deep blue velvet slops under his yellow velvet doublet with deeper gold sleeves. His legs were booted, and his hands wore well-used leather gloves. He pulled a small telescope from his saddlebag and swept the flat landscape with it. There was the odd windmill to break the monotony of the scene and a few short trees, all of which seemed to bend in the wind.

But the air was mostly still, and the sun shone. White, fluffy clouds drifted across the deep blue sky. The surrounding fields were green and gold with ripening wheat and pastures where sheep and a few cows grazed. Robin took a deep breath. There was a hint of wood smoke in the air, but she couldn't see from where it came.

"Do you see an inn?" Robin asked.

"I see the city," Roger said. He took the telescope down and pointed at the horizon. "You can just see the belfry over there."

Robin took a deep breath. The ancient city of Bruges was just over the horizon, and they had landed in late May 1584. The week before they left, one of the travelers had followed Donald's machine and found he had joined the Spanish army under the command of Alexander Farranese, the eventual Duke of Parma. The troops had just taken over Alst some weeks before, and other Belgian cities, including Bruges, were due to open their gates to the advancing army.

"Any guesses how close we are to the surrender?" Robin asked, although there was little likelihood Roger would have one.

"We'll know soon enough," Roger said, looking down the road away from the city.

Robin heard reins jingling and looked in the direction Roger had. A small party of three men on horses, with several others walking beside them, walked toward the city. The men on foot and one of the men on horseback suddenly went on alert as they saw Robin and Roger. Roger waved at them.

The party drew abreast of Robin and Roger.

"Hullo" called the leader from his horse.

He was a portly man and richly decked out in a red sur-coat trimmed with gold and balloon pants. He also wore a thick gold and jeweled chain of office around his neck. His hair was the color of dark wheat, with strands of deep gray running through it. He seemed a jovial sort, widely grinning through his pointed beard.

The second man on horseback was a tall, sallow fellow, with a long face and deeply etched lines. He wore a long black gown with deep purple trim and a richly jeweled crucifix dangled from a gold chain around his neck.

The suspicious man was a soldier of some rank, based on his rich clothes and sword at his side. His blue eyes alternated between sizing up Roger and Robin and sweeping the road and fields around them. The four men who were walking clearly looked to him for commands.

"Hullo," Roger replied. "I am Roger De Marais, of Bordeaux. My good wife and I are seeking shelter away from the Spanish troops coming this way."

The portly man laughed. "They've just made camp back that way." He pointed behind himself.

Robin tried to look worried, and Roger's eyes rose.

"No," Roger groaned. "We're trying to find a port to get home. We couldn't find a berth in Antwerp. They're all leaving, fearing a siege."

"Indeed," the portly man said. "But you need not fear joining us. You are outside the fine city of Bruges. I am Lord Mayor Jan Van Veldt. We have just come from a meeting with Parma's men. We open the gates and surrender the city tomorrow." His jovial face suddenly grew suspicious. "Have you reason to fear the Spanish?"

Roger smiled and shook his head. "Not at all. We merely want to get home. Our servants and luggage are not far from here at an inn. We came ahead to seek lodging in a safe place."

Lord Jan laughed again. "Well, you cannot get safer than my own little home. Join us, please. This is Bishop Dieter Wuyts and our sergeant at arms, Heinrik VanDen Melke."

VanDen Melke did not look happy but did not contradict Lord Jan. Roger got Robin seated on her horse and then mounted his own. Roger rode next to Lord Jan and Bishop Wuyts, with Robin and VanDen Melke riding next to each other.

"And what brings you to Flanders, Master de Marais?" Lord Jan asked.

"I am a wine merchant," Roger explained. "I brought our latest vintage up from Bordeaux for an English customer in Antwerp. I had also hoped to buy some textiles and other bits of finery to sell back home, but then the news came of Parma's advance on the Netherlands."

"Indeed, that was somewhat inconvenient," Lord Jan said with a chuckle. "However, we Catholics were getting tired of Calvinism and bloody sieges are terrible for business. Parma has been quite generous, too, promising no looting and that we can continue to govern ourselves as we always have. And as there will always be taxes to be paid to somebody, why should we care to whom they go as long as we are left alone to do business and prosper?"

"You seem to be very prosperous," Roger said.

"Well enough," said Lord Jan with a chuckle.

Robin thought that the look on VanDen Melke's face was less than approving. There was some tension between the sergeant at arms and the portly lord mayor, but Robin couldn't tell if it was because the more naturally suspicious sergeant didn't approve of Lord Jan's trusting nature or if there was some other cause. He smiled weakly at her every so often, but mostly he was engaged in watching the road for any hint of trouble.

"You are keeping such a careful watch." Robin said. "Are the roads that perilous along here?"

VanDen Melke smiled briefly and shook his head. "No, mistress. They are usually as safe as they can be, and perhaps safer than normal, thanks to the Spanish Army. I am an old soldier. I keep watch out of habit."

"Which, I am told, is how one gets to be an old soldier," Robin replied with a small smile and was gratified to see VanDen Melke suppress a laugh.

"Indeed it is, mistress," he said, quietly.

It wasn't long before the group saw the walls of the city rising above the canals and fields. The men at the gates seemed to be expecting the little group and did not express any surprise at seeing two new people. Robin found her nose twitching at the stench of the canals. Such smells were one of the few parts of time travel that she would be happier doing without.

Lord Jan's house was just off the main square, just beyond the old church with the precious relic of Jesus' blood. Bishop Wuyts had made his farewells as soon as they'd entered the gates, the cathedral being in another direction. VanDen Melke nodded at Lord Jan, then continued on his way, his men trailing after him. A groom appeared out front of the brick house and took the three horses, although Roger asked the groom to keep his horse at the ready.

"I must go back to the inn and retrieve my company," Roger said.

"Of course, of course!" Lord Jan said, smiling broadly. "We will see to the arrangements." He held out his arm for Robin to take. "Come, Mistress de Marais. We will refresh ourselves in the solar."

The brick house was actually two houses that had been combined sometime earlier in the century. The back walls had been built right up to the edge of the canal, and the combined house even had a floor that hung over the water. This was the solar. It was a bright room, with creamy white walls and several padded stools strewn about. As Lord Jan settled Robin on one, a young woman entered the room.

Lord Jan's face lit up with joy. "Ah, my greatest treasure! The prop of my old age! Anneke, come meet our guests. A merchant from Bordeaux and his wife, Master and Mistress de Marais. This is my daughter, Lady Anna."

"We are well-met," said Roger, bowing low over the young woman's hand.

"Indeed, we are, sir," said Lady Anna with a smile. She looked to be in her early twenties, with golden hair and bright blue eyes. Her dress was amber in color and richly embroidered and she wore a matching velvet cap over her loosely bound hair. "But, Father, I thought you had gone to meet the Spanish."

"We did," said Lord Jan, jovially. "We came upon Master de Marais on the road home."

"So why did you bring me home a married man?" Lady Anna asked with a sly smile.

Lord Jan laughed loudly as he gazed at his daughter fondly. "Quite the wit my daughter has. But you'd best keep a civil tongue in your head, or no man will want you."

Lady Anna bowed her head obediently, but Robin got the impression that the young woman would be perfectly happy if she went unwanted. Lord Jan looked around, saw a servant in the doorway, and waved at the small man in red and gold livery.

"Dries, tell Hester we have guests. Have her come so Master de Marais can tell her the size of his company and she can have rooms prepared. Oh, and bring refreshments. And have Master Ernst join me here. I must make some notes for the council meeting this afternoon."

Robin caught the slightest hint of a flush on Lady Anna's cheeks as the young woman sat herself down next to Robin and pulled some embroidery from the bag at her waist. Smiling softly, Lady Anna bent her head low over her work.

"It is not usual for merchants to bring their wives with them," Lady Anna said, lowering her voice so only Robin could hear her.

"He is most kind and I like to travel, so we are content," Robin said.

"Most women I know do not care to be separated from their children."

Robin sighed, as she would be expected to. "Alas, I have not been so blessed."

"You are lucky that your husband compensates by bringing you with him."

"I am, as you are in a father that so delights in you."

Lady Anna frowned. "He does but delights more in selling me to the highest bidder." She shook her head. "I am, perhaps, not being just. He is intent on finding me the best husband possible, and one that will benefit him as well, as I am his only living child."

"But your heart is elsewhere," Robin said.

Lady Anna winced. "I will do my duty as I should." She sighed. "But, yes, it would be nice if he saw the same good in a certain gentleman that I do."

Robin looked up as a young man with dark hair and intense green eyes came into the room. He ignored Lady Anna, who suddenly became completely absorbed by her embroidery.

"Ah, Master Ernst, young lad, come greet our guests, then we have dictation to manage," Lord Jan said.

Master Ernst bowed slightly in greeting at Roger and nodded at Robin. Dries, the servant, brought in beer and small savories and passed them around. Lord Jan, despite his concerns about note taking, remained and chatted with Roger while Master Ernst waited expectantly. As soon as Roger had finished his cup of beer, he announced he must go fetch the servants he had supposedly left behind. Lord Jan excused himself to Robin and Lady Anna and left, with Master Ernst following in his wake.

Lady Anna put down her embroidery and sighed in relief. "Enough of this nonsense. I have some instruments if you'd like to play some music. I even have a game or two that we can amuse ourselves with. Or, I do have some books if you can read in Flemish. You speak it very well."

Robin smiled humbly. One of the properties of the timetron was a language processor that enabled the travelers to hear and speak whatever language was being spoken, never mind that Robin only heard her native language. Roger had explained that it could be a little awkward if people were speaking several different languages, as it would be hard to tell which was which. But it made time travel possible in that even ancient languages were understandable.

"We come often to Flanders," Robin said simply. "I have learned to read Flemish and love to read."

"So do I," Lady Anna said. "I can read in Latin and English, as well. Oh, you must teach me to speak French. I would dearly love to learn."

"I will have to see if I have any books with me," Robin said, gulping. She thought fast. "The problem is, when I try to speak French when I am not at home and must speak Flemish or English, I get terribly muddled up and lose everything."

Lady Anna laughed. "Then I will not muddle you for the world."

An older woman servant stood in the doorway, expectantly.

"Oh, Hester," said Lady Anna. "What is it?"

"The guest rooms have been prepared, but Master de Marais did not tell me how many servants you have with you."

"He was worried about leaving them and our luggage," Robin said, feeling somewhat relieved that she knew how to answer.

She and Roger had gone over and over their story of leaving the servants behind at the inn, as they needed a good reason why they didn't have any. Only itinerant players and beggars traveled without servants in that time, and Roger had decided that it would be easier to trap Donald if they were of a higher social class. Robin had disagreed, but had to concede that being of the merchant class was considerably more comfortable.

She looked over at Lady Anna. "It made more sense to go ahead and find out where the Spanish Army was so that we could avoid them and maybe find a safer inn or better, a berth that could take us back to France. And even with me, we could travel much faster on our horses than we could with the cart and everyone else."

"You did not stay at the inn with your company?" Lady Anna asked, curiously.

Robin gave a little shudder. "My good husband will trust our cart master with his goods, but he does not trust the man with me. Nor should he."

Lady Anna nodded.

"Pray forgive, Mistress," Hester said. "But what is the number of your company?"

"Forgive me," said Robin. "I have my maid, of course, and her husband is our cart master. And then we have two more men to help. The cart is mostly empty, but we have two small clothes presses."

"Thank you, Mistress," Hester said and disappeared.

Robin returned to chatting with Lady Anna and found the young woman quite congenial. She was not unlike her father that way, but with an added grace and wit. Robin tried to let Lady Anna do most of the talking, but the young woman's curiosity was overwhelming, and Robin found herself answering all manner of questions, usually as vaguely as possible. She did not want to trip Roger up.

By the time Roger returned, Lord Jan had already had his meeting with the city's council and returned to the house. He joined his daughter and guest again in the solar, with Master Ernst hovering in the background. Roger was admitted and even though Robin knew what had really happened, she was startled by how dark and angry Roger looked.

"They fled," he complained after politely greeting the women. "The entire crew. They took the cart and clothes presses and headed south. Or something. They may even have made off for England.”

“What?” asked Robin.

“They were Huguenots!” Roger snapped. “In secret, of course. No wonder they feared the Spanish.”

“No wonder they loved coming up here,” grumbled Robin. “Could they have gone to Holland? I’ve heard some of their ilk have gone there.”

“Does it matter?” Roger snapped. “Thank God we’d already sold the wine, and I kept the money with me.”

“Then we are doubly well-met,” Lord Jan said, soothingly. “You can replace your belongings while we wait for the Spanish to take over, and then we can find you a way back to your home. In the meantime, enjoy my humble hospitality.”

Roger smiled gratefully. “Thank you, my lord. It is most kind of you.”

“Bah,” Lord Jan said with a chuckle. “We still do some fine weaving here in Bruges. We shall find a way to make this worth both our whiles.”

Lady Anna watched her father with shrewd affection, and Robin did not doubt that Lord Jan would find a way to profit from their loss. How that would affect Robin and Roger’s quest to find Donald, she did not know.

Nor did she get a chance to ask Roger about it until late that evening, when they and the rest of the household had finally gone to bed. The two had elected to share a chamber, and Lord Jan soundly teased Roger when he said he could help Robin undress that night. Lady Anna insisted that Robin take advantage of her personal maid in the morning. Finally alone, Robin eased herself onto the huge four-poster bed as Roger slid his hand under his doublet to get the small leather kit he had hidden there.

"I don't think I've ever eaten so much at one time," she groaned, holding her stomach. The feast had been grand with stews and savories and pies, crowned by a massive haunch of roasted venison.

"It's been a long while since I have," Roger said, opening a small flask. "At least I got a chance to drink some of this before dinner started."

"How much of that stuff do we have?" Robin asked after taking a sip of the cure-all drug phenyl tri-cloroacenol.

"Not enough for nightly feasts," Roger said with a sigh.

Robin shook her head as the warmth of the drug began to take effect. "We should probably save what we have for any real injuries. So, what do we do about finding Donald?"

Roger chuckled. "Such impatience. Don't worry. He'll find us. That's why we're wealthy merchants."

"That sounds so reassuring," Robin grumbled.

"Where are your timetron and handheld?"

Robin pulled them from the deep, hidden pocket under her overskirt. Roger stood on the edge of the bed and looked up into the top, from which the curtains hung.

"Plenty of dirt," he observed. "Probably as safe a place as any to hide these."

"Where are yours?" Robin guessed that Roger's timetron and handheld were somewhere close by, as well.

"Under the table," he said, nodding at the small piece bearing a pitcher and basin that stood under the room's window. "That should be good enough until we are dressed tomorrow."

With servants helping each of them to dress and the high likelihood that one or more would come and freshen their clothes in the morning, Roger had elected to hide the equipment overnight. It was a common practice, he'd explained. Members of the higher orders almost always had servants to wait on them, and it was fairly easy to procure one. Finding another traveler willing to take turns playing servant and master was considerably harder and didn't really help if one was going to establish a permanent persona in a different time.

Robin got up and tried to reach the ties of her bodice.

"Here. I've got that," Roger said, reaching for her.

Sighing, Robin turned her back to him. "What are we going to do about Lord Jan? Should we find our own place to stay?"

"Let's stay here for the time being," Roger said. "I pulled enough gold to support our story, so that won't be an issue. I'll try to put off buying any cloth, but if we must, we bring some cloth back. It wouldn't hurt to have some, anyway."

With her bodice unlaced, Robin slid it off, leaving the sleeves still tied to it. She could untie her riding skirt and the kirtle and petticoats underneath, but needed Roger to untie the corset over her long undergown or chemise. While Robin untied her garters and slid out of her stockings, Roger finished pulling off his stockings, slops and doublet. His shirt fell to his knees, for which Robin was grateful. Both her chemise and his shirt were of fine linen and somewhat sheer. Neither of them had anything on underneath. Trying not to look at Roger, Robin quickly got under the covers of the bed. Roger gave her a puzzled look but blew out the two candles next to the door, leaving a small one lit on the table under the window.

The next morning, as dawn peeked through the curtains on the bed, Robin heard the servants moving quietly about the room. Roger was still asleep. She looked at him, the soft glow of fondness filling her. They'd shared sleeping space off and on for over two months at that point, although they'd never undressed in front of each other. She wondered that he hadn't shown any real interest in doing anything else. He seemed to be fond of her. She debated making the first move, but had no idea how she would in a way that would make sense to him.

She waited long enough for the servants to shut the door, and then a few minutes more to be sure that they were not coming back right away. She was not surprised to find that hers and Roger's outer clothes had been taken away, with a fresh chemise and full kirtle with bodice for Robin and shirt and nightshirt (which was more like a robe) for Roger. Making sure that Roger was still asleep, Robin slid out of the bed and changed her chemise for the fresh one and slid into the kirtle. It seemed a little odd that she felt embarrassed about Roger seeing her almost naked when she'd been thinking about having sex with him. She shook the thoughts from her head. She had other things to concentrate on, such as making sure she could maintain her persona. It had seemed so simple when she, Dean and Elizabeth had been in the Seventeenth Century. Perhaps it was because she had Elizabeth to help, or more likely, she hadn't known enough to know what the potential mistakes were.

She paced for a few minutes, then found the small bit of embroidery she'd had in her saddlebag. She poked at it for several more minutes, despite realizing that she fully shared Lady Anna's distaste for the art. She was about to put it away when there was another soft rapping at the door. She went to it quickly and opened it, to the surprise of the three servants on the other side.

"Mistress," gasped the first softly. "You are awake so early!"

"I couldn't sleep," Robin said, just as softly.

"It's no matter," said the servant. She was a slightly middle-aged woman, accompanied by two young girls, carrying Roger's and Robin's outer clothes. "We shall have your bath ready right away."

"Please don't rush on my account," Robin said and then realized that what was a normal and expected courtesy in her time was unheard of where she was.

The matron either didn't notice or didn't care. She nodded at the girl carrying Robin's dress, and the girl hurried away down the hall. The other girl slipped into the bedroom and through the interior door to the dressing room beyond. She emerged a minute later and scurried after the older woman. A minute later, the first girl returned and invited Robin to follow her to the other dressing room. Robin followed, silently thankful that Roger was still asleep.

What she didn't know was that Roger had woken up almost as soon as she'd left the bed. He watched through the crack in the bed curtains, wondering and terrified. At times, it seemed like Robin was going to finally initiate their relationship. There was a naturalness to their being together that filled him with joy and impatience. Yet, other times, it seemed as though she wasn't entirely interested or that she expected him to make the first move, and that terrified him. If he made the first move and it was the wrong one, then it was entirely possible their relationship, whatever it might be, would end in utter failure.

Chapter Thirteen

The official surrender of the city of Bruges to the Spanish forces took place with some pomp in the middle of the town square. Robin and Roger hung back, observing and listening. There was some grumbling, but overall, it appeared the burghers were perfectly happy to have the change of power happen quietly and without bloodshed. Anything that kept business going was good, as far as they were concerned. Even though Bruges had declined from its heyday the century before, there was still plenty of business and trade to be done, and the crafters guilds and council members were eager to do it.

There was also a bit of tension over the next few days as the burghers collectively held their breath, waiting to see if the Spanish would keep the promise made by their commander, Alexander Faranese, the son of the Duke of Parma, that there would be no looting. But it soon became obvious that even the mercenaries among the Spanish troops were just as eager as the burghers for a smooth transition of power. Most of the foot soldiers camped just outside the city walls, while the officers chose to be billeted in a couple of the local inns.

"They are even paying for their own keep," Lord Jan told his household over another large dinner that Saturday evening, two days after the surrender. "Can you imagine? Soldiers paying their own way."

"Almost unheard of," Roger replied. "But a blessing for us."

He glanced at Robin, who remained virtuously quiet.

The next afternoon, after Sunday mass, Lord Jan came home with two Spanish officers. One was a slight man with an air of supreme confidence. His hair was dark, and his face was long and narrow with a patrician grace. The other man was tallish, with dark reddish-brown hair and a full mustache and neatly trimmed pointed beard. It was Donald.

Roger smiled blandly even as he noticed Robin's face tightening. It was no surprise. The last time she'd seen Donald, it had been incredibly traumatic. But it was what they were there for and, no doubt, Donald was fully aware of that. The trick would be to stay one step ahead of him.

"Master and Mistress de Marais, come meet my guests," Lord Jan said with a wave of his hand. "This is Captain... Oh, dear, Captains, I've completely lost your full names."

The smaller man stepped forward. "I am Captain Edouardo Munoz de Esteban Martinez, commander of the Spanish troops in Bruges. And this is my fellow officer, Captain Felipe Emmanuel Llanez de Garcia."

Martinez offered a small bow, then looked at de Garcia, or Donald.

"It is a pleasure to meet you," Donald replied. His eyes fell on Lady Anna, who had bobbed a small curtsey.

"Oh, and this is my beloved daughter, Lady Anna," Lord Jan said. "Master de Marais is from France and is on his way home there eventually." He smiled at Roger. "I thought it would be good to get to know our Spanish friends."

"An excellent idea," said Roger. He noticed Robin edging even closer to Lady Anna.

The talk was perfunctory. Captain Martinez was the younger son of a Spanish nobleman from Castile, while Donald hinted that his father was yet more powerful, but could not acknowledge Donald as his son.

"Have you a son in the army?" Donald finally asked Lord Jan.

"I have no sons living," Lord Jan said with a sigh. "But I am quite blessed to have my fair daughter, who is the prop of my old age."

"Indeed," Donald replied with a smile.

"You are not so old, Father," Lady Anna said. "And you hardly need propping."

Lord Jan chuckled. "We shall see. Perhaps you and Mistress de Marais would prefer to go elsewhere and talk about what women talk about?"

Lady Anna glanced at Robin, who nodded. The two bobbed small curtsies and left the room.

The conversation among the men centered on the atrocities committed by the local Calvinists, the likelihood of a siege occurring at one or more of the cities in the area, and the general agreement that such troubles were not good for business and to be avoided. Every now and then, Donald would slip in a question about Lord Jan's holdings and business. The Spaniards stayed through another long and heavy dinner, and Roger was exhausted by the time he and Robin finally got to their room.

"Donald's been eyeing Lady Anna all evening," Robin growled as Roger undid the laces on her bodice.

"I know. He's been trying to figure out just how rich Lord Jan is since he got here." Roger freed her from the garment. "He probably needs money. He had to leave awfully quickly."

"But he could rob somebody as easily as not." Robin shrugged herself out of her kirtle, then overskirt. She held up her hand to stop Roger's reply. "And, yeah, I get that it's not that easy to establish an ongoing persona. But he has two tactics that he uses over and over again. One is the witchcraft thing."

"He'll have a hard time using it here," Roger said. "It's clear we're well-liked."

"And the other tactic - trying to marry into what he wants. Or at least, creating a relationship." Robin sighed. "He reminds me of something my dad said about my mom. She loves the romance but doesn't really want a man in her life. It's almost like she's afraid of anybody getting too close to her."

"How does that apply to Donald?" Roger focused on getting out of his slops in order to hide that he'd seen the sudden flush on Robin's face.

"It's like he wants a relationship, but is afraid of it," Robin said. "So, he uses going after one to get what he wants, then abandons the relationship, even though that's probably what he wants the most."

Roger sighed. "Hopefully, that will come out when he gets treated."

"Or maybe we can use it somehow."

"Maybe."

Robin laid her dress on a stool. "So, when are we going to get his timetron blocked? Tonight?"

Roger shook his head. Robin was still very impatient.

"No," he said. "We'll give it until tomorrow or the next night. I have to get our disguises together."

"I've already gotten them," Robin said, a little testily.

Roger stepped back in surprise.

Robin shrugged. "I told Lady Anna it was my penance to collect clothing for the poor. She not only believed me, she helped."

"That was clever." Roger chuckled.

"You're not the only one who gets this game," Robin replied.

"No, I guess I'm not."

"Well then, are we going tonight?" Robin began pacing.

"Why? Trust me, he's not going anywhere or when."

"How can you be so sure?" Robin stopped suddenly. "Or do you know something about this that I don't?"

"Nope." Roger smiled. The only prior hints he had were about their relationship and there was no way of knowing when any of that would fall out, and he didn't dare push it one way or another. "It's just that Donald has two goals right now. One is to get himself settled as comfortably as possible. Which means he needs a permanent persona so that he can accumulate as much money as possible before he goes after his second goal."

"Let me guess, that second goal is getting revenge on us," Robin grumbled. "That's probably why we need to go after him tonight. It's like you said, stay one step ahead of him."

Roger sighed. "Okay. Do you know where he's staying?"

"No." Robin frowned, defeated.

"Neither do I." Roger crawled into bed. "We do have to get that bit of information." He sighed. "Look, he doesn't necessarily know that we followed him here. We could have just accidentally come across each other. It does happen. Either way, he's going to come after us before he runs from us. It's an elemental part of how his illness works. As far as he's concerned, he's all-powerful and more clever than any of us." Roger paused as he watched Robin reluctantly climb into bed next to him. "Are you okay?"

Robin shrugged. "I suppose so. I guess I'm just tired of being left out and lectured to. I know you can't help how men dealt with women in this time."

"You can still do a lot. You got our disguises for us."

"But I'm used to being in charge of things."

"So am I," Roger grumbled.

Robin groaned. "I suppose we shouldn't be so obsessed with running things then."

"Well, if you can make the effort for more equitable teamwork, then so can I," said Roger. "And I guess it is harder for you. So, should I focus on finding out where Donald is staying tomorrow?"

"Why don't we both do it?" Robin grinned. "I'm willing to bet I can find out, too."

And the next morning, Robin did. As she and Lady Anna sat in the solar, perusing Lady Anna's huge book of healing and cooking herbs, Lady Anna looked up and smiled. Master Ernst stood in the doorway to the solar.

"May I help you, Master Ernst?" Lady Anna asked.

Robin pretended to be interested in a page of the herbal.

"Your father begs me to tell you that he and Master de Marais will be elsewhere for the midday meal, so that you ladies may dine at your leisure."

"Thank you, Master Ernst." Lady Anna hesitated. "Do you know where they have gone?"

"To the Weavers Guild meeting. There are some concerns about the Spanish that your father wishes to answer."

"I see. Does this have anything to do with the visit from those two captains yesterday?"

"I believe so." Master Ernst smiled warmly, clearly glad for an opportunity to remain in the room. "They've been very well-behaved, but some of their lessers have been sniffing around as if they're looking for trouble."

"And what do we know about these captains?" Lady Anna asked. "Are they men of quality?"

"It would appear so." Master Ernst wandered into the room. "One of our own guild masters has traveled to Spain and has met Captain Martinez's father, and he is, indeed, a wealthy and favored don in his land. The captain himself is in the good graces of the Duke of Parma's son and has good expectations of a solid holding in the area. This is what Guild Master Op Tume says. Captain Martinez is most humble and speaks quite highly of the Duke's son."

"And what of the other captain?" Lady Anna asked.

Master Ernst frowned. "Captain de Garcia is new to the unit, but eager to prove himself. In addition, he seems to have a very full purse and is quite generous."

"And yet, you dislike him." Lady Anna's eyes sparkled with humor.

Master Ernst shuffled and cleared his throat. "We know too little of him."

"Do you know who's lodging them?" Lady Anna asked.

"And why would you want to know that?" Master Ernst asked.

Lady Anna laughed. "So that I can avoid any unwanted messages. We know which boys serve which inns. If I know where the Spaniards are lodged, then I can have those boys sent away before they deliver anything. And if I never got the message, then I can't be held accountable for not knowing what was wanted."

Master Ernst wasn't the only one impressed with Lady Anna's logic. Robin wasn't sure if Lady Anna had been planning her excuse or not, but the young woman was certainly aware that Donald was interested in her. Master Ernst, for his part, finally dropped his formal, respectful demeanor and grinned full out.

"You are such a clever one," he said admiringly. "Life with you would, indeed, be lively."

"I will be as good a wife as any man could want," Lady Anna said, blushing and ducking her head.

"Well," said Master Ernst. "Then it would be best if you avoided messages bourne by any of the boys from Master Reuchel's inn."

Robin smiled to herself. Later that afternoon, Robin suggested a walk around the city and Lady Anna was not only happy to go, she even suggested going by Master Reuchel's inn.

"I suppose I should be avoiding it," Lady Anna said, with a giggle. "But it wouldn't hurt to find out what we can about Captain de Garcia."

"Why?" Robin asked.

"So that I can convince my father that a marriage with him would not be in either of our best interests," Lady Anna said. She paused. "Father does love me and wants only the best for me. We just don't agree on what that is. As a dutiful daughter, I suppose I should be silent and trust him.”

"Well, love can be a very fickle thing," Robin said. "That is why we should trust our fathers to bring common sense to a very emotional process. Still, I believe that if a woman is to be the best helpmate she can be, her husband should be genuinely fond of her and she of him. I have two friends of my childhood who were sent into marriages with men they didn't care for, and neither household has prospered."

"Indeed." Lady Anna smiled.

Robin wasn't sure she should be interfering in what was, after all, a family issue. Not to mention that travelers were cautioned against trying to affect the lives of the people they were observing. Still, with Donald trying to get to her and Roger, anything that would keep Lady Anna safe from Captain de Garcia she was going to do. In addition, Robin was growing fond of Lady Anna and did not want to see the young woman hurt.

Outside the inn, Lady Anna wondered how they were to find out what they wanted.

"That's simple," Robin said. "We're still collecting clothing for the poor. Let's find the innkeeper's wife to find out if she either has something to contribute or knows of someone in particular need. We can go around to the back to do that and won't have to worry about being seen by Captain de Garcia."

"A most excellent idea," Lady Anna said.

They made their way through the muck of the alley behind the inn and found Mistress Reuchel in the inn's yard, supervising the maids as they washed linens. The matron immediately called for stools, a table, and tankards of beer.

"Come sit a bit and have a drink," said Mistress Reuchel, who was exceptionally stout. "'Tis a warm day and some beer will be refreshing."

"That's very kind of you, Mistress," Lady Anna said. "Have you met Mistress de Marais? She and her husband are my father's guests, having met with some bad fortune on the road. And despite her own misfortune, she's engaging in a work of charity. We are here to collect any useable rags you might have for the poor."

"That is a kindness, indeed," Mistress Reuchel said. "We've had a fair number of beggars at our doorstep these past few years. Not that I expect things to get better now that the Spanish are here."

"And why is that, Mistress?" Robin asked.

"Because they are no better nor no worse than any men," Mistress Reuchel said as a servant placed a small table and a pair of sturdy stools in front of the three women. Another hurried up with two tankards of beer. "Take Captain Martinez, for example. He's clearly a pious man, but he would not hesitate for a moment to lop off my head if he was so ordered. Or if he thought I was a Calvinist."

She made a quick sign of the cross over her abundant bosom.

"And Captain de Garcia?" Robin asked.

The matron huffed. "Him. He tries to act as though his purse is heavier than everyone else's. But he's a miserly one, he is. Whereas Captain Martinez is quick to offer a small coin to the girls who empty his night pot, Captain de Garcia doesn't offer anything and counts out the rent for his lodging grudgingly in the smallest coins possible.

He's quick to assume he's being cheated, too." She huffed again. "See what I mean? No better nor no worse than any others."

"Are they sharing a room?" Robin asked.

"Would that they were," Mistress Reuchel said with a heavy sigh. "They've taken two of my best rooms, on the end over the fireplace, one each. My good husband saw fit to offer them a lowered rate, too." She shrugged. "It will be nice to have those rooms rented for a longer time than usual, but I have two regular travelers who will not be so happy to move to one of the larger rooms with my other guests. And who's to say how long the Spanish soldiers will be here?"

"Do you know if either of the captains has a wife?" Lady Anna asked.

"Neither," said Mistress Reuchel. "At least, I have no reason to believe so. Wait. Captain Martinez did mention that he has been promised in marriage to a lass back home, but nothing formal has taken place. He did not seem unhappy about it. I expect that he's waiting until he has captured enough favors and perhaps some land from his lord, the Prince of Parma."

Robin blinked, then realized the matron was referring to the commander of the Spanish troops, and the son of the Duke of Parma. She wondered what information, if any, Roger was picking up.

Roger was not picking up much information at all. The weavers of the guild were a rather fussy group, interested in keeping the status quo at all costs. As no one could be sure how long the Spanish troops would be in the city, there wasn't much Lord Jan could tell them.

But his luck turned when he and Lord Jan were walking home and they encountered Captain Martinez, who invited them for a tankard of beer at a nearby inn. Local men crowded the room as they gossiped and did business over tankards.

"Is this where you're lodging?" Roger asked as the three men settled themselves over their beer.

Lord Jan's eyes rose.

"No," said Martinez. "I and Captain de Garcia are lodged at Master Reuchel's inn."

"I should have thought so," Lord Jan said. "It is the finer place."

"Yes," Martinez said, then took a sip from his tankard. "But the beer is better here." He paused suddenly. "Although I would beg that you do not tell my good host that."

"Your secret is safe with us," Lord Jan said with a chuckle. "So, all goes well with your superiors?"

"Yes," Martinez said. "I have just now received a message from His Grace, and he seems well pleased. We are to stay in place until all the Lowlands are back under the rule of Spain, but that shouldn't take too much longer. Then some of us will be given lands so that we can maintain order and get the taxes returned to the Crown."

Lord Jan smiled broadly. "Rumor has it that you are in an excellent position to be so honored."

Martinez shrugged. "It would be foolish of me to count on such a gift when there are so many who are worthy and, to be honest, perfectly happy to remain here rather than return to Spain."

"And you so wish?" Lord Jan asked.

"It really doesn't make much difference to me," Martinez said placidly. "If I am given lands here, I can make my way comfortably, but will not be able to go home. If I go home, I will be where my family is, but with all the vast comfort of a younger brother's revenue."

Which was to say little to none. Roger chuckled at the witticism.

"And you have no one in Spain eagerly awaiting the day her beloved will come and marry her?" asked Lord Jan.

"There is one to whom I am promised. But I received a letter from my mother today that said her eye has fallen elsewhere, not surprisingly, and is hoping that I will release her."

Lord Jan nodded and eyed Martinez surreptitiously. "What of your counterpart? Captain de Garcia? I haven't heard that he's likely to be left behind."

Martinez shrugged again. "He's too new to our company, I would think. Perhaps if we are forced to lay siege on Antwerp and he distinguishes himself there, he might be honored."

"You don't seem to care for the good captain," Lord Jan said.

Martinez glanced around himself. "He's not a bad soul. But, no, I don't. His letters of recommendation were perfectly correct, and I know of the gentleman who presented him. But I'm not confident that he is who he says he is. Of course, he doesn't entirely say who he is. He says he can't name his father."

"That's common enough," said Roger.

"True," said Martinez. "Still, one usually has some hint."

"And the gentleman who presented de Garcia?" Lord Jan asked.

"Don Tomas Rodolfo de Jimenez y Santa Maria. He is well enough known as a good man," Martinez said. "He has lands near Galicia, but spends most of his time in Madrid, at court."

Roger could see Lord Jan thinking it over and wasn't entirely reassured by what seemed to be surfacing in the portly nobleman's brain. It was only natural that Lord Jan would see a daughter of marriageable age as a mere asset, and while Roger didn't believe that Lord Jan was completely insensible to his daughter's preferences, there was no question the older man was looking to further his own interests. There wasn't much Roger could do, however. The purpose of time travel was to observe only and not interfere with the lives of the people being observed. The only time interference was allowed - and even then, it was frowned upon - was to prevent the untimely death of an innocent or a traveler. Given Robin's concerns about Lady Anna, Roger couldn't help but wonder if Robin was going to be able to remain unmoved in that situation.

He became even more concerned that evening as he and Robin prepared to go over to Master Reuchel's inn and reset Donald's timetron so that it would no longer respond to him. The operation itself was relatively simple and, with the aid of a handheld, could be managed in a matter of minutes. The problem was that it needed to be done with the timetron close by, as Roger was going to have to use brain wave transmission to do it. And because that also meant Roger was going to have to concentrate and watch his handheld, performing the operation during the day, when either Donald or others could observe, was impossible.

"They are clearly in love with each other," Robin said about Lady Anna and Master Ernst. "And I do not believe it's the temptation of forbidden fruit. They truly seem to enjoy teasing each other and things like that."

"We can't interfere," Roger said. "You know that."

"I know," Robin sighed. "And I'm not going to. I'm sure Lady Anna will find some way to encourage her father's will in her preferred direction."

Roger nodded. "Are you ready?"

Robin put one last bit of soot on her cheek, then looked at Roger. He looked rather forlorn, she thought. He had made himself distant again. He was worried about something, and it wasn't just their upcoming mission, although that was reason enough for concern. Robin sighed inwardly and smiled.

"Yes," she said. "Let's go."

The household and the rest of the city were deep in slumber. Even the beggars lay asleep in the dark doorways. The moon was in its last days of waning, and what light its tiny sliver gave barely added to that of the stars.

The door to Master Reuchel's inn had been bolted, of course. But Robin found an open window next to it. Hoisting herself onto the sill, she looked carefully around the main room. The fading embers of the fire cast a soft glow, and the room appeared to be empty, even of sleeping guests, although the tables had been left standing. Robin slid the rest of the way in as silently as she could, then hurried over to the door and unbolted it. Roger slid in and they shut the door.

There was a soft glow in his hands from the handheld. He looked up at the ceiling and shook his head. Robin tried not to roll her eyes. She touched his arm and pointed at the fireplace, then upstairs. Roger's eyes widened, but he moved over to the fireplace.

The coals inside had been banked on the back wall and were going out as Roger looked at his handheld and gazed up through the chimney. Robin watched as he touched the screen of the handheld again and again.

"Almost," Roger hissed, then groaned.

"What?" Robin asked.

"Something in my eye," he whispered. "Got it." He withdrew from the fireplace but stumbled. "Can't see."

Robin took his arm and led him silently along the wall toward the door. She felt the tread on the stairs above rather than heard it and began slipping along the wall across from the stairway where someone was coming downstairs. A soft chuckle identified the person as Donald.

Quickly opening the door, Robin pushed Roger outside, then hurried out. Half leading and half dragging him, she hurried down the street, only to hear the blast of a gun. Roger grunted and fell. Her heart in her throat, Robin slid down next to him, then rolled the two of them into a doorway where another beggar groaned in complaint.

Donald walked toward them, but by that point, Master Reuchel and his household had been aroused and they prevented Donald from going further. Robin held her breath as the servants ran past them, looking for the supposed burglars, then hurried back to the inn. She waited a few minutes longer, then checked Roger. He was not only still alive, but conscious.

"Are you all right?" she whispered.

"Well enough," he replied. "My leg hurts, and I've still got something in my eyes."

Robin helped him up, and the two staggered back to Lord Jan's house, arriving just as the cock began its pre-dawn chorus. They were able to get up to their room without anyone seeing them, and Robin hurriedly got Roger undressed, washed up and into bed, before quickly cleaning herself up, then getting into bed and closing the curtains as tightly as she could. She picked up her handheld and waved it over Roger's leg. The glow lit up the bed, and Robin could see the small hole in Roger's thigh, gently oozing blood.

"It looks like you've got a ball in you," she told him. "But it doesn't look like it's hit bone or is anywhere near an artery. You want me to dig it out or seal it up?"

"Seal," whispered Roger. "It will heal faster."

Robin silently let her breath out. She had been hoping he'd choose to seal the wound. She hadn't been looking forward to doing surgery. She got out the small ampule of disinfectant and the even smaller bladder of the sealant. Sealing the wound also had some risks, mostly of developing an abscess at the site of the ball. But surgery with minimal sterility was also risky and still an option if the abscess developed. Robin fervently hoped it wouldn't as she dosed the hole as liberally as she dared with the disinfectant. She fed Roger a bit of the phenyl tri-chloroacenol, then poured the sealant on the wound, taking care not to get any on her fingers.

A minute later, she heard the door to the room open and movement on the other side of the curtains. Roger had heard it, too. Robin turned off her handheld. They looked at each other, holding their respective breaths. Robin, fortunately, had gathered their disguises and hidden them at the foot of the bed, but the last thing they needed was for a servant to notice that something was not as it had been. The maid, presumably, was bringing their freshly brushed outer clothes and fresh underclothes. Robin still held the bowl with the sooty clean-up water. Eventually, the maid slipped out of the room.

Robin sniffed, her eyes almost overflowing in her relief. She slid out of bed and emptied the bowl into the chamber pot, then slid back under the covers. Roger sighed. She slid her hand over his forehead. It was warmer than it should have been.

"Damn," she whispered.

"Fever?" Roger asked.

Robin nodded. "It feels like you've got one."

"It's just as well," he whispered. "It will give you cover for getting the disguises out of here and for the bloodstains on my shirt."

"If I can just keep them from sending for a doctor," Robin said, sliding down next to him.

"Are you all right?" Roger asked her.

"I'm fine." She shivered. "Just scared, I guess." She swallowed as she realized what was really bothering her. "We almost lost you."

"Not really," Roger said. "It could be a lot worse."

"I don't want to think about it being a lot worse," Robin said with a sniff. "I don't want to lose you, Roger."

"I suppose being here by yourself could be a little worrisome."

Robin snorted. "I could manage just fine by myself and have, may I remind you." She shook her head. "This is going to sound silly, but I really don't want to. Possibly for the first time in my life, I don't want to manage by myself."

She looked at him. "We make a darned good team, I think. At least, when you're not trying to run everything."

Roger chuckled ruefully. "As you have just proven tonight."

He looked away from her.

"Why do you do that?" Robin fought to keep her voice low. "Every time it feels like I'm getting close to you, you pull away. Am I that terrible?"

"No," Roger groaned, still focused on the crack in the bed curtains. "I can't tell you, is all. Something must happen. I can't do it and I can't tell you what it is."

Robin snorted. "Well, how much longer do we have to wait? Because I'm getting really crazy with all these mixed messages."

Roger looked scared. "What do you mean?"

"I don't know." Robin flopped back onto the pillow and glared into the darkness above them. "I mean, I really like the way we've become friends. We seem to have a lot in common. And I'm all for going for more, but I don't really understand hooking up in your society. So, I don't want to push for anything. And sometimes it feels like you'd really like to, as well. But then you pull away."

"When you say hooking up, do you mean it as in your natal time? An intimate, but casual liaison with no commitments?" Roger seemed to hold his breath.

Robin felt her heart sink. "Actually, no. That sounds awful." She rolled over and looked at him. "I'm not real comfortable with the commitment thing. But just jumping each other when convenient sounds vile, too." She rolled onto her back again. "Sometimes I think I'm falling in love with you. And it's not that I don't want to. I just don't know how good I'd be in a relationship. I haven't done that well before."

Roger stared up into the shadows above them. "Why do you think that is?"

"I wish I knew." Robin frowned. "That's not right, either. The last two guys I fell for were both really, seriously unavailable. Dean says that's fear of commitment. But the last time I really tried to make a relationship work, that didn't work, either. I did everything right, too. But it turned out, he wasn't that into being with other human beings."

Roger chuckled. "Well, if you'll pardon the older but wiser routine."

"I don't know if I should."

He sighed. "I can't say that I'm an expert, but I have managed two long-term relationships in my life. The first ended mostly because of the secrets I had to keep as a traveler. We'd stayed together even though she couldn't get pregnant. She knew I did traveled but didn't want to herself, and in the end, couldn't accept that there was a part of my life that was completely closed to her. And I couldn't blame her for that."

"And the relationship after that?"

Roger swallowed. "She got accepted to join an interplanetary colony. She'd thought she'd been rejected, and we were about to start trying to procreate when they found a place for her on a new project. I didn't want to go. That addiction to time travel, you know." He frowned and shrugged. "And, as an academic, I really didn't have much to offer the colony, so they didn't entirely want me. They already had more than enough teachers and what they needed was muscle. We both knew at the time that we'd never see each other again."

"There's no way for her to come back and visit?"

"Possibly. But since I'm not there, she must breed, if at all possible, which means another man in her life who needs her commitment to him and whatever children they have." He turned to look at her. "But I guess what I'm trying to say is that both of the issues in my past relationships happened because I couldn't share traveling."

"You couldn't share your passion with them." Robin frowned. "I wish I knew what my passion was."

"It's not time traveling?"

"It is now." Robin sighed. "It's just that all my life, I've never felt like I fit anywhere. Even at the end of high school, and we were supposed to be thinking about what we wanted to do for a living, I couldn't make up my mind. Nothing seemed right. That's when my mom tried pressuring me into studying pre-med, then going to medical school. And it did kind of sound like fun. Mom thought I was resisting her suggestion because it was her suggestion. She didn't get that it just wasn't right for me. Engineering wasn't, really, but neither was history. Although I had more fun in my history classes than any others. And working with Dr. Frawley. Even before I came to your time, I was looking at my life and my business and thinking that I'd achieved everything I'd set out to do. What the heck was I supposed to do with the rest of my life? And now that I think about it, how do you share your passion in life when you don't even know what it is?"

"Well, it's not as though time travel was a potential career path in your time," Roger pointed out.

"No kidding." Robin frowned. "But it's not that, exactly. It's about me being true to who I am, to really following my heart. I had it bad for Dr. Frawley. I just thought I had a thing for older men. But it wasn't that. It was me finally following my heart. When I picked up the timetron for the first time. Yes, it knew me, but it also felt more right than anything else." Robin rolled onto her side, facing Roger. "It was as though it really knew me."

"We knew it recognized you."

"But it was more than that. I felt connected to it."

"Connected?" Roger looked at her, a little puzzled.

"Yeah." Robin shrugged. "I didn't even realize I'd taken it. But then I figured out how it worked and tried it. And it was great. That's why I tried to bring Elizabeth back to her natal time. I probably shouldn't have, but it was possibly the first time in my life something felt absolutely right. Does that make sense?"

"It does, and it doesn't." He glanced at her. "You've obviously got some unusual connection to the timetron." He looked away again. "I don't know what it is."

"What's going on, Roger? You're pulling away again."

"I know. I have to." He glanced at her again.

Robin suddenly frowned. "You know something, don't you? About us."

"Just enough to get us into really big trouble," he said finally.

Robin rolled onto her back. "And something has to happen first before you can tell me about it. I wish I knew what it was so I could make it happen."

"You don't want to do that. Trust me."

"Maybe I do." Robin folded her arms across her chest. "Because right now, I'd really like to fall in love with you.

Correct that. I'm already in love with you. And I'd sure like to do something about it. But if there's this mysterious problem between us..."

Roger rolled over and snuggled up to her. "Not any more there isn't."

"What?"

Roger reached up and lovingly kissed her. Robin felt her heart lurch as her breath slipped away at the feel of his lips on hers.

"I can't tell you what all I know," he said. "Only that the safest way for me to deal with it was to let you make the first move."

"Me, huh?" Robin tried to glare at him and couldn't. "So, I take it I've made it."

"Yes, and about freaking time, too."

Robin bent her head toward him and finally kissed him, her body tingling as his hands found their way under her nightgown. Suddenly, it didn't matter that he'd been injured and had a slight fever. The two burned with a different warmth and soon they were fulfilling all the desire they had held back.

Chapter Fourteen

Some hours later, Robin was dressed and fed, and moving about the house, supposedly gathering supplies but disposing of disguises at the same time. Somewhere in between her trips to the kitchen and maids sliding in and out of the room to bring food and soup, Robin caught a couple knowing smiles, as if the servants were finally seeing something they'd expected to from a couple that chose to share the same bed night after night. Robin felt herself flushing every time one of the maids smiled and chuckled.

Roger, however, remained oblivious to the change. As befitted someone with a fever, he slept most of the day. Robin remained close by, reading, or doing embroidery, or wondering when and how Donald was going to come after them. Fortunately, Roger's fever broke early that evening and by the next morning, he was alert early and happily reaching for Robin.

He started when Robin pulled away from him.

"No!" Robin gasped and smiled. "I definitely want to make love. But I forgot to ask you something yesterday."

"What?" Roger felt the relief fill him.

"What about birth control?"

Roger chuckled. "A legitimate concern, but I promise you won't get pregnant until we both decide it's time."

"Oh."

"It's part of the culture in my natal time." Roger squeezed her. "Do you want to go over it now or wait until we're closer to that commitment?"

Robin shivered a little. "How about when we're closer?"

"I am happy to wait." Roger kissed her again, and the lovemaking went on from there.

Later, as Robin got dressed, he laid back in the bed. It had been good to finally resolve that part of his worry, aside from how good it felt to be in love again. The die had been cast. If the relationship was headed for the rocks, at least he could be reasonably certain that it wouldn't fail because he'd pushed things along too soon based on the bit he knew about their future. Nonetheless, even though one couldn't usually trust the first flush of romance, Roger felt an unaccountable security with Robin that he'd never felt before. And while no relationship was ever perfectly easy and Roger could tell that this one would be even more difficult in many ways, there was something different this time that filled him with joy. He didn't understand how or why, but he accepted the feeling.

But that afternoon, Roger's high of romantic euphoria came crashing to earth. Donald was once again in the house solar, visiting Lord Jan and eyeing Lady Anna. While Roger stayed on the periphery, Donald paid Lord Jan gentle compliments that had the older man laughing.

"You should be aware, my lord," de Garcia said warmly. "You are considered as good a catch as your lovely daughter."

"I am far too old," Lord Jan replied with a solid chuckle.

"Not for a comely widow, and I've heard tell among the guilds that there are a couple ladies with considerable wealth who wouldn't mind aligning their goods with yours."

"Both of whom are old scolds who would sooner have me under their thumbs than not," said Lord Jan. "But you are kind in your observations."

Roger held his tongue, once again surprised and appalled at just how charming Donald could be when it suited his purposes. Roger was almost taken in by Donald's compliments even as he knew how hollow they were. It was no surprise that Lord Jan couldn't see Donald for what he was.

Worse yet, Captain Martinez was also paying Lady Anna considerable attention. Robin did not look pleased, and Roger could not miss the dark looks that Master Ernst aimed at both the Spanish captains. Then there were the silent pleas for help Lady Anne kept sending in Robin's direction.

"We're not here to get involved," Roger reminded Robin a short time later while strolling the street outside the house.

"We are here to keep Donald out of trouble," Robin said. "Besides, Lady Anna is getting really worried. Lord Jan keeps talking up the two captains and pointing out their respective virtues. She just now asked me how to answer him."

"And what did you say?"

Robin glanced around. "I didn't. I was hoping you had some ideas."

Roger sighed. "I'll talk to Lord Jan. But the best I can do is push him away from Donald. We aren't allowed to interfere."

"I understand," said Robin. "But if Lady Anna asks me directly for help, I can't simply refuse, Prime Directive or not."

"I know," Roger sighed. "We'll figure something out. Let's go in. It's getting close to dinnertime."

That evening, as the nightly feast wound down, Roger found a minute to talk quietly with Lord Jan.

"I noticed the Spanish captains seem quite taken with Lady Anna," Roger said, smiling.

Lord Jan guffawed. "Either one would make an excellent match for all of us." He suddenly grimaced. "If only I could convince my sweet daughter of that. Headstrong, that one is. Just like her mother. And with her head filled with ridiculous notions of love. In what way does a mere girl know anything about what is important for a marriage?"

"She may know more than you think," said Roger. "Lady Anna does not strike me as the foolish sort."

"That she is not," Lord Jan smiled with pride. "Alas, that also means she has a tongue on her, and it has gotten about. It's made it very hard to find a good young man for her. If I can get one of these Spaniards to take after her, there is hope she'll have a good husband yet."

Roger sighed. "I do hope you are taking Captain Martinez's concerns about Captain de Garcia into account."

"I am. Although, if he ends up with a good enough bit of land, why should I worry?"

"A man who lies will not treat your daughter well and I know you are not insensible to her welfare."

"It is my primary concern." Lord Jan sighed. "And I suppose one must consider more than mere wealth. But we don't know for certain that Captain de Garcia is lying."

"You could send to Spain to ask about his letters of reference. It would only delay things a couple of months."

"True." Lord Jan frowned again, then dismissed it. "But I must confess, Captain de Garcia seems perfectly charming to me. I do not understand why you and Captain Martinez do not."

"Perhaps it is because we are not as useful as you are to Captain de Garcia," Roger said with a smile. "Good evening, my lord."

Roger walked away, but he could sense Lord Jan's discomfort.

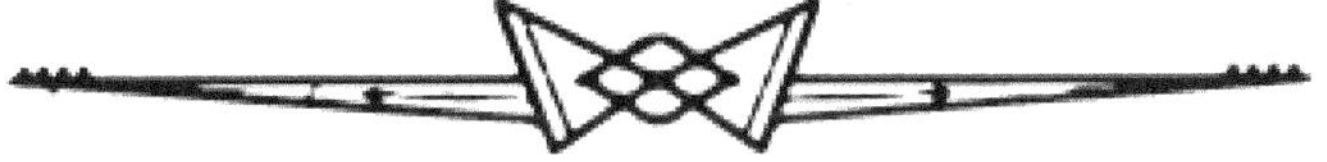

Two days later, the small town was abuzz with the news that the Captain de Garcia had secured a small holding about two leagues to the east of the city. The old knight who held the land had no living sons, and there had been great speculation as to who would inherit it once the old man died. Several of the wealthier guildsmen had even attempted to buy the holding from the knight, only to be soundly rebuffed. How the Spanish captain had managed to purchase the land, no one knew.

"I don't doubt there was some sort of illicit trading involved," Lady Anna complained to Robin that afternoon as the two sat in the solar. "But what am I to do? This makes Captain de Garcia ever so much more appealing to my father, and I'm very afraid."

Robin patted the girl's hand. "I know it's troublesome, but your father isn't completely sold on the captain. My husband has been whispering in his ear. We'll have to hope that makes the final decision."

Later that night, in their bedroom, Robin confronted Roger.

"We've got to do something," she said, pacing the floor. "I don't doubt Donald used some mind game on that knight."

"He probably did," Roger said with a sigh.

"What if he does the same to Lord Jan?" Robin glared at him.

He sat on the side of the bed, frowning. "It's possible, but it will be a lot harder to do with Lord Jan. Games and even brainwave interventions don't work that well with strong-minded people and Lord Jan, fortunately, falls into that category. He is only eager to make a deal with the Spanish because that will help Anna's and his future. He is looking to her care."

"If Donald weren't such a charming slime ball, Lord Jan would see that Donald is not interested in Anna's care."

Roger sighed. "He might be. If he's truly trying to establish himself here and stay in hiding, then he might be."

Robin looked at him. "Yeah. Right."

"Our job is not to leave him here, anyway," Roger said. "Which means we can't let him marry Anna. But that's all we can do."

"Can't we at least present Master Ernst as an alternative?" Robin blinked her eyes. "He works really hard, and he does love her."

Roger shrugged. "We may as well."

The next day, as he and Lord Jan again walked the city after yet another meeting and discussion regarding purchases Roger might make to bring back to France, Roger decided to make his case. Captain Martinez had greeted them pleasantly, then went on his way.

"Still favoring one of the Spaniards for Lady Anna's hand?" Roger asked.

"Of course," Lord Jan replied. "Shall we head back to the house?"

"By all means," Roger said. He paused, then smiled. "It has not escaped my notice that there is a third, very worthy young man who has his eye on your daughter."

Lord Jan sighed. "Young Ernst."

"You don't like him?"

"Oh, no. I'm quite fond of the boy. Almost as fond of him as Lady Anna is."

"Then why are you not considering his suit?"

"He hasn't made one, for starters." Lord Jan shrugged. "Although that only speaks well of him, in my opinion."

"That he lacks a title?"

"Bah. That does not worry me." He sighed. "You must understand that if I haven't outright offered Lady Anna to one of the Spaniards, it is because I do want to consider Master Ernst. The problem is, he has no property or real wealth. He is Master VanDen Melke's third son, you know. What little property our good sergeant-at-arms has will go to the eldest, of course. The second has already joined the French army in the hopes of acquiring some. I cannot bequeath my lands to my daughter and her husband as I have two good strong nephews ready, and the eldest of those has another three sons yet. I will, of course, leave all my money to Lady Anna, but that is barely half my wealth. With a good holding or sufficient wealth, that compensates for the loss of my lands. Master Ernst has neither and Lady Anna's wealth is thereby cut in half, and I do not want that for my daughter."

"I suspect she does not see it that way," said Roger. "And he is a worthy man and already works hard and well in your business affairs."

"Oh, indeed, he does and has helped to increase my fortune." Lord Jan sighed. "I don't doubt he would continue that work, but will it be enough to care for my greatest treasure? I can't say that it will with any confidence. Alas, it might surprise you to know, our fortunes in this, our fine city, are fading and have been for some time. A good strong holding will keep Anna the best, and now that Captain de Garcia has one, he makes a most attractive prospect. Captain Martinez will surely be awarded a holding as well. It is in Lady Anna's best interests that I choose one or the other of them."

"Captain Martinez, perhaps," Roger said. "But she is your daughter. You must dispose of her as you see fit."

That evening a messenger arrived from Captain de Garcia inviting Lord Jan and his household to see his new property and dine with him on the following Wednesday. Lord Jan immediately accepted, which made for several very tense days in his house.

"He means to serve me up to that miserable man," Lady Anna groaned the day before the visit, as she had all the days prior.

She and Robin were in the solar, supposedly practicing music, but Lady Anna prowled the room, completely unable to sit. Robin could barely stay seated herself. Yet, she and Roger had come up with a plan that should, at the very least, save Lady Anna from Donald.

"My lady, your father loves you," Robin said. "He does not want to see you unhappy. And nothing has been settled."

"But this is the final test." Lady Anna picked up a bit of embroidery and threw it back down on the stool. "You've heard the servants gossiping. Captain de Garcia has spared no expense, and you know how much Father loves a good show."

"Then we'll have to give him one," Robin said quietly.

Lady Anna looked at her, surprised.

Robin sighed. "It is not my place to interfere with how your father wishes to see you wed. My husband and I are only your guests. But as you have, we have noted that Captain de Garcia seems to have more of an eye on your father's wealth than to your well-being. Also, my good husband has noted that the captain has a temper. If we can expose him as a man who will not see to your care, then I doubt your father will allow a deal to be struck."

"But what if he does, anyway?" Lady Anna sniffed. "I don't want to take the veil. But I will sooner than let Father marry me off to that... That..."

"I understand," Robin said.

There really wasn't more to be said. Robin tried to stay calm for Lady Anna's sake. But there was no guarantee that Donald's rage would discourage Lord Jan. In addition, the last time Donald had been enraged, Beeman had died as a result. Robin could only hope that Roger would be able to contain his brother before something truly terrible happened.

The next morning, the group plodded along on their horses, accompanied by Master VanDen Melke and four men-at-arms. Lady Anna and Robin both rode on their own horses. Lady Anna looked as though she were headed for a funeral rather than to meet her probable future husband.

"Father asked me to accept Captain de Garcia's suit," she told Robin with a sniff. "I didn't say anything, but how can I? Father assures me that I'll come to love him. I don't see how I ever will."

"I understand," Robin sighed. It was the common assumption that couples would either learn to love each other or achieve some sort of detente. And it, apparently, happened. But like Lady Anna, Robin was hard pressed to see how.

Lord Jan had seen his daughter's dour mood and did not look happy. He was clearly caught between insuring his daughter's welfare financially and her happiness. Knowing how fickle a heart could be, Robin didn't doubt that the older man was at odds with himself.

The small square tower rose over the flat landscape. It was surrounded by fields intersected by canals. Cows grazed contentedly in one field. Not much further on, a small forest stood, the road bending around it. As the group grew closer, they saw a moat surrounding the tower fed by one of the canals. The drawbridge was down, and two men wearing the colors of Spain stood on either side of the portcullis, ready to receive the guests.

Donald was so focused on impressing Lord Jan that he was even pleasant to Robin and Roger and welcomed Master VanDen Melke. The castle had been well kept by its prior owner, and Donald had taken care to see that the wall hangings had been beaten and the floors strewn with fresh rushes. He insisted on taking Lord Jan and his party through the tower's first three floors, and it was a solid, but clearly comfortable place to live with huge fireplaces, cushioned stools and benches, and plenty of fine wall hangings. The several servants were attentive, but Robin caught an undercurrent of nerves among them. All to the better, Robin thought. If Donald wanted and insisted on everything being perfect, it would make things easier for her and Roger.

She watched Roger, wondering when the needling would begin. He had decided to take his time - that patience nonsense again. Robin marveled at how it was possible to love someone so much and still want to knock him upside the head.

Finally, Donald brought everyone downstairs to the second story, where the dining hall was.

"You will note how fine the tapestries are," Donald said to Lord Jan.

"Yes," said Roger. "Obviously, the knight who owned this place before you knew quality work when he found it."

Donald glared briefly at Roger. Robin smiled inwardly. The needling had begun. It was a delicate dance, indeed. Roger continued suggesting that everything in the household had come from the previous owner, rather than Donald's own work. Donald's smile grew progressively tighter. Robin saw a bit of old food stuck to the table near her place.

"Oh, dear," she told Lady Anna, supposedly softly enough to not be heard. "It would appear our good host needs a new housekeeper."

Lady Anna giggled and looked around. Donald was just within earshot.

"That's assuming he wants to pay for one," Lady Anna said. "You've heard the rumors."

Donald pretended he hadn't heard, but was clearly more on edge.

The guests were seated at a long table, with Donald sitting at the head, Lord Jan on one side and Roger on the other. Robin sat next to Roger and Lady Anna next to her father. Master VanDen Melke sat on Robin's other side. He had avoided joining in the needling, although Robin suspected he wanted to.

A small crew of servants served the guests pheasant, goose, and a swan stuffed with sparrows. They also offered a joint of lamb, alongside various vegetables and rich sauces. There were plates on the table rather than simple bread trenchers and silver goblets filled from great pitchers that contained either ale or wine. At one point, Robin excused herself for a moment. She waited until the servant bearing the pitcher of hearty red wine was close to Donald, then made her way back to her seat on the other side of the table just as the servant with the pitcher passed behind Donald. She turned, as if to say something, and not quite accidentally knocked the pitcher with her elbow. It was full, and as the pitcher fell, the contents poured all over Donald's head.

Robin fell back and slid toward her seat as Donald jumped to his feet, his face red.

"You fool!" he bellowed, turning on the servant and grabbing him by the neck. "How dare you!"

He knocked the servant to the floor, then picked up the man by his shirt front and punched him several times in the head.

The other men were on their feet in seconds.

"Captain de Garcia!" yelped Lord Jan.

"I'll teach this idiot to pour wine on his betters!" Donald roared, punctuating his words with more punches.

Roger and Master VanDen Melke hurried over and held Donald back. The servant scurried away. Donald got control of himself, dusted himself off, and smiled tightly at Roger and Master VanDen Melke.

"Pray forgive me," Donald said. "Please, be seated and let us continue our feast."

"Far be it from me to tell you how to run your household," said Lord Jan, settling into his chair. "But a little kindness toward your servants might better serve you. It was clearly an accident, and you were not greatly harmed."

Donald glared at Robin and Roger, then smiled at Lord Jan. "Indeed. I shall consider your words most carefully."

Lord Jan returned the smile, but it did not look as though he believed his host. In fact, the rest of the meal passed in awkward chatter, and as soon as Lord Jan could do so without seeming rude, he decided it was time to leave.

Donald pretended to be good natured about it, but as he came over to help Robin onto her horse, he smiled cruelly.

"You'll pay for this," he hissed at her. "Trust me, you will."

Robin swallowed and smiled. "Pray forgive me, sir. I do not know what you are talking about."

Donald glared as he helped her into her saddle. There wasn't much else he could do. Without a functioning timetron, he was forced to establish himself as best he could. Overtly attacking Robin and Roger would only force him to run some place else, and that would make it harder to gain the wealth Donald needed to be comfortable. At least, that was the theory that Roger was operating under, and it seemed to be working that way.

Lady Anna watched her father a little fearfully as they began the ride back to the city. Lord Jan, for his part, kept to himself until they were well away from the tower. Then he glanced back down the road they'd come on and sighed deeply.

"I believe we have had a narrow escape," he said to Roger.

"Yes," Roger said. "It seems the Captain was doing his best, but I would not have liked to deal with another outburst like that again."

Lord Jan snorted. "Indeed. However, I was also talking about the captain's worthiness as a groom for my daughter. I'm afraid, Master de Marais, you were right in your assessment of the captain."

Robin, who was riding with Lady Anna behind Roger and Lord Jan, smiled privately to herself. She glanced behind her at Master VanDen Melke. The sergeant-at-arms usually rode first, to be ready for whatever potential bandits might lie in wait, but the old soldier was not going to assume that Captain de Garcia was going to simply let the party go. Nor had he apparently heard Lord Jan's statement about the captain. Lady Anna had, and she smiled at Robin, her eyes glowing with relief and joy.

Chapter Fifteen

Robin woke with Roger's hair tickling her nose. She yawned. It had been a difficult night, filled with strategizing, worry, and fierce lovemaking, almost as a shield against whatever plan Donald might come up with. All they could be certain of was that Donald was angry and at his most dangerous.

They got up and dressed early. Roger declined to go about the city with Lord Jan, as he usually did, in order to stay with Robin and Lady Anna. Lady Anna was in a gay mood. She had been saved from her worst fear and, like her father, did not realize that had only increased the threat from Donald rather than lessened it. Robin shivered as she looked out the window of the solar.

It was after lunch when Lady Anna excused herself and didn't return to the solar. Robin held her breath. They all used the necessary because it was, in fact, necessary, and just because Lady Anna hadn't come hurrying back after a few minutes didn't mean she wasn't safe. Robin looked at Roger. Neither were interested in raising a hue and cry over nothing but waiting could be deadly.

Finally, Robin could stand it no longer, and from the look on Roger's face, he was equally ready to act. He nodded at Robin, and she left the solar and found the housekeeper Hester.

"Her ladyship has not come back from the necessary," Robin said. "Is she well?"

"I would expect so," Hester said, narrowing her eyes a touch. "Two Spanish soldiers arrived just a few minutes ago. They had a message from her father that she was to accompany them. So, she did."

"Where did they go?" Robin asked, her heart thumping wildly.

Hester shrugged. "Toward the city gates, I think." She frowned suddenly. "I would have thought they would have headed toward the city square or some such meeting place."

"Whose soldiers were they?"

Hester gulped. "They didn't say. We assumed they were from Captain Martinez. It is well known that he is seeking her hand. Do you fear some harm has come to her?"

"It's possible it was just as you say," Robin said. "Although it seems rather odd that her father would summon her this way. I will call Master de Marais. We'll go in search of her and if anything is amiss, we'll raise the alarm then."

Robin turned to find Roger right around the corner of the hall. They didn't say anything but hurried to the street. Roger turned down the street that led around the city square to the city gates.

"If Donald is kidnapping her, then he'll need to get her outside the gates as fast as possible," Roger explained.

"I got that," Robin replied a little testily. "Are you sure we're not running into a trap with Anna as the bait?"

"Probably," Roger sighed. "But what else can we do?"

"Good point."

They ran outside the city gates just in time to see a horse galloping along the road beyond, with Lady Anna tied onto the pillion seat behind the horseman. But before Robin could cry out, a rough hand covered her mouth. Next to her, she saw Roger tumble to the ground. Robin tried to wriggle an elbow into the ribs of the man who held her, but he pinned her arms firmly to her sides. The next thing Robin knew, she'd been gagged and tossed onto a rough pillion seat, then tied to the horseman in front of her. She wondered where the city guardsmen were, but as the horse beneath her leaped into a gallop, she looked back and saw one of them groggily getting to his feet.

Even at a full gallop, the ride to Donald's tower seemed even longer than it had when they'd walked the horses there the day before. Robin fought to keep herself erect and her back steady against the bounce of the horse's gallop. Already, she could feel the muscles in her back and neck stiffening. There were two men, the one she'd been tied to and a second, riding just behind them, both with the dark hair and beards of the Spanish soldiers.

The two horses eventually clattered into the tower's courtyard and Robin nearly fell off as the horsemen she was tied to pulled his mount up short. Three more Spanish soldiers surrounded them and the rope binding Robin to the horseman was quickly cut. They roughly pulled her from the pillion. But as they led away the now unmounted horses, she and the four men surrounding her stood and waited.

It was then that she heard Donald bellowing at two other men, Lady Anna standing erect between them.

"I should open your bellies and hang you up with your own guts!" Donald screamed at the men. "How could you make such a stupid mistake? I was very clear. Use this one to get the older woman outside the gates, then take the older woman!"

The men surrounding Robin looked at each other as if they weren't sure they should say anything. They had no need to. Donald had barely finished clouting the men next to Lady Anna when he descended on Robin and the men surrounding her.

"It's about time," Donald snarled. He looked back at Lady Anna.

Robin silently thanked her stars that Anna was there. The young woman's presence was possibly all that was keeping Robin alive. Finally, Donald pointed at Lady Anna.

"Take her upstairs," he ordered the man next to Robin. "I'll take this one for a few moments, then join you there. The room you prepared this morning."

The man nodded and roughly took Lady Anna's arm with another man taking her other arm.

Two other men pulled Robin into a small room on the bottom floor of the tower. Donald sent the men away.

"I want your timetron," Donald said.

"I don't have it," Robin said. It didn't matter whether she gave Donald the timetron or not. He wouldn't be able to use it. But she had to protest, or he would become suspicious.

Donald punched her in the side of her head, knocking her flat with the fury of his blow. A second later, he was under her skirt, searching frantically. Groggy, Robin tried to pull away, but Donald found what he wanted, tore it off her, then kicked her in the side for good measure.

He slid the small black box into his breeches, then summoned his men. They dragged Robin up to the attic and threw her inside a small room. Robin fell face first. Rolling onto her back, she cleared her eyes and looked around. The room was bare, with rough planks for floors. The walls were unfinished, the stone of the castle walls left bare of any tapestry. Light slid in through the tall, narrow windows. Lady Anna sat in a corner, blinking back tears.

"We are undone," the girl whispered. "He must be angry because Father won't give me to him."

"That's not helping his temper," Robin said, wincing. Her side hurt where she'd been kicked, and she still felt groggy from being punched in the head. She looked at Lady Anna and wondered what the girl had understood in the courtyard. "Do you understand Spanish?"

"No," said Lady Anna. "When I arrived, it seemed clear that the captain was not happy to see me." She shook her head, confused. "But that doesn't make sense if they took me because my father refused him. And why did he take you?"

Robin shrugged, not sure whether to explain that she was the target. She groaned softly and tried to get up.

"You're hurt," Lady Anna said, scrambling over to another corner. "Rest a moment. I'll get you a drink. There's a water pitcher here and bread. And a bucket for our slops."

Robin looked at the small pitcher, platter, and bucket. "Looks like he decided that he needs us alive for the time being. That's good news."

Lady Anna's eyes lit up. "Maybe we can use the pitcher to hit somebody if he comes in."

"Assuming that pitcher is strong enough to knock someone out, how do we get out of here?" Robin asked. "I saw at least six men, plus Captain de Garcia. Do you think they'll let us just leave?"

Lady Anna sank into herself and sniffled. "No. We are doomed."

"We are not doomed." Robin sat up gingerly, then slowly got up.

The room was essentially a corner of the tower that had been walled off with rough wood. Just outside the room were the stairs and another doorway. Robin closed her eyes for a moment, trying to remember what the tower looked like from the outside. The four stories were built as a square. At the top, there were crenellations surrounding a smaller room with a peaked roof. Robin looked up and saw the peak with its crossbars above them. She walked over to one of the windows. On the wall underneath were several gaps between the stones where bits of mortar had fallen out, and the stones were fairly rough as it was. Robin hoisted herself up on one such stone high enough to look out and down. Sure enough, there was a narrow walkway running along the inside of the crenellated wall.

"Can you climb?" she asked, slowly letting herself down.

"When I was a small girl, I would climb the walls of my father's castle," Lady Anna studied the wall. "These walls are even rougher. But how are we to climb in our farthingales?"

Robin looked down at the stiff, hooped petticoats the two women wore under their skirts.

"We'll leave them here," she said, smiling.

Roger blinked his eyes. Fortunately, he had the small medical kit and had taken a dose of the phenyl tri-chloroacenol, so his head no longer ached. Better yet, he realized, he was concerned, but not overly worried about Robin's welfare. That would make it easier to stay calm and make a good plan. Lord Jan was in a complete panic as he relentlessly paced the solar. Master Ernst and his father, Master Van-Den Melke, stood silently watching.

"But he has taken my daughter!" Lord Jan screamed at Captain Martinez, who was also standing by.

"I agree that it seems likely that de Garcia did," the captain replied calmly. "But we do not know that for certain. All we know is that some of our soldiers were involved. We don't know in whose company they were."

"Can't you keep a better account of your men?" Lord Jan bellowed, his face growing alarmingly red.

Captain Martinez shrugged. "I have questioned my men, and they were not involved. But there are several companies in the area. And even if it was de Garcia, I can't take up arms against him."

"But he is in violation of your general's orders." Lord Jan quickly turned his back to Martinez and Roger, but not before Roger saw the tears on the man's cheeks.

"My lord," Roger said, trying to keep his voice calm and soothing. "Perhaps I can find a way to discover where the ladies were taken, and then we can try to plan a rescue with our own men."

"How can you stay so calm?" Lord Jan yelped. "Your wife was taken, too, and there is no little affection between you."

"I know," said Roger, his heart leaping into his throat. "But staying calm is her only hope."

Lord Jan hung his head. "It is." He looked at Captain Martinez. "Can you ask among your fellows? The gatemen were very sure that they were attacked by Spaniards."

"I will do so," Captain Martinez said. He sighed. "If Captain de Garcia has taken the ladies, then perhaps we can appeal to him, find some way to give him some of what he wants."

"Not my daughter," Lord Jan snapped, then recovered himself. "But you're right. It would be best to find a peaceful resolution to this."

"By your leave, my lord," said Roger. "I would like to go and find out where my good wife and your daughter are."

Lord Jan waved him off. Roger left the room, followed by Master Ernst.

"Master de Marais," he whispered softly. "I am certain that Captain de Garcia is behind this."

"I know he is," said Roger, not adding that he knew why, as well.

"Then I will help you rescue them," Master Ernst said. "We must go quickly before the captain decides to do them harm."

Roger bit his tongue. Something inside him knew that Robin had not already been killed. But Donald would soon find out that he was just as locked out of her timetron as he was of his own. Hopefully, Donald would realize that keeping Robin alive made more sense than not. He got confirmation of that almost immediately. He and Master

Ernst had barely opened the door to Lord Jan's house when a young page came running up.

"Do you know Master de Marais?" the boy asked. "I'm told he's staying here."

"I am he," said Roger.

The boy handed him a small piece of parchment, folded over and sealed. Roger handed him two copper coins and waited until the boy had run off to open the parchment.

"Is that?" Master Ernst asked anxiously.

"It is, indeed," Roger said, reading over the parchment. Donald demanded that Roger re-connect his timetron, in veiled language, too, which meant that Donald was still hoping to stay in the area. But what to tell Master Ernst? Roger took a deep breath. "He wants my wealth. I guess he thinks that the townspeople will have less of a problem with me losing my money rather than losing theirs."

"And his orders are not to loot the city, but they don't seem to say anything about not looting any strangers here."

Roger smiled tightly at the young man. "Good point. We'd best talk to Lord Jan and your father. The sooner we act, the less likely the women will come to harm."

The two men hurried back to the solar.

"It is confirmed," Master Ernst announced. "Captain de Garcia has Lady Anna and Mistress de Marais."

"He does?" Captain Martinez growled. "That is in direct defiance of His Grace's orders."

"I am the target," Roger said. "He is seeking my wealth as the ransom for both ladies. My guess is that he is holding Lady Anna as a guarantee that I will be sufficiently pressured to give up my money. As I am a foreigner, he is not technically looting the city."

Captain Martinez winced. "Which will make it that much harder for me to send men from my company to rescue the ladies."

"We must send a parlay," Lord Jan said quickly. "You were quite right, Captain. We'll find a way to get him some of what he wants. And don't worry about your wealth, Master de Marais. We will make this profitable for all of us."

"My Lord," said Roger softly. "You have seen Captain de Garcia's temper. A parlay will take time and I gravely fear that time is the one thing we do not have. The longer it takes to resolve this, the greater the chance that the captain will become enraged and lash out at the women. Master Ernst and I can join with his father and his men."

"You don't mean to attempt to attack that castle, do you?" Lord Jan turned pale. "Even assuming you could succeed, it would guarantee the ladies' deaths. And where would you get the siege wagons and trebuchets?"

"And an attack like that would give my fellows an excuse to lay siege to the city," Captain Martinez said. "Or at the very least, loot, since you would be violating the terms of the surrender."

Lord Jan gasped and sank onto a stool. "No. There will be no attacks. I absolutely forbid it. We will attempt a parlay. Captain Martinez, can you help me bring it about? You know Captain de Garcia best."

"He's a proven mad man!" Master Ernst cried.

Roger silenced the younger man by putting his hand on Master Ernst's arm. Roger glanced at Master VanDen Melke and the two nodded. With Lord Jan absorbed in setting up the parlay, Master VanDen Melke led Roger and Master Ernst from the room. They met downstairs in the front study. Bare of all but a large table, it was a room that Lord Jan primarily used in negotiating business. The early evening sun filtered in through the windows.

"I expect that I shall be required to be part of the parlay party," Master VanDen Melke said. "But it's getting late, and they won't be able to ride in the dark. Therefore, we have until morning to do what we can."

"A stealth attack?" Roger asked.

Master VanDen Melke nodded. "It's our only hope of breaching the tower. I have been a guest there many times while the old knight was still sensible, so I know it well. The primary problem is that it was built to be easily defended. There's no cover for several hundred yards around it. The moat is a good fifteen feet across and at least another twelve feet deep. One bit of grace that we have is that is it kept running fresh and clear."

"Then one of us can swim it," Roger said.

"I will," said Master Ernst. "But the walls. How am I to manage them?"

"They are easily climbed," said his father. "All you have to do is find a window next to an empty room, then you'll be inside."

"But how will I find them?"

Roger shrugged. "Probably the hardest room in the place to get out of." He looked at Master VanDen Melke. "The dungeon?"

Master VanDen Melke shook his head. "It's almost always flooded. My best guess would be the room at the top of the tower. It's easy to guard, with only one door, and one would have to get through the entire tower to leave it. Unless one climbed down."

"Which means I will need to create a considerable diversion," Roger said.

Master VanDen Melke nodded and the three bent over the table to devise their plan.

Robin was still feeling achy as the sun sank below the horizon. She and Lady Anna had taken off their farthingales and had ripped the fabric to strips, leaving the hoops bare. Their skirts had been kilted up into their belts. They were as ready as they could be for several different scenarios.

"Do you think they'll come?" Lady Anna asked. She paced the room relentlessly.

"I don't know," Robin said, bending over and stretching to keep herself from stiffening up. "The waiting is the worst part."

Robin thought not knowing what Donald was planning was somewhat worse than waiting. The absolute optimal plan would be for them to capture each of the soldiers and Donald, one by one, then take a horse or two and leave the castle through the gate. Robin thought the odds were rather long on the two women being able to capture six trained soldiers plus their rabid commander. The next best plan was to wait until most of the tower occupants were asleep, then slowly climb down the tower wall. But they were ready if the soldiers wanted to play nasty games or something else equally unpleasant. They were not in a good situation, but Robin had decided it was far from hopeless.

In fact, no matter how dire the situation seemed, Robin felt oddly reassured. She couldn't explain it. But then she wondered if Roger was sending her some brainwave message through the timetron, although how he could have when she didn't have hers, she didn't know.

The one thing she did not expect, though she realized she should have, was the loud banging on the tower gate shortly after darkness had fallen. Robin listened at the door. Down in the courtyard, men yelled. Robin heard Donald screaming something. She wasn't sure what until she heard the pounding of feet up the stairs.

"They're coming for us," she hissed at Lady Anna. "Get ready."

Anna grabbed a farthingale hoop and leaned against the door as Robin backed herself up next to the opening. The guard on the other side cursed and pushed the door open, poking the ax end of his pike into the room first. Robin grabbed the pole and pulled hard. The man stumbled just long enough for Anna to whip the hoop over his head as Robin wrenched the pike away. Anna got the guard's arms pinned, knocked off his helmet and whacked him across the head with the slops pail.

Robin faced off with two more guards, both carrying swords. Swinging the pike, Robin knocked the first man's sword from his hand, then hit him on the side of his head with the pole. Anna was ready with another hoop. Robin then faced off with the third guard, who charged her. She swung the pike again and caught him in the chest. Another swipe of the pike to his head and he crumpled.

With the three men immobilized, Robin helped Anna finish tying and gagging them, taking just enough time to be sure the men would not get loose easily. Then Robin led Anna down the stairs, but stopped short at the first landing.

"Do you hear that?" she whispered to Anna.

"They're yelling at someone," Anna said.

"Someone's creating a diversion." Robin looked back up the stairs. "We'd better get back up there and see what's going on."

"We can't go out that way anyway," Anna said, retracing her steps.

Once up the stairs, they went to the door that led to the battlements. Robin raced around to the front of the tower. Sure enough, Roger and a few men stood just outside the gates, taunting Donald. Robin shivered, but ran to the back of the tower. Anna was already over the edge and slowly crawling down the wall. Robin eased herself over the edge and, taking a deep breath, started fumbling with her foot for holds. They were almost halfway down when they saw Donald above them, screaming.

"Jump!" hissed a voice below them. "Land in the moat and I'll fish you out."

Robin looked down, trying to see where the voice was coming from, but it was too dark. Landing in the water would be dicey, with their heavy skirts ready to soak up water and pull them down. Robin hoped Anna would think to slip out of her overskirt once she hit the water.

Taking a deep breath, Robin pushed off the wall and felt the rush of air in her ears, then the choking sting of icy cold water. She sank to the bottom and landed on her feet. Pushing with all her might, she reached the surface to find that she was close to the outer edge of the moat. One gasp of air, and she fought her way to the grassy bank.

Anna was having a much more difficult time. At first, it didn't seem as though she would surface, but her head broke the water, at last. Robin heard another splash and saw someone swimming toward her. Only Anna had sunk again. Robin was about to push off and help when the second swimmer pulled Anna's head up out of the water.

"Here's the plank!" someone on the bank hissed.

Robin felt strong hands on hers and looked up to see Roger standing over her.

"You're here!"

"The others have taken over the diversion," Roger said, grabbing her wrists and pulling her up onto the grass. "Once I saw you up at the top of the tower, I figured I might be more useful here."

Nearby, Anna and Ernst were being hauled out of the moat by Master VanDen Melke and a couple more men. There were several horses nearby, each carrying plenty of blankets and hot possets of ale and honey. Fortunately, the summer evening air was relatively warm and, for once, there wasn't a breeze from the ocean.

Soon, everyone in wet clothes had been wrapped in blankets, and the small group mounted and galloped back to the city.

Chapter Sixteen

Lord Jan's household remained in an uproar the next morning over the rescue of Lady Anna and Mistress de Marais. As they sat in the solar, Lord Jan hovered over his daughter, who was still coughing a bit after her dunking, but was otherwise in good health and spirits. Roger didn't quite hover over Robin, but stayed quite close. Captain Martinez arrived early with news.

Because the rescuers did not actually attack Donald, Captain Martinez could not accuse them of breaching the terms of the surrender, especially since it was obvious Captain de Garcia had. Captain Martinez also brought them the disquieting news that Captain de Garcia had first killed three of his men and then fled with the other three.

"I do hope that we've seen the last of him," Lord Jan said.

Robin looked over at Roger. He looked somewhat puzzled, but couldn't say anything at that moment.

"I do not know," Captain Martinez said. "I do fear that we have released a new set of thieves in the area, though."

Everyone shuddered at the idea of four more men with no real allegiance roaming the land, ready to terrorize and plunder whomever crossed their path.

But then there was a knock on the outside door of the house and Master VanDen Melke and his son Master Ernst were announced and admitted to the solar.

"My good young man!" Lord Jan ran across the room to embrace Master Ernst. "Master de Marais has told me how you saved my beloved Anna from drowning. What would I do without you? How can I repay you?"

Master Ernst stepped back from the older man and swallowed.

"You can give me the hand of your daughter in marriage," Master Ernst said quietly. "I know I do not have the wealth you wish for your daughter. But I assure you, sir, that no one will care better for her."

"You have proven that, indeed," Lord Jan said, his eyes blinking again. "And since your father is here, let us go down to my study where we may discuss the terms of the contract, then summon the bishop to announce the banns this Sunday."

Lady Anna gasped in joy but was prevented from rushing over to Master Ernst because her father was ushering the young man out of the room. So, instead, Lady Anna turned to Robin.

"Is it true?" Anna gasped. "Did I hear my father correctly? Ernst and I are to be married?"

Robin nodded, her own throat thick with emotion. "It does seem so. I'm so happy for you, my lady."

But as happy as Lady Anna was, she remained on edge until the contract had been signed and the bishop summoned. After all, it was possible that her father would change his mind. But fortunately, that didn't happen, and almost immediately after the contract was signed, the household erupted again into joyful chaos. Bishop Wuyts had not only agreed to posting the banns, the betrothal would take place that Sunday in front of the church doors before Mass.

Which meant that a feast had to be planned in short order to celebrate the event. Lord Jan encouraged Robin and Roger to stay for the festivities, and Roger happily agreed.

That night, as they got ready for bed, Robin sighed.

"So, now what?" Robin asked as Roger undid her bodice. "I find it a little hard to believe that Donald just took off for parts unknown."

"He hasn't gone far," Roger said. "He needs a working timetron too badly."

"For what?" She slid out of the bodice and sleeves and set them on the table under the window.

"Our greatest secret. Remember?" Roger eased himself out of his doublet and set it aside.

"You mean the cell growth thing?"

"Yeah. Unless he time travels, he is eventually going to get old and die. Can you imagine Donald settling for that?"

"Point taken." Robin frowned. "So maybe we should go on the road to draw him out."

"I was thinking the same thing. But let's wait until after the feast." Roger pulled Robin close to him. "I almost died of terror when I saw you push off that wall last night."

"So, you've said." Robin snuggled in. "Trust me. It wasn't my idea of a fun way to go swimming. But I can't tell you how glad I was to see you on that bank. I had no idea how I was going to get out of that moat."

The two cuddled for some time before sleep overtook them.

Sunday dawned bright and dry, with billowing white clouds drifting across a brilliant blue sky. Tables had been set up and laid under the sprawling trees in the nearby garden next to the canal.

Robin walked with Lady Anna to the church, both wearing richly jeweled gowns. Men-at-arms, as well as several women from the nearby houses surrounded them. Roger and Lord Jan had arrived at the church first, along with Master Ernst and his entire family, including his older brother and his wife and children. Lady Anna all but ran up the steps of the church, where the bishop blessed the young couple, and Master Ernst placed a simple ring on Lady Anna's left forefinger. Then everyone entered the church, where they heard the solemn High Mass. After mass, it was time to feast.

All the city's notables were there. Captain Martinez had brought some of his soldiers, partly to honor them and partly to keep guard. Servants brought platter after platter heaped high with meats and sweets and all manner of vegetables to the tables. Two huge kegs of beer were breached and poured from generously.

As the afternoon wore on, Robin felt herself relaxing for the first time in days. It was, she realized later, the perfect time for Donald to strike.

He appeared as if out of nowhere, galloping at full speed through the party. Shrieks and screams tore at Robin's ears as people scrambled to get away from the hooves. Robin saw Lord Jan lying on the ground, blood glistening on his brow. Lady Anna and Master Ernst rushed to his side. Roger stood on a table nearby and, as Donald's horse made its next pass, Roger jumped on behind Donald. That was all Donald needed, and he kicked his horse into a run, heading away from the city.

The cries softened into sobs. Several people were injured, but the worst seemed to be Lord Jan. Robin walked quietly alongside as a crew of men-at-arms gently took him to his house on a litter. Once Lord Jan had been transferred to his bed, Robin cleaned the wound carefully and when she could unseen, scanned Lord Jan with her handheld unit then dosed the wound with some disinfectant cream she had in her medical kit. If she stayed firmly focused on caring for His Lordship, it was to avoid thinking about what was happening to Roger.

"Do you think he'll live?" Lady Anna asked anxiously as darkness finally fell on the house.

Robin looked at Lord Jan. He was breathing evenly and did not have a fever. His skull had not been fractured, either.

"Fortunately, the gash is not deep and seems to have stopped bleeding," Robin said. "When I talked to him a few minutes ago, he was alert and knew where he was and what had happened, which is a very good sign. And he has not taken a fever. So, I think he will. It's never certain, of course. But he looks good."

Lady Anna sniffed. "How could Captain de Garcia do such a thing?"

"Anger is a cruel master," Robin said. "In any case, I will wake your father up every so often to make sure he continues to do well."

Robin was profoundly glad that Donald had not gotten her handheld unit, and when Lady Anna had left her father's side for a few minutes, Robin quickly looked up treating a concussion and discovered that waking the patient up every couple of hours was not necessary if the brain wasn't bleeding. She quickly scanned Lord Jan again, and his brain was fully intact. She hid the handheld and waited for Lady Anna to come back.

It was getting close to midnight at that point. Lady Anna said she'd watch her father and Robin went back to her room feeling alone and useless. Except that she felt a strong desire to go after Roger. That was ridiculous. Even Captain Martinez had men scouring the fields and woods in the area. How was her sneaking out and getting on a horse going to help? Except the feeling kept getting stronger.

Robin waited only a moment longer before finding Roger's everyday wear and slipping it on. The house was deep in slumber, and she moved as quietly as she could to the stables and found Roger's horse.

Roger held on for all he was worth as the horse continued its gallop across the fields and roads. With Donald focused on keeping the horse on track and Roger focused on staying on, the two didn't have a chance to say anything. He wasn't terribly surprised when the horse approached the tower and clattered across the drawbridge into the yard. Donald pulled the horse up short, and Roger tumbled to the hard-packed dirt of the courtyard. Darkness was falling fast. Donald dismounted and used some future technology to light a couple of torches. His horse ambled to the stable. Roger got to his feet as Donald studied him.

"Well, you played true to form," Donald said finally. "Roger to the rescue again."

Roger shrugged. "I suppose."

"Of course, the question now is, do I just kill you and be done with it, or let you live a little longer?"

"I believe you'll be better served if you leave me alive," Roger said. He kept his voice calm, but his stomach roiled.

Donald smirked. "Once again, my dear big brother, the Great Roger York, is looking to his own self-interests."

"And yours," Roger replied. "I came here to rescue you."

"From what?" Donald snapped.

"From yourself. Your surgery has failed you."

"What if it's my free will to be here?" Donald rolled his eyes.

"Your free will has clearly been compromised."

Donald hesitated for a fraction of a second. That was good, Roger decided.

"I'm fine," Donald snapped. "I know who I am and what I'm doing."

"Donald, we've had our disagreements, and many times, your complaints were and are valid. But it's never been a blood sport before. Now, it is." Roger sighed. "Something is terribly wrong. It's not anything you've done or didn't do. But you're not the same person I grew up with. The same man I would trust with my life."

Donald snorted. "There's a good one. You've never trusted me with your life. No one has since Eric. You've all wondered."

"No one wonders. Not Cricklan. Not me. No one. What happened to Eric was beyond all our control." Roger swallowed.

Their father's death had been a sore point since it had happened so many, many years before, in the early days of time travel. If anything, ignorance had killed Eric. But Donald had thought at the time, and apparently still did, that he was to blame for the death.

"Donald," Roger continued, not at all sure he should. "I'm here to help you. Whether you believe it or not, I care about you. I want to see you healthy and alive and the man I know and love."

Donald suddenly roared and rushed Roger. Somehow, Roger was ready, but it didn't help much. Donald got his hands on Roger's throat. Roger gasped for air as his vision turned black. He thought of Robin. He so desperately wanted to see her again, to be with her again. Somehow, that thought propelled his knuckles into Donald's biceps.

Donald howled and let go just long enough for Roger to press forward. Donald fell on his back and Roger fell on top of him. But that gave him enough of an advantage to rabbit punch Donald in the side of his head. Donald was stunned for just a moment, but that was plenty of time for Roger to apply a sedative squeeze on Donald. Technically, Donald should have done the same to Roger, but it was an only too obvious sign of his illness that he hadn't. Donald slumped.

Breathing heavily, Roger got up and fumbled for his medical kit. Donald was going to need a much stronger sedative to keep him out until Roger and Robin could get Donald back to their natal time.

In the meantime, Roger thought about Robin as he searched the tower for a good room where he could make sure Donald would be comfortable but unconscious, until he and Robin could appropriately head "home."

It was well after midnight when Roger trussed Donald up in one of the nicer bedrooms. He was wondering how to leave the castle secure when he heard hoofbeats in the courtyard below. Feeling oddly safe about the sound and yet realizing that the intruder could be a threat, he hurried downstairs and cracked the door to the main tower to peek out.

Robin was getting off the horse and looking around. He slid into the courtyard.

"There you are," she said.

"Yes. What brought you here?"

Robin grimaced. "I'm not sure, really. I just had this feeling that you needed me and wanted me here. I thought it was that mind reading thingie going on with the timetron."

"Really?" Roger grinned. "It probably was, although I've never seen it work this far away before. Huh."

Robin gasped. "So, what do I need to do to rescue you?"

"Uh, you don't. Donald is securely trussed and sedated for the next thirty-six hours or so."

"What?"

"Yeah. You seem to have missed all the fun."

"Fun?" Robin roared. "I have been worried sick about you! This is not fun. It's not even close."

"Bad choice of words?" Roger hoped his smile looked apologetic.

"I'll say it was." Robin swallowed and got a grip on herself. "So, now what?"

"We get back to Lord Jan's, say goodbye, then come back here and transport."

Chapter Seventeen

The next morning, Lord Jan was walking around, but conscious and happy that the incident the day before hadn't been worse. Robin and Roger found him comfortably seated in the solar on a small bed with a high, padded headboard.

"I'm told you come to say goodbye to me," Lord Jan said.

"I'm afraid so," Roger said. "It's time we were on our way back home. It will take several weeks, and I need to be home before it's time for the grape harvest. We've done well here, though, and I thank you for it."

"You're very welcome, indeed," Lord Jan said.

"They can't have left yet!" Lady Anna's voice was raised in worry as she burst into the solar. "Oh, you haven't. Thanks be. I did so want my chance to thank both of you and to wish you well."

Robin and Roger accepted everyone's good wishes and a small cart filled with woolens and other goods, along with an extra horse to pull it.

"What are we going to do with all of this?" Robin asked as they headed around the city toward the tower.

"Store it until we or someone else needs it," Roger said. "We used to try not to bring things home, but we found having clothes and animals from various times and places was pretty useful."

Dark clouds were piling up, but the rain held off as they trotted along. Once they arrived at the tower, the two tied up the horses, then searched the building for anything Donald may have hidden. Robin found her timetron and the one Donald had been using in his bedroom. Donald's handheld was in one of his pockets.

Donald was still unconscious. Robin and Roger hefted him up and brought him to the cart, then collected the horses.

"Are we all touching?" he asked Robin, although he didn't need to.

"Yes," said Robin with a chuckle.

Then the sucking pressure and blackness began and ended almost before Robin could cry out.

They arrived in the huge field next to the time center. Roger checked his handheld, then pressed the screen.

"Hello, Roger," came Cricklan's voice from the handheld.

"We're right outside," he told her. "And, yes, we've got Donald. Along with an extra horse and a cart with all sorts of fun things."

A second later, Cricklan appeared with two other men. Then men took the horses and cart. Cricklan held onto Donald and the three transported into the Time Center. Alayo was waiting and helped Cricklan get Donald dressed into more timely night clothes. Roger and Robin elected to go to his home and change there, which raised Cricklan's eyes for a moment.

"I'll check in with you when we've changed and rested," Roger told his mother.

"Yes, do." Cricklan did not say more, but her eyes rested on Robin for several moments.

Robin squirmed, but there really wasn't time for more. Roger transported them back to his apartment in Paris. Robin ran for the cleaning room.

"What?" Roger asked.

"Shower," Robin yelped. "I need a shower!"

Roger laughed. "Mind if I join you?"

"I only mind if you slow me down." Robin tore at the bodice and sleeves.

She had to wait for Roger to undo her bodice and stays, but in no time, she was turning on the tap. As the hot water cascaded over Robin's shoulders, she groaned happily.

"I don't think I will ever take showers for granted again," she sighed.

Roger laughed as he got under the water with her, then sighed with pleasure. After drying off, they made love with achingly glorious slowness.

Sometime later, Roger stirred and picked up his handheld.

"That was fast," he muttered as he sat up in the bed.

"What?" Robin sat up next to him.

"Donald's already in surgery," he said. "Usually, it takes a day or two for psycho-neural scans to register, but Donald's abnormality showed up almost immediately." He sighed. "I hope he's all right."

"Yeah." Robin looked away.

Roger sighed. "You're angry at him."

"You think?" She frowned. "Look. I know he's your brother. I know he wasn't always like this, that it was this whatever in his head making him do it. But, damn it, he's caused so much pain and misery. He hurt my mom. He's almost killed me several times. He could have killed you. Don't think I missed those bruises on your neck. He killed Beeman." Robin blinked back tears. "It just feels like he's getting off scot free with a nice, clean brain. I want to be merciful and all that, but right now, I want to lock him up and throw away the key."

"That's to be expected, I guess," Roger said with a sigh. "But he's not getting away scot free. He will have to spend time in a holding room until he can prove that his condition has been healed, and he will never be able to time travel again." He reached over and gave Robin a hug. "But I understand. It may take some time to work through this."

Robin looked at him and smiled softly. "I will. I'm sorry to be such a downer right now. It's time to be happy. We're safe. We're back. You haven't got any Board out to get you."

"And you're still not home." Roger reached over and touched her cheek. "Would you like to go back?"

"I have no idea," Robin said. "I mean, I don't want to disappear and never see Dean and Elizabeth again. Or the rest of my family. But I really don't have much to go back to. Work is pretty much a wash and kind of problematic now that I know more physics and technology than I should. Not that I'm doing much design work. I'm mostly babysitting engineers these days, and I hate that." She paused. "And if I go back, where will you be?"

He laughed. "Right next to you. I'll just establish a new persona, that's all. Just like you will in my other lives. We've got plenty of time to explore, you know."

Robin closed her eyes and sniffed happily. "Oh, thank heavens. I kind of figured we'd be together, but had no idea how we'd work out when or where."

"We'll live in lots of different times and places." Roger pulled her closer and held her. "Now, why don't we get dressed?" He stopped. "I should probably not be assuming this, but are you okay with eventually forming a family unit with me and having kids in our time rather than yours? I mean, if it comes to that?"

"Huh?" Robin asked, completely perplexed.

"It's what you would call marriage in your time," said Roger. "Basically, a contract to join economically and raise children. We don't have to continue our relationship. You're still a traveler, no matter what. But if we do continue, we are going to have to think about breeding, that being something of an issue now."

"Well, there's the height of romance," Robin said with a laugh. "Shouldn't we just live together for a while to decide if we're compatible and then do the contract thing?"

Roger thought about it, then shrugged. "I suppose." He grinned. "I just want you so badly, Robin."

"I want you, too, Roger," Robin said. She touched his cheek. "Let's get dressed and see how your brother is doing."

They transported to the hospital and met Cricklan in the waiting room near the surgery center. Cricklan paced, stopping to check a hologram screen every few minutes, then waving it away.

"It's going well," she told them. "They've located the abnormality and are applying the new neurons."

"Good," said Roger.

Cricklan looked the two of them over. "So, you two connected on this trip."

Robin flushed as Roger dropped his arm over her shoulders.

"Yes, we did, Cricklan," Roger said, laughing. "Which should come as absolutely no surprise to you."

"I was wondering how long it would take," the older woman replied, somewhat acerbically. She gazed at Robin. "You do realize there are implications involved here, don't you? About the population?"

"We're not that committed yet," Robin said, wincing. "But I don't mind having children here rather than in my home time. Assuming we get to that point."

"Naturally," Cricklan said. "Well, when and if you're ready, you'll be a welcome addition to the family." She threw Roger a warning glare, then waved a hand to bring up the hologram screen and peered at it critically. "They're going to be working for several more hours yet."

They continued pacing, looking at holograms and waiting until they were officially informed that Donald was out of surgery. Robin was with Roger when he and Cricklan finally got to visit Donald in his resting room. Donald barely seemed aware of who he was, let alone Roger and Cricklan. The caregivers decided that what Donald needed most of all was rest without any input and shooed the three out of the room.

Roger pulled Robin aside. "Listen, I appreciate you hanging around while we wait to see how much brain Donald has left, but it's got to be pretty hard on you. You need to take a solo trip, anyway. Why don't we do this? You go to your home and get settled in, more or less. Don't worry about your job for the time being. We'll figure that out when I get there."

"So, you're coming?" Robin asked.

"Make it a day or two after you get there, but of course." He pulled out his timetron. "Trace the coordinates on here."

"Why aren't you coming with me?"

"I have to go visit you first."

"Huh?"

"Remember the visit I made right after the baby was born? When I set your timetron to meet up with me when I was in trouble?"

"Oh, right." Robin grinned. "You were pretty handsy then. If only I'd known."

Roger chuckled as she reached around and tweaked his backside.

"And you know why that doesn't work," he teased. "Anyway, I've got to get that taken care of as soon as possible before I forget too much. Otherwise, it gets too crazy-making wondering if I'm doing things right."

Robin thought for a moment, then traced the coordinates and date she wanted on the machine, focusing on an image of her house in Pasadena and a date in the middle of September.

"I hope I've given Dean enough time to cool off," she said, suddenly shuddering.

"Well, we'll find out soon enough," Roger said. "Either way, I'll be there."

Robin smiled, then Roger brought them back to his apartment for one more evening of lovemaking and closeness.

The next morning, Robin slipped out of bed before Roger was awake. She cleaned up and found some clothes that were reasonably close to what she'd worn in her own natal time. After eating breakfast, she picked up her timetron, then went over to the bed where Roger was still asleep. She sat down next to him and gently prodded him awake.

"Yeah?" he mumbled.

"I'm taking off." She bent down and kissed his lips. "I'll see you in a couple of days, then?"

"Absolutely." Roger smiled. "I don't want to spend any more time apart from you than I have to."

They kissed once more, then Robin tore herself away. She stepped back, took a deep breath, looked at her machine and thought of home.

She gasped as she landed in her bedroom. It was mid-day, but the house was warm, as if the air conditioning hadn't been turned on. The suitcase she'd brought to Las Vegas sat next to the closet. The house was silent, but her bureau had been freshly dusted, and the floors swept. She pulled her mobile phone from her pocket. It was working again, but very low on power.

After putting it on the charger, she texted her brother and Elizabeth. Elizabeth responded right away that she and the baby were out for a walk and that Dean was at school. Robin took another deep breath and found a pair of jeans and a t-shirt, put them on, and went to turn on the air conditioner.

A few minutes later, she looked out the front window as Elizabeth hurried up the walk, pushing a stroller, her face flushed in the heat. Robin checked her weather app. They were in the middle of another heat wave. She sighed.

Elizabeth entered the house a moment later, backing in with the huge three-wheeled stroller. She still wore a full dress that hit her mid thighs and tights. But in concession to the heat, her dress had short sleeves. She'd pinned her hair up under a kerchief.

"Hi," said Robin, a little hesitantly. "Can I get you some water?"

"That would be lovely," said Elizabeth. "And there's a bottle of water in the fridge for the baby, too."

With the baby removed from the stroller, Elizabeth followed Robin into the dining room. Robin brought in the glass and bottle. Elizabeth took the glass first and drank deeply.

"Thank you so much," she said, setting the glass down on the table, then giving Robbie the bottle. "When did you get in?"

"A few minutes ago," Robin said. "How have you and Dean been?"

"We've missed you, of course," Elizabeth said, coming over and giving Robin a hug.

"Not necessarily, the way I left things."

"Oh, nonsense," Elizabeth laughed. "It was the heat of the moment. We were all overly emotional, what with getting married and Donald and all. At least, you had someplace to go."

"How's Mom doing?"

"Quite well. She was hurt and angry at the way Donald left things, but she's back to normal. Dean says she must not have had that much invested in the relationship, which makes sense."

"How's Dean?"

Elizabeth smiled and rolled her eyes. "Working all the time. If it's not his job, then it's schoolwork. He's determined to do well for our sakes. It will be better when we move closer to the campus."

Robin bit her lip. "You're moving?"

"Not until next quarter," Elizabeth said. "But we got a very good rent on a couple's unit for grad students. It will be closer to school and Dean's work, and I'll have other young mothers to talk to." Elizabeth made a face. "Perhaps." She looked at Robin shrewdly. "How was your trip?"

"Quite illuminating," Robin said. "I can't talk about much."

"Did you meet with Roger?" Elizabeth's eyes glowed.

"Yes." Robin felt her face flushing and knew she did not need to say more on that score. But she did. "I guess we are now what we here would call an item."

"You look so happy," Elizabeth said softly as the baby squirmed and made soft baby noises.

Robin smiled. "I am. He'll be here in a few days, maybe a week or so."

Outside, Robin's BMW pulled into the driveway and, a minute later, Dean burst through the door.

"I just saw your text," he announced, sweeping her into a hug. "I'm so glad you're here! I owe you an apology. Really."

"I'm sorry, too, Dean," Robin said as he released her. "But it turns out there was more going on with Donald than we knew."

"I'm so glad I got home early," Dean said. "I mean, I've still got some reading to do for class, but let's go get lunch together."

"Why not?" Robin asked, feeling somewhat lighter in mind.

Roger did not turn up on the day Robin had entered the timetron. He turned up two days early. Robin had only been home a day at that point and was a little startled when he landed on her doorstep.

"Plus minus three days," she said, after giving him a long hug and kiss. "But I'm so glad to see you."

Elizabeth was out walking Robbie and Dean was at his job. The mid-morning air was cooler than it had been, the heat wave having finally broken the night before.

"I'm so glad to see you," Roger said. He had a suitcase with him, presumably with clothes. "Wow. This place is small. Do you want me to go to a hotel?"

"Not really. Do you mind sharing my room and the bathroom with Dean and Elizabeth?"

"I'm not going anywhere you aren't," Roger said, sweeping her into another kiss. "Unless you want me to."

"No," said Robin, feeling a little giddy. "I'd rather be with you."

They got him settled in Robin's bedroom.

"We'll have more room in a few months," Robin told him. "Dean and Elizabeth have a student apartment they'll be moving to in January."

"This is just fine," said Roger. He stopped and looked at her. "We have to do some planning and figuring out our lives here, but I have some interesting news for you."

"What?"

Roger was about to explain when Elizabeth returned home, and then there was the baby to coo over and lunch to make. Then Robin's mother came over to visit, it being Friday afternoon. Elizabeth explained quietly to Robin that Marlene had spent the past two weekends in Pasadena to play with the baby and ostensibly give Dean and Elizabeth a little time to themselves. Marlene was a little cautious about Roger at first, but then saw how happy Robin was. She offered several scenarios for the couple and would have continued planning for them, but Dean came home and there was more visiting.

Roger sat back with a slap-happy grin and occasionally played with his handheld, which looked remarkably like an iPhone. Robin was glad to see that Elizabeth was sucking on one of Robbie's diapers even when Marlene frowned. Elizabeth finished cleaning up the baby's spit up and put her to bed.

Finally, finally, Marlene decided it was time to go to her hotel and Dean and Elizabeth retreated to their bedroom. Robin shut the door behind her and Roger.

She grinned. "So, I guess this is officially happily ever after," Robin said.

"I suppose," Roger said. "Or reasonably close." He smiled. "Let's face it, happily ever after does not exist. We still have to make our commitment to each other, perhaps here and definitely in my time. But I'm feeling confident in our long-term odds."

"So am I," Robin leaned in for a lazy kiss.

Roger pulled away a bit and sat on the bed. "We do have an interesting problem, though."

Robin sank down next to him. "What do you mean?"

"It's Donald."

"Is he okay?"

"He was doing very well when I left." Roger winced guiltily. "I stayed there an extra day or two because Cricklan asked. But Donald is completely lucid, feeling awful about his behavior, which he actually remembers. But there's something else. He was pretty upset because he's convinced he's the father of Elizabeth's baby, even though he can't figure out how he impregnated her."

"Maybe because he didn't?" Robin said.

"He didn't." Roger smiled. "But he said he did a DNA test on one of the baby's diapers, and he came up as the father."

"That's what he was doing," Robin said suddenly. "It was when we were in Las Vegas. He checked his phone, only it must have been his handheld, then suddenly dumped Mom and asked if Dean was sure about being Robbie's father."

"That would have been right before he went after you three in Bath and London." Roger looked a little guilty again. "I hope you don't mind, but I went ahead and did the same tests tonight on Dean and the baby, and there's no question Dean is Robbie's father."

"So why would Donald think he was Robbie's father?" Robin asked.

"I saw Elizabeth sucking on a corner of one of Robbie's diapers," Roger said.

"She does that all the time," Robin said, then stopped. "Which means Donald didn't necessarily test Robbie's DNA."

"Exactly." Roger looked at Robin. "He must have tested Elizabeth's."

Thank You for Reading

I do hope you enjoyed the book.

If you can do me one small favor, please. Can you go to one of the social media/retail profiles below and leave a short review? It doesn't need to be a lot, just honest.

BB bookbub.com/profile/anne-louise-bannon

f facebook.com/RobinGoodfellowEnt

g goodreads.com/author/show/513383.Anne_Louise _Bannon

in linkedin.com/in/annelouisebannon.com

🐦 twitter.com/albannon

Coming Soon

The final book in the Time Travel Trilogy – ALL THE TIME IN THE WORLD

This novel is currently being written, but there's more action, and lots more time traveling, as Robin and Roger try to figure out how they are going to live, which gets even more complicated when Robin meets a teen-age girl who is the daughter she hasn't had yet.

Other books by Anne Louise Bannon

I'm so glad you liked this book! Check out my other novels, available in print or ebook at your favorite retailer:

Old Los Angeles Series:

Death of the Zanjero

Death of the City Marshal

Death of the Chinese Field Hands

Death of an Heiress

Operation Quickline Series:

That Old Cloak and Dagger Routine

Stopleak

Deceptive Appearances

Fugue in a Minor Key

Sad Lisa

These Hallowed Halls

My Sweet Lisa

A Little Family Business

Just Because You're Paranoid

Freddie and Kathy Series:

Fascinating Rhythm

Bring Into Bondage

The Last Witnesses

Blood Red

Daria Barnes:

Rage Issues

Mrs. Sperling:

A Nose for a Niedeman

Brenda Finnegan:

Tyger, Tyger

Romantic Fiction:

White House Rhapsody, Book One and Two

Fantasy and Science Fiction:

A Ring for a Second Chance

But World Enough and Time

And I would be honored if you left a review for this and any of my books on the below sites. It really helps.

bookbub.com/books/these-hallowed-halls-operatio n-quickline-book-6-by-anne-louise-bannon

goodreads.com/book/show/59695574-these-hallow ed-halls?from_search=true&from_srp=true&qid= mtoiwM2ryT&rank=3

Connect with Anne Louise Bannon

Thank you for sticking it out this long! Please join my newsletter. It's the best way to stay up-to-date on my upcoming projects, blog posts and even the occasional game and giveaway.

You can sign up for the Robin Goodfellow Newsletter here: http://eepurl.com/zH0Ab or by visiting my website, annelouisebannon.com

And don't forget to connect with me on your favorite social media platforms:

BB bookbub.com/profile/anne-louise-bannon

f facebook.com/RobinGoodfellowEnt

g goodreads.com/author/show/513383.Anne_Louise
_Bannon

in linkedin.com/in/annelouisebannon.com

y twitter.com/albannon

About Anne Louise Bannon

Anne Louise Bannon is an author and journalist who wrote her first novel at age 15. Her journalistic work has appeared in Ladies' Home Journal, the Los Angeles Times, Wines and Vines, and in newspapers across the country. She was a TV critic for over 10 years, founded the YourFamilyViewer blog, and created the OddBallGrape.com wine education blog with her husband, Michael Holland. She is the co-author of Howdunit: Book of Poisons, with Serita Stevens, as well as author of the Freddie and Kathy mystery series, set in the 1920s, the Old Los Angeles series, set in 1870, and the Operation Quickline series, plus several stand alones. She and her husband live in Southern California with an assortment of critters.